The Last Chatelaine

By the same author

On A Thin Stalk
Shrouded Legacy
Straws upon the Surface

The Last Chatelaine

A.M. Story

ROBERT HALE · LONDON

First published in Great Britain 2011

ISBN 978-0-7090-9307-7

Robert Hale Limited
Clerkenwell House
Clerkenwell Green
London EC1R 0HT

www.halebooks.com

2 4 6 8 10 9 7 5 3 1

Typeset in 11/14.5pt Sabon
Printed in the UK by the MPG Books Group

For Christopher Farmer – February 1941 to September 2009

Prologue

Shrieks she didn't recognize as hers pierced a distant air; running feet rang on stone – another wretch being hauled through the same hell.

'Just kill me, get it over with.' She tried to writhe but strong bonds held her legs. 'Aaaah.' Again the knives, only this time they left them in, twisting and forcing like crowbars – stabbing, prising. Through ruptured skin, the burden was wrenched from her body. A geyser of hot sticky fluid gushed like a severed artery. Surely that was all of her, all out, all gone. How they would gloat over her entrails.

What she had shed was swathed in a towel, the last sinew severed. Summoning all her strength she extended her arm and through muffled doubts, the bundle was brought. They helped her raise her head, witness the naked, bloody, wrinkled form of what she'd done. Someone whispered: 'Think of it as a pain removed – like an appendix.'

Afterwards, she drifted in and out of consciousness, unsure where she was, afraid it was heaven and He'd discover her sin; certain it was damnation and she could smell herself burning.

Chapter 1

This fiasco was gathering the hallmarks of a first class spoof faster than the windscreen was collecting flies. Elaborate Red Nose Day stunt, practical joke ... or one hell of an advertising junket? Since no one would hire a private detective, a country estate and a vintage Bentley, just for my benefit – mine was obviously a walk-on part in a far grander scheme.

I had blinked my way out of Warwick station with trepidation.

'Wow,' the man in front of me whispered, stopping so abruptly I almost disappeared up his exhaust. 'A 1935 six cylinder Sedanca de Ville, if I'm not mistaken.'

In gleaming white, the vision sported sleek curves, wide running boards and a half hood. Eyes fixed in disbelief, the man circled the motor with measured steps and bent knees, swivelling his head owl-like as he made the turns, expelling entranced air through reverent teeth.

Borrowing importance from the vehicle against which he lounged, an ageing spiv with a Teddy boy haircut bore aloft the ripped side off a cardboard box on which was scrawled *Macenna* in wobbly letters. His appraising look as I walked towards him made me cringe.

'I'm Synnove McKenna.'

'Frank Channing.'

'Where's the car?'

He swung out an arm with a 'tadaaa' flourish.

With a more agreeable companion, the drive would have been exhilarating. Early summer, hedgerows freshly painted and the smell of hay breezing through the open top Bentley; upholstery redolent of a bygone existence; thick worn leather, straps to hang on to. This was motoring. Apart from the views from its motorways, I had never seen South Warwickshire and I was enchanted. Soft rolling escarpments worn to comfortable contours by millennia of weather, swallows riding the air currents and a distant cuckoo, lent my day a magical quality. I could almost wish it were real. Prompted by a signpost indicating Blakesley, childlike I asked: 'How much further?'

'Ten minutes.' He turned in his seat to look at me. There was no rear view mirror. 'Goes like the clappers, doesn't she? There's three and a half litres under this bonnet. My granddad used to drive her for the old girl.'

'Were you her chauffeur too?'

'No fear. Got my own business.' He fished in a top pocket with two fingers and handed me a card over his shoulder. *Frank Channing, Motor Dealer*. 'If you're looking for a bargain or want to hire Sybil here, you let me know.'

'Couldn't the usual driver come?'

'Hasn't been no driver since her ladyship passed away.'

I had that wrong then. I thought Jean Edwards's notes had said everything should stay as it was. Mind you, among many other laughable strictures, that one had struck me as particularly impractical.

Channing went on: 'Barry fired them. Sixteen in all, there were. Eight here and eight in London.'

'Who's Barry?'

Channing guffawed. 'Who's Barry? Only the geezer what runs this place.'

'But you kindly volunteered to pick me up ... since the will stipulates it. I see.'

We wheeled in through an impressive entrance flanked by imposing stone pillars, each topped with a snarling griffin. Long grass and old man's beard held the wrought iron gates permanently open, yet beside them a brightly painted lodge displayed neat rows of well-hoed vegetables.

The Bentley waltzed its way through undulating parkland. Cows ceased grazing to stare desultorily, jaws unceasingly mobile like ill-mannered gum chewers. Half a mile further on, deer swivelled alert ears at the engine's purr. Through a second gate we skirted an overgrown copse before diving into dense shrubbery and emerging at a disused fountain where brazen nymphs gambolled shamelessly with half-goat creatures. We turned through ninety degrees to commence the final approach.

'Stop. Stop the car. Let me out.'

Channing did as requested. I scrambled from the rear seat, clutching at my throat, unable to swallow. 'Where the hell is this, really?' Mesmerized, I stood on the gravel, leaning against the chassis for support, racking my sketchy knowledge of stately homes: Woburn, Tyntesfield, Chartwell. It was unlike any of those; neither had we driven that far from Warwick ... nor passed along any strange platforms.

The building was probably a shell, its innards tragically consumed by fire; or a trick of technology – a photograph back projected on to a giant screen. Or even an ingenious stage set, constructed from cardboard and papier mâché, with which one of my more creative employees was toying at my expense. I was sure the plot would reveal itself the minute I walked through that recessed entrance into nothingness. Everyone would laugh and clap and I'd remember it was my birthday, or April Fool's Day or St George's Day. Except ... it wasn't.

A glittering chateau emblazoned on the Cotswold countryside, the house was breathtaking. Doubting my vision, I closed and reopened my eyes for fear I was dreaming; like Dorothy on those billious paviors, or Hansel and Gretel sighting the gingerbread cottage. With a frontage to rival Blenheim, Sanderling's stone glowed liquid gold in the sun, each corner marked by a fairy tale turret complete with conical green-tiled hat. Pagoda-like wings stretched back to infinity and intriguing balustrades entwined themselves around dual columns which flanked a porticoed central section.

Hoping the Channing individual had failed to register my loss of composure, I pieced together my vestigial dignity and climbed back into the vehicle, determined to show whoever was behind this charade, that I too could play games. Think they could pull my strings, did they? Make me jig on a stick while they giggled like schoolgirls behind their hands? Bring it on. I hadn't come all this way to falter at the first shock.

After our unscheduled stop, Channing crawled the motor car down the drive, while I stared straight ahead, confident the mirage would disappear as we drew nearer. The grounds on either side of the approach were overgrown with waist high grass and self-sown seedlings, the gravel interspersed with clumps of vegetation.

As I alighted, a man emerged from the doorway encased in tight velvet trousers, magenta jacket and a frilled shirt open to the navel displaying a garrish gilt medallion on an orange chest. He extended a hand weighed down with the largest pinkie ring I'd ever seen.

'Pleased ter meet yer, doll; Barry Fentiman.' Bracelets jingling he waved a hand towards the edifice behind him. 'Welcome to Sanderlin' Manor.'

If I was the one cast as proprietor, who was this upstart? He'd definitely overdone the costume. No one could take such a ludicrous character seriously. Was this an attempted coup before I'd even set foot in the place? My first obstacle?

Two or three other staff, all young, casually dressed and probably foreign, shuffled outside; Fentiman introduced them. In role, I inclined my head in their direction but made no attempt to shake hands or converse. Glancing up I noticed a crest and a motto carved ten feet up in the stone: *Sola Nobilitas Virtus* – Virtue Alone is True Nobility. Not an aristocratic establishment then – hadn't they believed in divine right?

Our footsteps echoed through the stone porch as I followed Fentiman out of the light ... into a sumptuous gallery. It must have been fifty yards long. The tall windows I'd thought painted on stood draped in acres of heavy silk; sturdy oak floors sported the densest of Turkish rugs while priceless sideboards, occasional tables and Louis XV chairs adorned the sides – every inch of surface filled with intricate objets d'art. Above tall portraits of elegant ladies, fruit hung from a ceiling frieze, ripe targets for the cherubs swinging from the plaster ivy.

'Right wonderland, innit?'

'The entrance hall, I presume?' Assumptions shredded, my internal switch gear had gone into spasm.

'Yeah. The old lady was about to update the 'eatin' when she turned up 'er toes. So only an 'andful of rooms are still furnished. She'd packed the rest up. Shipped it off site somewhere.'

Blinded by opulence and bewilderment I dragged myself from the Gainsboroughs and followed Fentiman to the right, passing through one of the many double height doorways into a sitting room with comfortable, chintz covered sofas. I strode across to a desk in the window, clutching at the reality of an outside view. Neglected terraces and overgrown box hedges led to the end of the world. Built – I now accepted, solidly – on the side of a hill, the garden ended at a low cliff; beyond which a vast lake stretched to the horizon.

I turned. 'Why are the grounds so neglected?'

'Too much to keep up. That's the problem 'ere, see.'

He led the way out of the sitting room, back into the hall and along into the base of one of the turrets I'd noticed from outside. Edged with ceiling to floor windows, corded hand rails and carved pilasters, a curved staircase slinked out of sight like a red velvet cobra. I shook my head to dislodge the mist.

Fentiman stopped on the first step. 'Same 'ere. All this cleanin' and repairin'.' He continued on up and I followed.

'So you've been managing the place?' We'd arrived on a broad landing which must correlate with the hall beneath.

Striding ahead, Fentiman pointed down a corridor. 'That leads to the west wing. All shut up.' Strange, the floor there looked cleaner than the one on which I stood. He flung open a few other doors and closed them again swiftly, muttering: 'Not safe,' affording me only a glimpse.

'Mr Fentiman,' I called, thoughts of jests and spoofs fading faster than the damask in the window seats. I was damned if I was going to run after this popinjay.

'Yes, love?' he sauntered back, rattling.

'I am not your love, and I asked you a question. Do you manage the place?'

At close quarters I judged him younger than I'd first supposed from his dyed hair and exaggerated suntan. 'For the last two years;

that's why I say, it's a lot of work. Everythin' crumblin', weeds sproutin' everywhere; not enough people.'

'What happened to the staff? There were over fifty in the house alone.'

'Suddenly know a lot don't we, love,' he looked out of the window idly. 'Walked out after the old girl croaked.'

'Why?'

'Search me.' We moved on; past a suite of billiards rooms, more empty lounges and closed doors and down a matching staircase to the one up which we'd come.

'You've no idea what it takes to run this place.' Neither had he judging by the state it was in, rife with rubbish and dust, the grounds unkempt.

'I hear the countess managed very well.' Back on the ground floor I headed for that first furnished sitting room. I'd liked that – more personal than the grander halls and staircases. And I liked the view. This time it was Fentiman who followed. 'And the estate itself, the farms?'

'Run themselves; nothin' to do there.'

Odd, so why did other people employ estate managers, land agents and the like?

'Charlie's been sellin' the stuff that doesn't.'

'What?'

Fentiman threw himself into a deep settee, legs wide apart, chin squashed down on his chest, grinning. 'Look, doll, there's no need to worry. You play ball with us and we'll see yer right.'

I grabbed the telephone. 'Does this work?' the dialling tone purred in my ear; my first normal sound in half an hour. 'What's Poulson's number?'

Fentiman supplied it without moving.

A woman confirmed Poulson was in. 'Don't bother transferring me, I'm coming over.'

'How are you goin' to get there, doll? Frank will have gone for his lunch.'

I deduced from the jingling behind me that he was following me to the front door. Keys still in it, the Bentley Sedanca stood where

Channing had left her, pulled up to the entrance like a poster for Beaulieu.

Arms folded, Fentiman lounged against a pillar as I slid into the driving seat. It had been a long time, but it felt good.

'You can't drive that thing, you stupid cow.'

Was that a promotion or demotion from 'doll'?

'Ain't no syncromesh, no power steerin' neither.'

I would strip the leather off my heels but it was a small price to pay for freedom and the sight of Fentiman's face as I gunned the engine, still warm and hence easy to start. Manoeuvring the beauty around, I double declutched through the gears and glided up the drive, faultlessly negotiated the fountain and rolled on through the fields to the gate. Dad had been given a neglected Racing Bentley when I was little, the sort with a strap over the bonnet. On weekends I'd sat for hours watching him painstakingly bring her back to life. Said it kept him sane, especially after Mum died. When I was old enough he'd taught me to drive her. We even did the Brighton Run one year.

Once on the open road I put my foot down and the responding whoom under the bonnet snatched at my heart. I sped along that country lane reborn, wind tugging at my hair, dappled sun licking the bonnet. The artist who'd designed this beast had relished the feel of horseflesh; galloping along the road with smooth and majestic motion the Sedanca's muscles rippled and her flanks shone.

How I wished I still had Dad's racer. After he died, Russell said keeping it would be ridiculous; I could hardly drive it around London and where did I think I was going to keep it? 'Be reasonable,' he'd said, 'if you don't sell it, it'll just sit in a garage somewhere and decline into the wreck it was when your father found it.' Did I want that, he'd asked ... making my wish to hang on to the object of Dad's love and hard work sound either shameful or stupid.

Lost in pleasure I almost missed the turn to Blakesley but I managed to brake in time and proceed at a more sedate pace into the village. Bolstered by this double shot scotch strength of unexpected exhilaration, I marched into Poulson's office. He had his feet on the desk which he did remove – albeit with insolent slowness – but that must have exhausted his energy because he declined to stand.

'Sanderling is a disgrace. It was meant to be kept as the countess dictated.'

'Not possible,' Poulson drawled.

'I want to see the countess's will,' I sat down.

'I'll send it on.'

'Now.'

'I'm really not sure where it is,' he said, relighting his pipe to avoid meeting my gaze.

Whilst he had both hands thus occupied. I moved around to his side of the desk and started opening drawers.

'Hey, you can't do that,' he struggled to his feet.

I straightened. 'We'll see what the Law Society has to say about that. Have you even bothered to file for probate yet? If so, as a beneficiary, I can get it from there.'

He gave in, bent to a lower drawer and tossed a heavy envelope on to the desk. 'Of course I've spoken with them but it'll take years to sort out.'

Which gave his mate Fentiman plenty of time to gut the place.

'And I want to see the inventories – this afternoon.' Inheritance tax had done for many large estates – so why should Sanderling survive the ransacking. What had I expected? A fairy tale?

Chapter 2

With nightbirds chirrupping in the aviary and the sun dipping behind the escarpment draping the west terrace in dusk, the countess breathed in the magnificence. Her heart fluttered at the enormity of it. The estate represented her whole existence, everything she cared about was here, wrapped in its glowing stonework and rolling acres. She had sacrificed all else to preserve the place, devoted her life to its continuation; so Sanderling's worth was beyond reckoning – less would be unthinkable. Yet she had failed to safeguard the one thing she would not be present to oversee – the future.

The last, and most important duty she had to perform was to appoint the next mistress of Sanderling; find the person who would follow in her footsteps, maintain the respect, keep the traditions, look after the estate workers – as she had.

The solution to the current generation's ills lay in the values abandoned since the war. Values Sanderling had so enshrined in its fabric that everyone associated with it prospered. She deplored today's lack of honour; money and power were all that mattered now. What basis was that for the exercise of judgement? What heathen rules were those to live by? She'd spent the last fifty years, stemming the tide of man's decline. And at Sanderling she'd succeeded. Sanderling must continue as it was, else what had it all been for?

Sighing, the countess lowered herself slowly on to the seat. A tortoiseshell shadow snuggled its furry substance around her legs, dug its head into her foot, warming her. Absent-mindedly she tugged its tail. 'What are we going to do, eh, Hildegard? Can't you whisker up an answer for us?'

Ninety this year – without an heir. She should have tackled this before. But making a will was an admission of mortality, though in all conscience, even she must allow that the time had come. The problem was no less intractable now than when she'd preferred to ignore it. Of course, she could keep on doing that and eventually it would cease to be her concern. But abdication was the antithesis of everything she believed in.

The National Trust had been her first thought. 'Would you install someone here permanently ... a family?' she'd asked the woman who came to see her.

'Oh, no. Not somewhere as grand as this. We'd need a caretaker, of course.'

'As in a museum, you mean?'

The countess had conducted the woman into the ballroom overlooking the south terrace. Sullivan followed to throw back the drapes, padding across the curved parquet in his morning coat just as had the gentlemen in tails, palms extended in invitation. The orchestra perched on the dais to her right and the strains of the foxtrot drifted out into the night while the dancers in patent pumps and sweeping silks, glided across the boards, spilling into the garden.

Of course the National Trust couldn't be expected to keep up her way of life. How could they? Sanderling wouldn't be a home any more. No one's existence would be bound up in it, tied to it as she was, by umbilical cord. The countess had waited for Sullivan to escort the woman from the room before waltzing slowly over the floor, arms outstretched to her imaginary partner.

So what was the answer? Weren't there people who could trace families back for generations, find a distant relation? She must talk to her solicitor about it. Poulson would know what to do.

The countess hid her initial shock when Poulson brought the detective to Sanderling. Plain, unremarkable ... unnoticeable even. About five feet five inches tall with mousy hair cut short with a fringe, a pleasant but by no means pretty face – flat bone structure, thin mouth with a dash of pink lipstick and a kink in her nose suggestive of a break at some time. She wore a navy-blue two-piece of doubtful origin, a white blouse and no jewellery; the sort of woman one might chat to in a waiting room.

Carefully formal even after all these years, Poulson made the countess a little bow. 'Lady Foxhill, may I present Miss Jean Edwards. Miss Edwards is a private investigator. She has spent many years working undercover for the police.'

'And what have you learned?'

The woman pulled a file from a nondescript holdall. 'I've been through the usual sources plus catalogues in the British Library and the Public Records Office, the manuscript depositories and the records here to which you allowed access,' she paused. 'And I've come up with a possibility.' She rose and handed the countess a half sheet of paper.

The countess glanced at it and froze. She peered at Mr Poulson and back to the paper. 'You are seriously telling me that ... this person,' she tapped the paper, 'is my relative?'

'Yes.'

The countess's limbs went limp. Only decades of practice saved her from the ignominy of fainting.

'I didn't think you'd want ...' the detective faltered, 'so I haven't gone through the details.'

'Well, that's that then,' the countess whispered.

'I'll make a start on the will next week, shall I?' Poulson had relaxed.

'You'll do no such thing, Mr Poulson. I meant the trail has run cold – isn't that the expression you people use? It means I have to find another way.' As Poulson spluttered, the countess turned to the detective. 'Do you have notes?'

'Only these,' Jean Edwards held out the file.

The countess took it and threw it wholesale on to the fire, employing the poker to ensure every page was consumed.

Three weeks later, Sullivan showed the detective into the drawing room. 'I have asked you to return because I have another task for you,' the countess said. 'I want you to find someone for me.'

Jean Edwards perched on the edge of her seat looking uncomfortable, whether with her surroundings or the statement was hard to tell. 'But I thought—' she glanced at the long since cleared fireplace.

'I've decided that reliance on an heir, even a known quantity, is a lottery – at best a game of hazard, often with unhappy consequences. You have only to review the fate of so many aristocratic families to see that.' The countess glanced at Edwards who remained silent; that's what attracted her to the woman. Observant without being nosy, intelligent but with plenty of common sense, by all accounts. Best of all, she oozed integrity. Which was crucial. A lot was going to depend on this woman's judgement and determination.

The countess rose, motioning the well-mannered Edwards to stay where she was. 'My parents died in 1941 and I have run this estate ever since. It is self-sustaining, makes a good profit – and, I'm proud to claim, is well managed.' She turned to Edwards. 'Even in your field I'm sure you understand how difficult that has been in these changing decades. The juggernaut of today's so-called progress has reached such a pace that children grow up believing they have a right to untold riches for little or no effort, and will commit all manner of dishonourable deeds to that end. Allegiance has moved wholesale from what is right to what is expedient. Those who would ordinarily have behaved decently are left wondering where goodness gets them in a world of grab-as-grab-can, and our existence is devolving into bestiality.'

She stood with her back to the room, surveying the parkland. 'Do not misinterpret me, Miss Edwards. At the risk of lecturing you for hours on the subject of equality, I do not believe I am better or worse than my fellow men. All I know is I have been given a job to do and I do it to the best of my ability. I simply expect the same of others. We have all been allotted our place and, within moral boundaries, must make what we can of it.'

She turned back. 'The estate has managed to resist this decline. Sanderling stands as a bulwark against such disaster – an example of how things can be. Our family motto supports our aim – virtue alone really is the true nobility, Miss Edwards, otherwise, luxury corrupts.'

'What do you want me to do?'

The countess crossed to her bureau, opened it with a key

suspended from her belt and extracted a closely written page of foolscap. 'I have drafted a list of criteria. It consists mainly of the qualities required to run Sanderling as it has been run.' She handed the sheet to Edwards. 'I want you to find me the person who fits that description.'

Jean Edwards read through the list with neither sound nor expression. When she had finished she raised her eyes. 'I will need to understand what's behind each of these stipulations.' She glanced down. 'For instance: "*Women*'s size and approximately five feet eight inches tall. Preferably of dark colouring"?'

'The same as me. Yes, I can see why you might be puzzled.' The countess sat down as the tea arrived. When the maid had left she continued. 'It's best to inherit a few clothes; otherwise you look just too nouveau.' She could see this was a new concept for Edwards. 'And it's important that the new chatelaine adopt the lifestyle of the 1930s. To maintain a tradition she will have to play a part, one to which she wasn't born. Have you ever indulged in amateur dramatics, Miss Edwards? I imagine in your job, disguise is an everyday necessity?' Edwards nodded. 'Then you'll understand that infiltrating the character, moving the right way, thinking along certain lines ... becomes much easier once you don the costume.'

'You're ruling out the possibility of a male candidate, then?'

'For centuries, succession in the Foxhill family has been through the female line. Since I now have a choice, I see no reason to change that.' The inscrutable Edwards betrayed no opinion. 'I suggest you come to stay for a few days so you can familiarize yourself with our regime; see at first hand what uncommon sort of person it's going to take.'

'I've left it too late haven't I, Bertie?'

'You could've made your mind up earlier, trained 'em up yourself.' Lord Danhanbury wacked vehemently at the undergrowth with his walking cane.

They were sitting side by side on Bertie's bench, overlooking the lake which separated their two estates. 'We're headed for a recession. If for no other reason, it's been too good for too long. What used we to call it, the *law of averages*? People seem to have forgotten that, haven't they?' the countess mused.

'Gone the way of *moderation in all things*. Dashed unfashionable nowadays. We need to restore the old code.' Two years her junior, the right honourable Lord Danhanbury, otherwise known as Sir Bertram Fanshawe-Parker, had been the countess's dearest friend for most of her life. In yellow cords, an old tweed jacket, check shirt and woollen tie he affected the uniform of the modern country gentleman. Never married, Eton and the Royal Navy had absented him for many years in her youth, but he'd always been there when she needed him.

'If I don't find the right woman to take over, Sanderling will be crippled. All that I've worked to preserve will be thrown away.'

'Put like that, I'm glad I shan't be here.'

'Oh but you must be, Bertie. I'm relying on you.' She clasped his hand, squeezed it, let go. 'Who else is going to keep an eye on things for me, help my successor?' The countess's cat rubbed around both sets of legs. 'Besides, Hildegard will need you.'

She pulled a silk handkerchief from her sleeve and fanned her face with it. 'There's so much still needs doing. The restoration programme is only half way through and I fear I won't be here to see it finished. The plumbing and heating systems need replacing and while they tell me the wiring has a few more years of life, the dislocation involved is so great we should do them all together. Apparently we need a new fire precaution system too which will entail lifting every floor and covering every wall with fire retardant paper. We've started on the packing....' She shrugged, 'I feel as though I'm packing for a journey. Still, I can hardly object to that if it prevents what happened to the original Sanderling; razed to the ground so grandfather said.'

'Sounds rather like Sleeping Beauty to me, being stored away ready to be reawakened,' said Bertie, wistfully. 'Do you have to do all this now? Why not just enjoy—'

She placed her hand over his. 'Dear Bertie, I shan't be here much longer and since there may be a hiatus before someone takes over, that's precisely why it is important I pack things up. My jewellery is going too.' She turned to face him. 'But I must find the right person;

not only someone who can manage the place but someone who shares my convictions.'

'You don't think that's a rather tall order?'

The countess studied him sideways, for rather longer than was customary. 'What else can I do? Have them sell the estate when I'm gone? After all I've sacrificed, let it fall into the hands of a pop star ... or a developer?'

Bertie blanched. 'Just supposing this crazy idea of yours works, what will happen then? You're advocating inheritance by the fittest?'

'And why not? Plato thought it was a good idea, designed a whole society around it.' She didn't want to be challenged, she had no choice.

'I remember. Where only the old soldiers were allowed to mate with the young maidens, marrying prowess and experience with physical perfection....' Bertie gazed at his feet, tapped the cane thoughtfully against his toe. 'Don't you think someone as strong-willed as you describe might want to do things their way? What if the new Lady Isabel Foxhill departs from her script?'

'She won't.'

Chapter 3

After dinner one evening, the countess and Jean were sitting on the terrace with Hildegard keeping her distance. 'Now I've visited a tiny part of your estate, seen how you work, I think I've a grasp of the considerable managerial skills required ... and I appreciate that Sanderling is unique; but don't you think our changed times might dictate a more empowering approach?'

The countess turned in her seat to look directly at Jean. 'Miss Edwards, if Sanderling were run on different lines, I could afford to employ only half the work force.'

Jean would have to let that go for the present though she feared deep down that only the countess could carry off such a regime. Once she'd gone.... She moved on. 'You stipulate an age of 35. Is there any particular reason for being so precise?'

'I'd have thought precision would make your job easier. Either she's 35 ... or she's not.'

Did the countess have in mind an actual person? Jean felt like the prince in the fairy tale, though armed with significantly more than a glass slipper. The trouble was, at least the person he sought had existed; Jean enjoyed no such assurance. 'Forgive me, Lady Foxhill, but I wonder if you're looking for someone in particular whose details you know but maybe not their whereabouts. If that's so, it would be an awful lot easier if you just—'

The countess rose. Hildegard raced to her side. Jean could have sworn the cat glared at her. But instead of the acerbic reply she expected, the countess answered softly: 'If only there were, Miss Edwards. If only there were.'

'You also say the person should preferably not be a member of the aristocracy,' Jean paused. 'Wouldn't someone used to this sort of life find it easier to make the transition? An ordinary person might feel overwhelmed by the trappings before they'd even started.' A glance at the countess's drawn face told Jean the criteria were not to be challenged; that she was pulling the cat's tail too hard.

'Miss Edwards, when you've met as many of them as I have, you'll realize that as a bunch the aristocracy are indolent, flighty and corrupt. Hence W.H. Auden's opinion of the 1930s as "*this low, dishonest, decade*". He was referring to a licentious ruling class where everything was covered up and hypocrisy ran riot. Sadly, today's openness has served only to expose those transgressions, not improve them. So, as a class I consider them unsuitable.'

Jean nodded, mentally red-pencilling the nation's notables. 'And single, no children? You don't want her to have any help, someone to lean on when things get difficult – which they're bound to at first? What happens if she wants to marry later on? Are you relegating her to a life of chastity?' Jean was looking forward. Assuming she could find her, how would she ever persuade this paragon to abide by the terms?

'Of course not; what she does later will be her affair. But if she has children or a husband when you find her, then she won't be free to make her own commitment ... whatever she may say to you.' The countess sat down again. 'You do understand that no one must know of this task I've set you. That's why I've not told Poulson any detail. He's very old and not too well at present and I don't trust that son of his. There must be no competition for this role; no chance that someone might hear of the criteria and adjust their credentials to suit ... or cheat their way into it in any way.'

Jean nodded. She scanned the final cryptic sentence on the sheet. 'The one which really puzzles me is this last one.'

'Don't you like mysteries, Miss Edwards? That's why I've hired a detective,' the countess bent to caress the cat, 'isn't it Hildegard.' She went on almost dreamily: 'It's what in modern parlance you might call a tie-breaker. The one clue that if you're backed against the barn door by a bull, will guide you in the right direction. It may be something, it may be nothing. Don't let it concern you overmuch.'

*

The idea may be eccentric, but when Jean considered some of the idiots who inherited fortunes earned over centuries and blew them in one spin of the wheel at Monte Carlo, the countess's method sounded amazingly sensible. And banning any form of competition – no advertising, no interviews – avoided the possibility of misrepresentation. Though it placed great trust in Jean's honesty.

By picking someone whose characteristics fitted the Sanderling ethos and leaving them to it, the countess, either by design or circumstance, may just have hit on the approach most likely to result in her wishes being met. And found a way to govern from beyond the grave.

It took Jean twelve months to arrive at thirty names – by which time every candidate was now one year older. For the first time since being engaged by the countess, Jean telephoned to Sanderling. 'We have a shortlist but now they're all thirty-six. Do you want me to start again?'

'That will be satisfactory,' came the faint reply.

Relieved, Jean's teams constructed a picture of the candidates' backgrounds, affiliations and beliefs. Anything which might indicate the women's suitability ... or otherwise. Thus the list was narrowed down to seven of the most capable women Jean had ever come across.

Nearing the end, two candidates stood out; their dossiers were feet thick and Jean's staff had been working on them for months. Jean travelled to Sanderling to consult the countess. 'I've brought the results so far for you to look at Lady Foxhill; detailed information on the two women whom we deem the best fit.' She handed the countess two heavy manila folders.

The countess sat with the files in her lap, hands folded on top of them, gazing into the fire. The clock ticked on the mantelpiece, noisy accompaniment to the machinations going on in the old lady's head. Just when Jean was wondering if she'd nodded off, the countess rose, hugging the information Jean had given her. 'It is late, Miss Edwards, please leave these with me until the morning.' On her way out of the room she turned, brow furrowed. 'You will make sure, won't you?'

Having lain awake for several hours, keeping vigil with the countess in spirit at least, Jean overslept. She awoke to find a tray beside the bed and a maid tugging at the curtains – with difficulty – one hand rubbing her eyes. Jean hauled herself to a sitting position. 'What's the matter?'

Force of habit wrenched a curtsey from the girl. 'Beggin' your pardon, Ma'am, only ...' Jean waited. 'It's the countess, Ma'am,' the tear-riven face searched Jean's in anguish. 'She'm proper poorly, Ma'am.'

Jean sped along the labyrinth of corridors following the girl's directions. Arriving at the suite she tapped and stepped into a high-ceilinged sitting-room decorated in the Regency fashion – burgundy striped wallpaper, French furniture, a magnificent view of the lake – now hastily converted into a nursing station. Two uniformed women whispering over a chart barely registered her presence. An elderly man dragged himself through from the main bedroom carrying a briefcase; Mr Poulson, the countess's solicitor.

Rheumy eyes took a second to focus on Jean. 'Ah, Miss Edwards, Lady Foxhill is asking for you.'

A doctor, equally ancient, followed him out of the bedchamber. 'Had some sort of a seizure,' he said, in answer to Jean's raised eyebrow. 'Don't tire her.'

Jean's feet sank into the Aubusson as she approached. Perched on a raised platform the countess was dwarfed by voluminous bed hangings which mirrored the window swags. Jean's two folders lay open on a bedside table and a familiar bundle of tortoiseshell fur stretched prone against the countess's legs. The old lady beckoned to Jean before collapsing against the pillow. Jean shouted for the nurses. Her hand still on the cat's head, the countess opened her eyes and whispered, 'St Hildegard's.'

Jean backed away as the nurses leaned across the bed in concern. Unnoticed she retrieved the folders, stuffed in the scattered papers and retreated.

Chapter 4

'*You will make sure, won't you?*' What about? That Jean found the right woman to fit the criteria, the right woman for Sanderling? Or that whoever was chosen would indeed inherit the estate? Did the countess fear someone might try to prevent it?

She must see Mr Poulson. Did the search end here – perhaps with the countess dying intestate? No one had expected her to go so suddenly. Had Jean unwittingly hastened the day by bringing the dossiers?

The papery skin on Mr Poulson's face was even more pallid than when Jean had last seen him. Manfully he struggled out of his old leather chair, which creaked in sympathy, although by the twinges in his face his chivalry cost him dear. In response to Jean's question he said: 'Lady Foxhill telephoned me around midnight, told me to come over first thing. You don't ... didn't, argue with the countess, as I'm sure you've discovered. I wouldn't have gone if I'd realized how ill she was, but she insisted on seeing me.'

'Did she ask you to alter anything?'

'No. She just wanted to update me on what she'd asked you to do; so I'd not let her wishes be undermined,' he peered at Jean. 'I knew she was conducting a somewhat unorthodox search for an heir when I drew up the will, but I was unaware just how unorthodox ... and of course I assumed that when a person fitting the exact requirements couldn't be found, she'd amend her will. Now of course, the final decision rests with you,' he winced, whether through pain or apprehension, Jean couldn't tell. 'I don't like it, Miss Edwards, it's most irregular.'

'So what exactly does the will say?'

'I suppose it's alright to tell you, since, as executor, it's my duty to ensure you do your job.' He extracted a large envelope from the bottom drawer of his desk and tipped out a sheaf of long legal papers. 'You'll understand that this is a condensed version; the estate papers to which it refers fill a whole room at Sanderling. To answer your question simply, it says I have to wait. I must suspend all action save that of the maintenance of the staff and functions of the estate as is, until you find the person you have been instructed to find. Give or take some relatively minor bequests, that person will inherit Sanderling and all that appertains thereto.'

Jean sat back, hands and arms hanging limp over the chair arms. She'd never really thought the countess would do it. 'Phew.'

Mr Poulson allowed himself a grimace. 'My sentiments entirely, Miss Edwards.'

'Can the will be challenged?'

Mr Poulson steepled his fingers, considered for a moment. 'I think it unlikely. Particularly since the countess hired you to find her next of kin two years ago and promptly rejected that person. Had that not happened then it would have been possible.

'So what if I can't find this person?'

'The way the will is worded, we have to keep on until we do. It's not if, it's when. So for the sake of the estate and its future, the fundamental reason for the countess's scheme, I hope you produce this "heir" sooner rather than later, Miss Edwards. Estates without a helmsman soon run into the shallows, if you'll excuse the yachting metaphor.'

'You think I should hurry up.'

'Don't you?'

Chancing to be in the area three weeks later, Jean called into Poulson's office. The receptionist showed her through.

'The old boy died last week. I'm Charles Poulson, you'll have to deal with me now.' Fat, florid faced and puffing incessantly at his pipe, Poulson Junior made no attempt to stand as Jean entered.

'As Lady Foxhill's executor in my father's stead, I've appointed a management company to look after the estate.'

That was sensible, you couldn't leave a place like Sanderling to run itself. Jean imagined Poulson Junior was looking for the quickest and easiest way to shift the responsibility of Sanderling off his desk. 'I'll carry on with my search then and let you know when I've found her.'

'Not so fast. What's happening about the Frobisher girl? She looks the best bet to me.'

How did he know about her? From his father via the countess presumably. It would have been just like the countess to double check, ask Poulson Senior to look into the two women ... as well as Jean. 'Really, what makes you say that?'

'It's obvious, woman, we need spend no more time on the subject.'

'You reckon she fits the criteria then?'

He leaned back again, replaced the pipe. 'Ah, yes, the criteria. What did you say they were?'

'I didn't.'

He smiled; a grin of gamesmanship. 'Look, my dear, whether you like it or not, I call the shots now. So whatever my father knew—'

'He didn't.'

The blue fug of pipe smoke turned to freezing fog as the spoilt child levered his weight out of his father's old seat and wobbled around the desk. He stood looking down on Jean, gesticulating at her with his pipe stem; tempting her to tip him on his broad posterior with one well-practised move. 'I'm warning you. Don't come the privileged information bit with me. What are the criteria?'

'I am not at liberty to tell you ... and I don't like being threatened, Mr Poulson.' She stood, forcing him to back away. 'I have been charged with a duty which I intend to carry out. I suggest you do the same.'

Chapter 5

Poulson Junior's clumsy attempt at promoting Natalie Frobisher ruled her out in Jean's mind. It certainly appeared he'd sounded her out – probably come to some arrangement with her. Besides, whilst on paper she more or less fitted the criteria she'd never been Jean's favourite – too grasping.

That left Synnove McKenna. In her earlier investigations, Jean had traced the woman's career through a succession of blue chip companies to the launch of her own sales outsourcing firm, McKenna Associates, in 2000. Exploiting the boom in flexibility – where companies hire in expertise only as required, allowing them to expand or contract with the market through avoiding fixed assets and permanent staff – McKenna's had prospered. And whilst the ephemeral foundation of Synnove's clients contrasted with the overstaffed, traditional and stable life at Sanderling – the success of McKenna Associates proved she could run a business.

In case she'd missed something, Jean quizzed Sharon, the field operative who'd done the original fact-find. 'Tell me about her background again. She came from Essex?' Jean sat down.

'Not exactly. Squadron Leader McKenna followed his own father into the air force. His father was killed in the war, but McKenna Junior died of a heart attack six years ago. So she was moved around a fair bit as a kid.'

Sharon perched her bottom on the corner of her desk and flipped the pages of a looseleaf notebook. 'Her mother died of cancer when Synnove was seventeen. From all accounts, Mrs McKenna was a socialite – enjoyed the costume balls, the tennis, the golf and the tea dances you used to get on air bases.' Jean pictured a lonely little girl shunted from place to place with a father frequently absent and a mother more interested in her own pursuits.

'Grandparents?'

'None left. The McKennas were from Perth; moved to England looking for work, I imagine. I can draw you a big tree of them all if you like?' Jean shook her head. 'Synnove McKenna seems to have had little to do with them. Her mother's side is sketchy but nothing very interesting. Came from Cumberland. No wonder she hankered after the bright lights.'

From the moment she'd learned of Synnove McKenna's profession, Jean had been concerned. Visions of a gung-ho personality turning Sanderling into a theme park with Kiss-me-Quick hats, pony rides and a gift shop, kept her awake at night. But closer delving into McKenna Associates had revealed an altogether different perspective. Far from her preconception of foot in the door, blarney-fuelled purveying of non-necessities, the selling in which MA indulged was strategic rather than opportunistic – consisted of discovering what was required and meeting that need. Much as Jean was struggling to do for the countess.

Jean had to find someone who sat between the extremes of entrepreneurship – the cold calculator who would see Sanderling only as a business and the unworldly, who'd be too soft to run it. She was looking for steel – in the proverbial mink muff.

Sharon swung her legs to the floor, stood up with a sigh.'We could keep up the surveillance for a few more weeks but I honestly don't think we'd learn much more. Other than the odd row, and who doesn't ... there's not much to tell. Boring life if you ask me. You should see that flat though; talk about stark. Nothing on the walls except acres of white paint – like something out of *Doctor Zhivago*.' Her choice ... or his? Or simply the product of too little time spent on domestic niceties.

Sharon went on: 'She's usually home by nine; often her boyfriend's still in the City and goes on to a club. Sometimes goes home with other women.'

'Do you think Synnove knows?'

'Could be what the rows are about. Anyway, she's not exactly a saint. We've seen her having dinner with some very tasty men in some very nice places.' Sharon paused, grinned. 'But she doesn't stay out all night, likes her beauty sleep.' Sharon consulted her watch. 'Talking of which....'

Jean locked the doors and sat in her office with the light off, feet up on the desk, thinking. Russell Prince, Synnove's partner, was a charmer with an inflated ego. Educated at a minor public school, he had risen on the upcurrent of City fund managing. Along with some savvy pals he'd formed a hedge fund business before branching out on his own. Since his partners had been academic introverts with doctorates in mathematics and workaholic lifestyles, Jean put the rift down to a personality clash. In a buoyant market, Prince had continued to flourish; personally investing in the obligatory block of flats, his Ferrari, a Jeep and currently ... flying lessons. And he'd put up half the money to establish McKenna Associates.

His philandering and Synnove's other admirers should have cheered Jean. Maybe they had one of these open relationships she'd never understood. Or, after five years, had their involvement run its course, burnt itself out? Wasn't that goodness for Sanderling, no ties?

Intuition had saved Jean's skin more than once and the better acquainted she became with Synnove McKenna, the more worried she grew. What had drawn Synnove to this man? An error of judgement? A weakness for chancers? What hold did he have over her? The business presumably. The Sanderling inheritance would solve that.

Bereft of the countess and the sage advice of Poulson Senior, Jean felt the weight of decision keenly. 'You've done all you could humanly do', she told herself. 'There are no clanking skeletons in understairs cupboards; nothing nasty behind the arras. The woman was born for the role.'

Chapter 6

'I've found someone who fits the countess's criteria. All that remains is for you to invite her to Sanderling.' Jean made it sound as effortless as possible.

'Damn fool nonsense. Bloody woman, I've never heard anything so ridiculous,' Charles Poulson leaned forward, coughing out stained air like a steam train. 'And I'm not at all sure it's legal.'

'Your father had no such qualms.'

'Well he's not here now, is he.'

'You only have to write a letter,' she allowed the edge in her voice. Over two years had passed since the countess's death, and while every minute had been well used by Jean, still she felt guilty. Sanderling shouldn't be left unattended. Poulson had not once chased her, never inquired as to her progress or chivvied her in any way. At the time she'd been grateful; now his disinterest struck her as ominous.

'Write to Synnove McKenna, invite her to Sanderling and explain the countess's will.'

'You could have failed to find anyone,' he muttered. 'Or picked someone you knew would last five minutes – like that Frobisher woman.'

'What makes you think I haven't? We all have our commitments to fulfil, Charles. I am obliged to carry out my part in it. Admittedly it's taken me a while – sorry for that,' she grinned again.

He stared at her for longer than normal. 'All right, all right. I'll write.'

*

Two weeks later, Jean phoned again. 'When's she coming up to Blakesley?' she asked Poulson's secretary.

'She's not.' The secretary spoke as if Synnove had declined an invitation to attend the harvest supper. Jean waited, confused. 'After Mr Poulson wrote, I rang to inquire as always. She said she hadn't time to come and would speak to him on the phone. She asked what it was about but I didn't know. When I told him, Mr Poulson shrugged and said that was that, then.'

'Put me through to him.'

After a few clicks Poulson came on the line. 'Why haven't you informed Synnove McKenna about her legacy yet?' She heard the pipe go into the ashtray.

'Not that I have to explain to you, but she doesn't want to know.'

'That's because you haven't told her what it's about.' What the hell was Poulson's game? He couldn't possibly inherit himself.

'For your information, I have told her. She thinks it's a stunt ... and I agree.'

'Ha, it matters not whether you agree, you have been solemnly charged with carrying out a task. What are you playing at?'

'I've told you before, your work is done ... and you've been paid. What happens from here on is none of your concern.' He hung up.

You will make sure, won't you. Jean suspected that she, and only she, stood between Poulson and his determination to ignore the countess's wishes. Whatever his goal, Jean must move fast – before he sold the place in its entirety, put in a developer or committed some other irreversible felony.

Exploiting her old police credentials, Jean Edwards wangled an appointment with Synnove at her offices that evening.

For a woman's, the room was remarkably impersonal: pale green velvet pile carpet, an antique desk and chair and a stunning walnut break-front cabinet in one corner, its perfection marred by overflowing piles of books stuffed in at all angles. The impression was far from sterile, but the room could just as easily have belonged to a man – with clues to his background, family and hobbies equally absent. Had Synnove adopted male ways in order to succeed in their world? Was she secretive … or just businesslike? Did she not have much of a private life?

Jean took the proffered seat by a low table, Synnove the settee opposite. She certainly fitted the countess's sketchy description in terms of height, size and colouring with the added advantage of being arrestingly attractive. Chisel-jawed, she had dark eyes and prominent cheekbones; ear-length curly hair framed her face. Not unlike the countess in those pre-war photographs … or the young Jessica Mitford. Immaculate in heels, navy-blue pencil skirt and silk shirt, a suit jacket adorned the back of the leather armchair behind her desk. She sat on the sofa, swinging one foot, waiting; the expression on her face curious but relaxed.

'I'm sure everyone asks, but where did the name Synnove come from?'

Synnove laughed. Not unapproachable then. 'My mother's idea. Always thought she'd been born too late; would have preferred her heyday in the 1920s and 30s.' She shifted in her seat. 'Now, what can I do for you?'

'My name's Edwards. I'm sorry to barge in on you like this. I confess I'm no longer a police officer but a private detective … with an offer to make.'

'Go on,' Synnove replied, warily.

Jean opened her bag and brought out a fresh copy of the countess's criteria. She laid it on the coffee table in front of Synnove who picked it up and began reading.

Jean wandered over to the window and stood with her back to the room thinking of that aristocratic old lady, wondering if she was watching.

'This is ridiculous,' Synnove glowered at Jean. 'What sort of stupid joke is this?'

'Charles Poulson, Poulson and Sons, solicitors – didn't he explain?'

Synnove frowned. 'The man who wrote asking me to get in touch? No. I'd no idea what he wanted and I haven't had time….' So Poulson had lied. Synnove tapped the sheet in front of her. 'This is me, isn't it?'

'I think so, yes.' Jean sat down again. 'I was handed that list and asked to find a woman who fits the criteria and who was thirty-five years old when I started. So you can see how long it's taken, over two years.'

'What? Any woman, or a specific one? Why me? I've never heard of this place,' she glanced down, 'this Sanderling.' Synnove leaned back, her mouth forming various shapes in readiness but no sound emerging. Eventually her brow lightened. 'This is one of those crazy TV things, isn't it?' she whirled, as if seeking hidden cameras and grinning presenters. The walls stared stoically back. She bit her lip. 'I have to say you had me fooled for a minute there. Intriguing proposition, isn't it?'

'I'm glad you think so. How soon can you go?'

'You're serious.' Her eyes widened.

'The solicitor is the Countess of Hampden's executor – rather, his father was, but sadly he's no longer with us. Poulson Junior has been a little less than assiduous in his handling of the countess's stipulation ... otherwise he would have come to explain to you in person. Out of respect for the countess, I felt compelled to fulfill the mission on his behalf.' Jean now extracted a bound volume from her bag and handed it to Synnove. 'I've had the main facts collated for you to digest – about Sanderling Manor, the estate, how the countess ran it ... and what she wants you to do. A sort of "Is This Your Life?"'

Chapter 7

With the exception of one establishment tucked between Covent Garden and The Strand, whose banquettes were as well stuffed as the quail on its menu and whose clients crossed oceans for its steamed steak and kidney, I'd grown blasé about fine restaurants.

Hollowed out after my extraordinary day, I leaned back against the cushions. Since the trip to Warwickshire and particularly since mid afternoon, when I'd read the will for myself and finally accepted its veracity, I had existed in a daze. Thin smoke whirled around me, dividing me from other people, isolating me. One minute I couldn't contain my excitement, the next, when I thought of Russell, I admitted doubts. Hence the meal at our favourite place – to put him in a receptive mood.

'Do they want you to sell their cars for them, then?' Russell asked, yawning.

'Which bit didn't you hear?' I made no attempt to hide the sigh, these days Russell always had something more important on his mind. 'I've been chosen to take over the Sanderling Estate. All of it; to run it.'

'McKenna Associates outsource sales campaigns; you're not estate managers,' he swirled his brandy around the bowl of his glass. 'Though, I guess there's no reason why you shouldn't pretend to be – if there's enough money in it.'

'This has nothing to do with McKenna Associates; it's me they want.'

'Sounds barmy to me. How long for?'

I fished my bag out from under the table, extracted the will and gave it to him. Draining what was left of the Fleurie into my glass, I kept quiet while he scanned the first page. 'Try page three,' I flipped forward for him, afraid he'd give up if the gist weren't immediately apparent.

'You mean you've inherited this lot?' finally Russell's tone took on the incredulity I'd waited an hour for.

'No, I just made it up to get your attention.'

He glanced at me, then back at the document. 'What do you reckon it's worth?' The pages flew backwards and forwards now.

'Can we go?' A crowded restaurant was not the place for this discussion. I'd chosen to break the news over dinner because I was bursting to tell him and because I wanted us to enjoy it together. Be thrilled. Instead, he'd paid scant attention to anything I'd said all evening and had awoken only at the mention of money.

Fresh from the bustling restaurant our apartment felt cold and empty in comparison with the lavishness of the sitting room at Sanderling. I closed the blinds; succeeding only in shutting out the blackness. Now all we were left with was white. Russell found decoration distracting. Wasn't that the point?

He brewed the coffee – because I wasn't trusted to do it right – and brought it into the lounge. We sat facing one another on cream settees. Shoeless, I propped my legs on the coffee table.

'I can't turn down something like this, can I?'

'Take a while to sell I daresay, especially with the property market as it is. We're only one blink from a loss of confidence and when that happens ...' he made a downward arc with his thumb and blew a raspberry. 'We'll have to break it up into lots; get more for it that way.'

'We could make Sanderling our base. Lots of people do that now. They keep a flat in London for when they have to be here, but otherwise opt to work from the country.' Even those who had grown up in the city, like Russell. His father had made a pile in property rental and Russell had been brought up in one of the wealthier suburbs, learning to measure worth by the length of someone's swimming pool or the height of their gates.

'I could set up some sort of balancing wager. Get people to bet on what they think it'll fetch ...' he leaned forward. 'Or come the last I could sell shares in it and then sell the company.' Russell blew on his coffee. 'I need to think about it.'

'It's truly beautiful; the most magnificent place I've ever seen. Like something out of a story.' I put my feet back on the floor; so intoxicated with Sanderling I wanted to return right away. 'It's no good me describing it, you'll have to come and see. How about tomorrow?'

'Whatever for?'

I stared at him. What an idiot I'd been not taking a camera with me. But then I'd suspected a scam, so recording my own gullibility hadn't crossed my mind. 'Because I can't expect you to comprehend what I'm talking about unless you see it. I didn't.'

'Aren't you getting a little carried away here?' he sipped his coffee.

Maybe I was ... wanted to be. But I'd have liked him to share my euphoria if only for an hour or two. I sat up straight. 'You said the idea of companies outsourcing their sales function was absurd – that McKenna Associates would bomb,' I remembered now, 'told me you'd taken out some kind of counter investment to make sure you didn't lose money.'

I'd been devastated when he'd told me that. Having assumed he loved me, had faith enough in me to invest in my idea – I'd discovered his so-called support was just another one of his complex shell shuffling manoeuvres where money was tossed around like a game of pass the parcel – or in his case, several games working the room in different directions. So far the firm had been very successful; so the dividends he was earning, and I'd like to think, consideration for me, had stopped him from withdrawing his stake.

'What's your point?'

'That you were wrong,' I turned away, reluctant to start a row at this time of night. 'That things aren't always about money.'

'Oh for heaven's sake ... what I do isn't about money. It's about winning, about playing; being ten strides ahead of the next punter.'

Hence the chrome and glass minimalism of this room; built-in cupboards for hiding away your personality. I liked things tidy but I liked the richness of life too ... whereas Russell boiled everything down to a scoreboard. At first I thought it was his way of concealing his feelings. I understood about that. Then one day, prompted by what – I can't remember – I wondered if he hedged his bets with me too.

Were there other partners scattered across London … just in case? I had pooh-poohed the idea, buried it. That sort of suspicion destroys trust, breaks up relationships for no reason other than the need for constant reassurance. Well, at thirty-seven I didn't relish dining alone, going to parties wearing the label: 'Career Woman – single – what a surprise', or behaving like an undignified 20-year-old playing the field.

I picked up my coffee, walked in stockinged feet around the end of the smoked glass coffee table and sat beside him on the other sofa. 'I know emotion doesn't come into it when you're buying and selling things, Russell but – well – I'm so overwhelmed by this Sanderling thing … I need to touch it some more.' I laid my hand on his arm. 'Couldn't we live there just for a while, see how we feel about it?'

'Don't be so bloody stupid,' he shook me off and rose, paced the floor by the window. 'Someone's having a good old game with you, aren't they. Old flame is it?' He turned to face her. 'I've got a lot on my plate at the moment, Syn. The markets are turning; probably in for a dive.'

'Isn't that good news for you; means you can buy back the shares you borrowed at a much lower price than you sold them for?'

'That depends what else I've banked on.'

'You could work just as easily at Sanderling. It's very quiet there.'

'Look, I can't begin to know what this nonsense is all about but the sooner you stop reverting to the little girl who thinks she's been cast as Cinderella, the better. It makes you look ridiculous. Huh, I can't believe you'd fall for something so pathetic.'

The words bit. There was no history of someone inheriting by criteria so the phenomenon didn't compute with Russell. If it didn't feature in one of his mathematical models then, incapable of thinking for himself, he automatically dismissed it. Uncertainty held no place in Russell's world. 'I know it sounds far-fetched, I thought so too. I was convinced it was a prank.'

I stood up, had to make him see. 'But it's not. I can show you the list of criteria they used, and I've met the private detective whose firm has spent over two years whittling down the possibilities to arrive at me.' I sipped the bitter expresso. 'You've seen the will ... if you'd only come with me to the property you'd understand how I feel.'

'So why pick you to inherit it then? Of all the fifty odd million suckers in Britain, why you? Because you fit some ludicrous criteria? Give me strength.' He marched to one of his obscured cupboards and poured himself a brandy.

I couldn't answer that.

He sat down with his drink. 'The more I think about it, the more it sounds like one of these scams that come through the post or they ring up about. "Congratulations! You have won umpty ump million pounds. All you have to do to claim your prize is to pay us half that amount for finding you...." '

'And if you're right, as long as we don't pay them any money what have we to lose?'

'Dignity? Reputation? Time? Take your pick. And don't bring me into this. You want to make a fool of yourself, you go ahead.' He leaned forward. 'Matter of fact it sounds like a good idea to me. You go on down to the country and neglect McKenna Associates – the company I have tirelessly supported you in. Suits me; I'll sell my shares tomorrow.'

'Is that what this is about? Are you short of money, Russell?'

'I've decided to go to Africa.'

Where had that come from? 'Oh good. You won't mind if I'm not in London, then.'

'You can do what you effing well like for all I care,' he took to pacing again. Was that finally the truth? Was that where they'd been headed this last couple of years?'

Having resisted so far, I went to the kitchen for the red wine. I couldn't have this argument dry. By the time I'd opened the bottle, poured myself a large glass and come back into the room, Russell was flicking through the channels on the wall-mounted TV – a practice he knew I detested. 'I'm not competing with that row. Are we going to finish this discussion?'

'I thought we had,' he muted the sound, but kept his eyes fixed on the flickers behind me. 'I'm going to Africa and that's that,' he shuffled his feet. 'I had thought you might come.'

I laughed out loud. 'Oh that's rich. So much for my neglecting Mckenna Associates then. You know full well I can't come. Anyway, how long are you planning on being away?' The bombshell of his intention was only just percolating; I barely believed it.

'They want me to set up the financial trading infrastructure for a fledgling African state; North Tamin, you know, the one that's been in the news. It's a pretty backward place, lots of tribal infighting and so on, but they're rich in rare minerals and now there's been a military coup. The new government has invited me to set up their finance systems.'

'Why you?' It sounded rude, but he'd just said worse to me.

'Because they know what I've done in the past, watched the funds that have been successful. It's obvious isn't it?' he leaned forward. 'They've seen the effect hedge funds can have on national economies. Well, these guys intend to get in first. Want me to make that sort of money for them.'

'You mean this coup is only so they can rape the country – with your help.'

He shrugged. 'So what? It's a fantastic opportunity – will put me up there with Soros and Buffet.'

'Then it seems the gods have singled out both of us, doesn't it.' Why was it, when I thought everything was going my way, something always happened to spoil it. I felt unreasonably resentful. I had been offered, no, given – entrusted with was even better – I had been entrusted with a manorial estate in the heart of the English countryside; could picture myself driving the Bentley, waltzing in the hall—Stop. There had to be a catch and since it wasn't yet evident it probably revolved around money. I put the glass down so abruptly I knocked it against the side of the table, severing its stem. Blood from my finger fell in thick teardrops on to the wooden floor.

Bandaging the nick with a tissue I asked: 'Do you think they do it on purpose? The gods I mean. Amuse themselves by watching us flounder?' Had the genie appeared to us both, granting our dreams – and omitting to mention that great dagger sticking up out of the table. 'When are you thinking of going?' I wanted to ask, when had you intended to tell me, as he clearly must have had some inkling of this before today. But then, I'd known about Sanderling for forty-eight hours – and said nothing.

Russell watched me gather the broken bits. 'This weekend.'

'And you expect me to drop everything, come out with you to some heathen—' Were the gods on my side after all? Perceiving the dilemma with which I would be faced, had they manufactured the intriguing magnet that was Sanderling to make sure I made the right decision. I abandoned the pieces.

Chapter 8

The following Tuesday, I packed a suit carrier, locked up the flat, promoted my extremely able second in command to managing director of McKenna Associates and drove down to Sanderling; smiling inwardly at how shocked the countess would have been at my travelling with luggage.

For several reasons I told no one I was coming. The easiest to explain was that I wanted no herald of my arrival; intending to catch them unawares, see what was going on. The more difficult to put into words was that until I actually arrived I wasn't convinced I'd go through with it ... although thirdly, and at odds with this last, I also feared that by stating my intention I'd spook those flighty gods into thwarting me in some way.

I parked the car outside that overgrown shrubbery and followed a track to the fountain, cutting off the corner taken by the Bentley. Not as fine a morning as before – leaden sky, an absence of birdsong, droplets from an earlier shower suspended precariously from low stems, targeting my neck, as though a bucket of cold water had been thrown over the whole idea.

Pale against the heavy clouds, like a sandcastle rising through wet shingle, Sanderling stood looking at me. Cramped by uncertainty, my feet tottered towards the house until I reached the edge of the lawns. Between me and the entrance portico lay an expanse of unkempt gravel the width of a football pitch; my personal Rubicon. I could turn now, saunter back down the drive like a sightseer, pretend the whole thing never happened.... Or I could gather up my lacerated courage and march in there as the rightful successor.

A bright red Ferrari similar to Russell's roared around the corner from the direction of the stables and screeched to a halt in my path. Caesar come to defend his unlawful territory. According him less than a nod, I crossed the divide towards the door. Fentiman caught up with me, bracelets jangling. 'Where you off to, darlin'?'

Desperate to gain the house before answering him, have the security of the citadel around me, I prayed the door would not be locked, forcing me to demand the key. Instead, it was propped open and as I entered a young man was coming the other way pushing a sack trolley with a large packing case on it. I stopped directly in front of him, antennae bristling.

'What's going on?' I asked in my mildest voice; grateful for my heels, which, together with a natural height advantage, meant I could look down on Fentiman.

His shifty little face assumed a wide-eyed expression. 'Oh just routine stuff. I told you, managing this place is a terrific undertaking; some nights I get no sleep at all.' He took my elbow in an attempt to steer me away which made me seethe. Who the hell did he think he was?

A large removal van swung in front of the house carrying the legend: Asquith & Sons, Auctioneers. I stepped on Fentiman's foot just hard enough for him to release my arm. The T-shirted young man scratched his face. 'What's in the box?' I asked. The man looked to Fentiman.

'Oh, just carpets for cleaning; we rotate them, send one to be restored most weeks.'

'To an auctioneer's?' I moved back towards the door staring at Fentiman who kept pace with me. 'If you wish to avoid embarrassment in front of these people you will send the van away ... otherwise I will.'

'You can't do that. I've got a contract,' Fentiman had turned tomato colour.

'Not any more you haven't. You had a contract as caretaker; not asset stripper. And you will recompense the estate for what you have stolen ... or I will sue your arse off.'

I went inside fast, kicked the wedge from beneath the solid door and pushed it shut, turning the key. I didn't kid myself for a minute that there weren't myriad other doors to the mansion also open – the gesture was a symbolic one.

Briskly I made my way to the only place I knew possessed a working phone – the sitting room overlooking the lake. Adrenalin pumping I was banking everything on the dictum that he who wants power must seize it. Not daring to relax lest my nerve desert me, I telephoned Poulson but he spoke before I did.

'Barry Fentiman's been on to me. He's very upset. What have you done?'

'Caught him stealing and told him to get off my property.'

The chink came across the wire as he put the pipe down. Were the feet still up? 'My dear girl, whatever your differences may be with Barry, I assure you—'

'Mr Poulson, I am now in charge of Sanderling, isn't that so?'

'Yes, but a single woman can't.... You'll need Barry to run it for you.'

I counted to five. 'Mr Poulson, the quicker you sort out probate, provide access to the working capital and take your nose out of my affairs, the sooner you can go back to your post prandial naps; do I make myself clear?' I hung up, insufficiently naive to believe I'd seen the last of Fentiman. He and Poulson would assume I'd be unable to manage and that I'd return to London within days, leaving Sanderling, once again, at their mercy.

I clearly remember that moment, looking out over the weed-infested raised flowerbeds and unclipped parterre of the west terrace to the lake beyond. Sanderling Manor had been rebuilt by the countess's grandfather on the site of its predecessor, a medieval castle belonging to his wife's family. The estate comprised three thousand acres, originally with ten miles or so of brick wall around it, from which, judging by recent aerial photographs, hundreds of thousands of tons of bricks had disappeared in the last few years. Outside the walls of the park lay another eighteen thousand acres along with several hundred tied cottages let to tenant farmers.

I allowed myself one unguarded moment of relish – a metaphorical twirl on the lawn while the servants weren't looking. And experienced my first inkling that the countess knew me very well. Not me exactly, but the person she'd chosen.

I stabbed at the button concealed in the fresco of the marble fireplace and two people materialized, a middle-aged man and a young woman. 'What do you both do?'

'Gardener, Ma'am.'

'And I was a scullery maid. Susan, Ma'am,' she bobbed a curtsey.

'What happened to the butler?'

'Mr Sullivan was very old; died shortly after the countess.' The girl gave a timid smile. 'Folk say he only hung on because t'wouldn't do to be goin' in front of 'er ladyship.'

'Where are the others?'

Susan shrugged. 'They weren't used to the way Mr Fentiman has of ... doing things, Ma'am.'

That didn't surprise me. 'Susan, you will show me round.'

She paused at each door, flinging it open and announcing its purpose. Those nearest the sitting room were still furnished; the dining room, a morning room; large drawing room for entertaining. After that the ballroom and the other rooms were empty. 'What's happened to the furnishings?'

Susan looked down. 'Some of it was emptied before her ladyship died, Ma'am. Ready for the restoration like.'

'Oh I see. And where are the contents?'

'Mr Fentiman asked me that, Ma'am. Got quite cross 'e did. But Mr Sullivan were the one who dealt with it.'

'And he's dead.' The girl nodded. Be grateful for small mercies, Synnove; at least rat-face didn't get his hands on them.

'Where did the countess sleep?'

'Above her sitting room, Ma'am.'

We retraced our steps and ascended via one of the curved red velvet staircases to the floor above. This was the wing I'd spotted in the distance, which Fentiman had said was closed up. Someone had been cleaning it. I pressed on; room after room was well attired, beds made up, towels on towel rails. It couldn't be where the staff slept, no personal belongings cluttered the surfaces, nor discarded garments on the chaises longues. 'Had visitors?'

''Otel,' Susan whispered.

'It's being used as a hotel?' I gaped at her. 'Who for?'

'Mr Fentiman's friends, I think, Ma'am.' I had the feeling Susan didn't altogether approve of Barry Fentiman.

'No more,' I said. 'Tell everybody this has stopped; as of now.' With what else had Fentiman been feathering his nest? I marched on, aware I'd made an important enemy. I'd no choice. Although I'd as yet little proprietorial feel for the place – it sure as hell wasn't his; I couldn't let him cream off everything saleable.

'So which are the countess's rooms?'

'They're not aired, Ma'am,' Susan muttered. A cluttered and dusty sitting room with a large fireplace and a desk against the window led through into a dark void. Susan threw open the shutters while I waited on the threshold. Just as well: discarded just inside the door was a folded carpet, left where it had been pitched out of its crate not half an hour ago, I'd venture. Cobwebs made bridges between the corona over the bed and the window hanging. Beautiful Louis XV chairs were upended on bathroom fittings, a hatstand pierced through one seat. The walls and cornices had begun to peel, the carved light wood panelling showed a sad lack of sheen and the room had about it a damp, neglected atmosphere – a dumping ground for when Fentiman fitted out the guest rooms.

'Why is this room in such a state? The countess's sitting room, dining room and the main drawing room, the other areas she herself inhabited, have been kept as she left them. Why not this?'

'I don't rightly know, Ma'am,' Susan hung her head again. 'You can't stay here, can you, Ma'am.'

I'm sure Susan meant nothing by that except the obvious but her words lit a fuse. 'Why ever not?' I looked at my watch; not yet noon. 'Susan. I'm going to give you your first big task. Enlist whomever of the others you need and get this room into a presentable fashion by this evening. I will be sleeping here tonight.'

Before I knew it, seven o'clock had come around and a dinner of sorts was plonked in front of me, in isolation in the dining room. Luckily I was far from hungry. I'd already inspected progress with the bedchamber and, to be fair, they had done a reasonable job. Susan had even found a fan heater from somewhere and used it to take the chill off the room. The dust and dirt had been removed along with the extraneous fittings – for the moment I cared not where to. Crisp bedlinen adorned the bed and the bathroom had been scrubbed.

I wouldn't have chosen that room, far too gloomy; but I was determined to demonstrate resolve. I viewed it as a stronghold and warmed myself with the thought that I'd commission my own when I'd time. Meanwhile I had appearances to keep up. By inhabiting the countess's room, maybe a little of her grit would rub off; I could certainly do with it.

What was Russell doing in Africa right now? I envied him the heat. At nine o'clock I checked the front door key was turned, assumed the staff had secured the rest because I'd no idea where all the doors were anyway, and made my way, shoes in hand, up that sumptuous, if still bit-strewn, staircase to the countess's suite. I brushed my teeth in a basin big enough to bathe in and having ensured the main door was locked, I collapsed into bed. Always a nervous sleeper, in a strange house where I'd no idea what went on, I didn't fancy being taken unawares.

There was no clock and stupidly I'd left my watch in the bathroom so I'd no idea what time it was. No light could enter those shuttered windows but I sensed it must be the early hours of the morning. I turned over and lay on my back in the dark, listening, glad there were staff somewhere in the house. What had woken me?

Chapter 9

The rumble came first, a deep pulsating tone reverberating through the mattress. Central heating starting up? I imagined I felt a movement but it must have been me tugging the covers. All the same I lay rigid, not daring to breathe let alone reach out to the light switch. The bedclothes undeniably tautened across me. There was someone else on the bed. A dead bird, fallen from the rafters? Except there weren't any rafters. Caution abandoned, I had to get to the light before they stopped me. Lurching for the lamp my shaking hands almost sent it crashing to the floor before I managed to turn it on.

At the end of the bed a large, fluffy, tortoiseshell cat with a knowing expression regarded me with slit green eyes. Tufts of fur grew out of its pointed ears, like a lynx, and its tail took up half its body space. The Cheshire Cat's aunt. I put out a tentative hand, more to determine its reality than for any other reason. The creature stood slowly and arched its back before advancing up the counterpane, its huge paws crevassing the silk. It stopped just short of arm's length from me, weighing me up.

Where on earth had it come from? The door was locked, I was sure of that. It must have crept in during the day when the room was being prepared and hidden under the bed or behind the curtains. I clicked my thumb and second finger together and the cat drew close, allowing me to massage her back. I welcomed the company.

In the morning, crushing the temptation to don casual wear I put on a crisp white shirt and navy skirt suit. How long would it be before I could relax in my own home. Home? Ha, it felt more like solitary confinement on a large scale.

The dining room was deserted, no breakfast; last night's things still where I'd left them. Realizing I'd no idea where the kitchens were I opened the front door and decided to circumnavigate the building from the outside. That way I should be able to locate the ground floor functions without getting lost.

Susan was standing at an eight feet long scrubbed pine table in the middle of a vast old-fashioned kitchen, pouring boiling water into a teapot. Dressers laden with china lined the walls; pots and pans littered the netting overhead. She jumped as I rattled the outside door; came to let me in. 'Oh Ma'am. They'm all gone,' evident distress had sharpened her country accent. 'I were just doin' your tea,' she sniffed. 'Exceptin' John the gardener an' me that is; beggin' your pardon Ma'am.'

I pulled out a chair and sat. Truth was I felt more comfortable down here. 'The other staff?'

'Yes Ma'am. Last night. Mr Fentiman came for 'em. Said they wouldn't get no wages if they didn't leave with 'im like.'

'Join me,' I invited. Consorting with the hired help was bad form but right now I had to talk to someone – and this willing youngster had one hundred percent more knowledge of Sanderling and the countess than I had. 'Whose is the cat?'

Biscuit half way to her mouth, Susan froze. 'There b'ain't no cat, hasn't been since the countess died. That's a tale.'

'What?'

Susan looked at her feet. 'Mr Fentiman's guests complained something furry jumped on them in the night, spat at them, clawed their hands and faces.'

I convulsed with laughter, unable to stop, my amusement out of all proportion to the joke but it felt so good. Susan gave me a sideways look and decided to move on. 'What do you want me to do, Ma'am?'

'Ring your old friends, see if any of the original staff would like to come back.'

This morning I felt alive. No longer the interloper, the new girl; treading so carefully for fear of upsetting those here before me and worrying about Fentiman. I knew little about *true virtue* but I was well acquainted with *carpe diem*. I intended to seize the day good and hard.

It would take weeks if not months to recruit permanent staff and I intended to be very particular – as I'm sure the countess had been. Meanwhile I needed help. I rang an agency who sent temporary staff that afternoon: a professional cook plus two or three assistants – if only to feed the temporary workforce: butler, laundress, chauffeur, maids, all of whose predecessors Susan said had either died or retired since leaving Sanderling. Realizing I'd no idea what I'd need, I asked for versatile characters in case other tasks took precedence. A landscape gardening crew agreed to come the following week to sort out the wasteland. I called Poulson and instructed him to expect the invoices.

I'd thought that due to the unemployment situation, at least some of the old staff would return. 'What, none of them? Are they afraid Fentiman's still running things?'

'Oh no, Ma'am. It's him 'as told 'em not to come.'

Intrigued since yesterday by a constant twittering from beyond the front lawn, I made my way from the sitting room via the west terrace along an overgrown gravel path, and with only one or two full stops and backtracks, I rounded the contour of a small hill to be confronted by an aviary.

I say aviary but it was more like a grand pavilion, built in an eliptical shape with two wings radiating from a central hall the height of a house. The netting of the cages was so artfully entwined with ornate wrought iron tracery that it blended in like the grille of a Rolls Royce or the fretwork on an Indian cabinet. Only three of the eighteen separate sections were occupied because the building sported a huge hole in the roof through which palm trees now grew, and most of the cages were mangled and twisted.

As I turned to go, the ground shook and a galloping grey topped the hill behind me. Casually dressed in jeans and a white shirt, a blond-haired man slid to the ground and held out his hand. 'Jolyon St Clair ... you've caught me in the act.' He swung a large sack down from the horse as it bent its head to crop the grass. 'I come about this time to feed the birds.'

Servant? Gardener? Ornithologist? 'I'm Synnove McKenna.'

'Yes, I know,' he laughed, dark blue eyes creasing with amusement at my puzzled expression. 'This is the countryside – forest drums sound every hour.' For the tiniest part of a second I was stupefied. Not for years had I felt attracted to a man on first meeting. Then, who wouldn't be? The first friendly face, and about my own age. It must be the strain ... and the unreal dimension everything had acquired. Hefting the sack he turned towards a door at the side of the structure. 'How're you getting on?'

What could I say? Help?

'Do you want me to carry on for a while until you find your feet?' He looked back over his shoulder. 'I live at the lodge so it's easy for me and it gives Rainbow a run.' He made it sound as if it were I who'd be doing him the favour. So he was the one who kept the lodge so neatly ... or was that his wife's doing?

'Rainbow?' The horse was white.

Another laugh. 'Oh he's colourful all right, but you only glimpse it in rain. Like one of those children's picture books – just add water. Cheers you up.'

'Yes please; I mean, please carry on, if you wouldn't mind.' With zero knowledge of birds I was scared stiff they'd die otherwise ... and besides, I could do with the company. The birds and I watched while he carefully unfastened then refastened each cage gate behind him, treading with agility through the jungle undergrowth to refill their bowls.

Having replaced the sack on Rainbow he looked at me for a second or two. 'Look, if there's anything at all I can do ... just let me know.' He swung easily up into the saddle, touched a hand to his temple in salute, gathered the reins and set off down the slope at a trot.

Better for my outing, I walked slowly back inside. The fresh air had done me good. I should make a point of getting out there every day for half an hour or so. Crossing to the sitting room, I rang Poulson. No matter how much I resented it, he was still my only real source of information. 'Mr Poulson, I still haven't had the inventories for which I asked, and I want a list of all the property I own.'

'There's no need for that, you know, the paperwork's all in the strong room over there and I'll let you have the listings when everything's tied up. Meanwhile—'

'Meanwhile I want what I ask for. For instance, I assume I own the lodge?'

'Well I'm still doing the paperwork but....' Fears that Fentiman and Poulson between them were selling off my property mushroomed in my head. 'You saw the will; the countess left it to Jolyon St Clair.'

As yet I hadn't got round to studying the several pages of legacies to staff and friends. Why should I? None of the names meant anything to me and, at the time, neither had the bequests. 'Oh, I see.'

'The countess was very fond of him.' Did I detect a nuance of pleasure in that remark? A hint of – 'so you can't have absolutely everything, you grasping bitch'. Matters were barely cordial between Poulson and I but we needed one another right now. He to avoid my reporting him to the Law Society if not the police, and me because only he knew the ins and outs of the Sanderling estate.

I hung up, the uplifting effect I'd felt at meeting St Clair dampened by a note of disquiet. But if they'd been that close, why hadn't she left Sanderling to him?

With the influx of staff the place began to open up; take on a more lived-in atmosphere. The temporary butler, Travers, proved a gem. He had served in royal households, understood every nuance of etiquette and, best of all, could play the piano. He remained a respectful distance from me at all times, both physically and metaphorically, but he knew how things should be done and was a great organizer.

I sent for the rest of my things – just in case I needed them while I was here. Which action forced me to explore the wardrobe facilities. In the five days I'd been here I had fallen into bed each night, exhausted; then in the morning, showered and gone down. Other than worry just how the cat got in and out of my bedroom and how it fed itself, I'd had neither cause nor time to return there during the day.

The dressing room comprised a series of chambers leading off the bathroom. Floor to ceiling cupboards in delicate wood panelling lined three walls of each section, the fourth was given over to picture windows fronting the lake; the same view as from the bedroom. In the centre of each area stood an artfully arranged ensemble of graceful couches, velvet footstools and cheval glasses. Cautiously I approached the first pair of cupboard doors. They slid open effortlessly, releasing a hint of cedarwood.

Brass rails at shoulder height held hundreds of garments; suits and costumes I guessed, though it was difficult to tell since they were well wrapped. I undid a couple of the nearest. One, a knee length loose-weave tweed suit in multiple blue checks was the sort of thing I would wear these days. Funny how fashion came round. The size was right too. Curious, I slid off my skirt and tried it on. A perfect fit. Still wearing the two-piece I opened a second pair of doors to find blouses and shirts – mostly white and blue. The next set had rows of drawers housing sweaters, organized by colour. And the fourth, to my surprise, opened on to a further corridor, lit by electric light and lined on either side with glass containers housing court shoes, walking shoes, boots and headgear of every description. No jewellery, though, and no sign of a safe up here, which struck me as odd.

At random I chose a pair of heeled pumps – unscuffed, probably unworn ... my size. This whole dressing room must have been solely for daywear. I walked briskly through the other rooms. The second was inhabited by summer frocks, silk scarves and bonnets. A third, sports and occasion wear – tennis dresses, riding outfits, swimming costumes in drawers; a fourth, evening wear.

My own private Harrods dress department with everything in my size and colour, to suit my shape. I couldn't resist. Selecting a backless floorlength shift in pale cream silk with matching silk slippers I slid it over my head. The effect was alarming.

Who was I? What was happening to me? I went back into the daywear room where the cat had commandeered my discarded clothes. Dazed, I sank on to the couch beside her. The situation was unnerving yet I felt comfortable, happy ... at home. Some of these clothes must date back to the thirties. What a pity Mum hadn't lived to see all this, she'd have adored it.

Could I really pack up and leave this place, pretend none of it had ever happened? Cinderella returns to her city apartment and no one's any the wiser. What would happen to Sanderling?

Stroking the cat, I could sense a warm evening, piano music filtering on to the terrace, the intoxicating scent of old-fashioned roses, curtains billowing in the breeze; the Lagondas and Sedanca de Villes pulling up at the door, gentlemen in white tie and tails, laughter issuing in peels from the drawing room. She'd picked someone her own size to carry on her life. That's why she'd insisted the Bentley be sent to meet me by way of introduction. I had been systematically seduced by an expert.

Chapter 10

January 1936: 'The King is dead, long live the King.' Bertie and Isabel were taking sherry in the library before lunch when the news of George V's death came through on the wireless. They stood silently to attention as the national anthem crackled over the ether.

After a respectful pause, Isabel switched off the set and handed Bertie his glass. 'We'll see some changes now, I'm thinkin',' Bertie said thoughtfully. 'David's an entirely different kettle o' fish.'

'Don't you think they lose that pioneering spirit once they join the powers that be? So far his personal peccadilloes have been indulged but now David is king he'll have to conform.'

'I don't see why a chap has to do as he's told once he's king. Surely, that's when he should be able to do as he likes.'

'How could you possibly understand, Bertie. It's a question of responsibility.' Two years his senior, Isabel frequently teased Bertie for his refusal to grow up. At eighteen, he retained a childishly benign view of the world.

'You'll see. Times have changed. Why, fellows I know couldn't care two hoots how many times she's been divorced. And neither do I. Will he make a good king is the important question – and from his showing so far, I'd say he will. The people love him.'

'All the more reason for him to set a good example then.' Isabel's tone was sharp because at heart she agreed with Bertie. *Sola Nobilitas Virtus*. Who cared what his beloved had done.

'Why shouldn't he be allowed to marry the one he loves? Other people can—' As pink edged up his neck, Bertie strode across to the window and stood with his back turned, gazing out.

'Precisely because he is king and has a duty to behave in an acceptable fashion. Just think what would happen to standards and values if we all did just as we pleased.' Bertie was right of course, nevertheless someone had to set an example – it went with the privilege of position.

Bertie turned to face her. 'Now, because of a load of stuffy anachronistic busy bodies the poor chap will have to make a decision. His throne or his heart's desire.'

'Don't be so dippy, Bertie. Decision indeed. He has no choice.'

'Oh yes he has. The papers are saying he can abdicate; give up being king.'

'Of course he can't. I ask you, whoever heard of such a thing? He must just make the best of it, that's all.'

Chapter 11

I harried Poulson into providing me with the inventory of cars compiled for probate. It read like a vintage catalogue. Runabouts comprised a 1931 Austin complete with dicky seat; two or three Ford Eight model Y family saloons, a 1939 Fiat, a 1938 Peugeot 2020 Berline and four 1935 Morrises. All collectors' items. Not to mention the more prestigious models of which the Sedanca de Ville was only one. Armed with this amazing document I went down to the garages.

Frank Channing emerged from halfway along the left hand block as soon as I entered the yard. On the right, curious equine heads peered over stable doors, Rainbow's white visage among them.

Watched by all those eyes I ignored Channing and stepped through the first open doorway. As with Fentiman, I was blowed if I was going to be conducted around my own property by an interloper. Hark at me. The difference was, I meant no harm.

The garage, as it now was, ran the length of the block, but in it were fewer than six or seven cars out of a total twenty-eight by my calculations. I lifted the corner of the nearest tailor-made cover revealing a sweeping maroon wing like an exaggerated eyebrow, the Delage D8-120 I reckoned. I ticked it off on my paper. The Sedanca stood next to it, without a cover. I felt the bonnet, still warm.

Channing had followed me inside. 'A beauty, isn't she?' he said proprietorially, smoothing her flanks. I wanted to knock his hand away.

'Where are the other cars?' I tapped the list.

'Out on loan,' he said, glibly. I waited. 'Barry knows all about it.'

I recalled him saying he hired out the Sedanca for parties ... before

I'd realized the car was mine. 'Mr Channing, I asked you a question. Now, where are they?' Had he and Fentiman sold the others?

Channing leaned nonchalantly against the car. 'I thought you wouldn't want to be worrying—'

'Where does the rent go from these loans?'

He shuffled his feet. 'I get a cut for having the motors looked after.'

'Get off my property.'

'You can't do that, I—'

'Before I call the police. You told me your grandfather was chauffeur here. For that reason, and that reason only I'm giving you a chance. Get those cars back in here by tomorrow night.' Renting out the cars wasn't actually a bad idea, but if it was going to be done it would be through Sanderling ... and me; not Fentiman Enterprises.

Poulson had told me the wiring, the plumbing system and the fireproofing were all in need of updating. The outside work had been finished but they'd been clearing the rooms inside when the countess died and Sanderling had gone to sleep. Putting aside the little matter of just where Sullivan, the old butler, had sent the contents, there was little point in replacing them without doing the work.

Amongst the papers in the countess's desk I came across an architect's report on the house. Since I was stopping, I had little choice but to embrace the upheaval and asked my assistant to get the architect, Roy Smithson, to come over. She reported that he had been impossible to track down.

'But he's only in the village.'

'Apparently he's always like that.'

'Well why don't you ... never mind, I'll go myself.' I'd take the Sedanca. If I was to be mistress of Sanderling – I would start by being eccentric, wasn't that expected?

I pulled the Bentley into the layby opposite the main stores. As I pushed through the door everyone in the checkout queue fell silent and stared. I smiled thinly, grabbed a magazine and joined the end. What had I done?

A bedraggled mother with a gaggle of children stood at the

counter, shoulders slumped. 'You think you can just pile up debt and not pay it off?' The shopkeeper raised her voice and appealed to her audience who shuffled in embarrassment. 'That's the trouble with people like you, isn't it – expect the rest of us to carry you.' One man tapped his foot impatiently.

'I haven't got it today,' the woman mumbled.

'My Dad, God rest his soul, was far too soft.' The shopkeeper scooped up the meagre few goods on the counter and dropped them in a basket behind her with a self-satisfied flourish. 'You pays yer debts and you can 'ave 'em. Not til then.'

The baby in the woman's arms began to cry, soon joined by the toddler in the pushchair. An older child tugged expectantly at a rack of sweets.

'And get your brats out of here.'

I could stand it no longer. 'I'll pay for those.'

All eyes turned. The shopkeeper scowled at me, tightened her lips but otherwise took no notice. Was rescue of the victim against the rules? The poor woman crept out and the elation I'd felt driving that beautiful car along the country lanes evaporated along with her.

Serving the next customer the shopkeeper went on in a loud voice: 'I sent her a reminder two weeks ago for a bill she should 'ave paid last year. Her sort shouldn't be allowed.'

Someone ahead of me muttered: 'It were never like this in the old days.'

When it was my turn at the till, in a whisper I tried again. 'Please let me pay that woman's bill.'

The shopkeeper slammed my change down on the counter and, avoiding eye contact with me, immediately turned to the next customer. 'Dad let some of 'em 'ave everythin' on tick and 'alf the time mislaid the paper 'e'd written it on, deliberate like,' she leaned over the counter. 'Well I've found some o' them chitties and they're goin' to pay or my name ain't Sheila Parsons,' she leaned back, a righteous smirk on her ugly features. She didn't want these people helped, she wanted them humiliated.

Thrown into a position I'd no idea how to handle and finding myself the target of rudeness if not outright hostility, a deep pool had opened in front of me. Outside the shop I breathed in fresh air. Should I ignore such scenes in future; adopt a haughty disregard for fear of trespassing on the proletariat's territory ... or being inundated with begging letters? What was I meant to do? Had I contravened some unwritten law by setting foot in the shop?

Leaving the Bentley where it was, I meandered down the street mulling over how I was to find the architect. Ahead of me, set back behind a small forecourt bedecked with bright red geraniums in half beer barrels was the Coach and Horses. A high central archway fronted a cobbled passage leading to the rear and currently housed a tall white horse occupied with a full hay net suspended from the wall.

I pushed open the door marked *Saloon* into a large low-ceilinged room furnished with dark oak tables and wheelback chairs upholstered with hunting scenes. Pewter tankards and gleaming glassware were suspended above the bar, the obligatory brass horn above the fireplace. A pleasant faced serving woman raised a practised eyebrow. Rummaging amongst a collection of half-empty bottles in a tub full of ice on the counter, I selected one and held it out to her. She took it from me. 'Do you know where I can find Roy Smithson, the architect?'

The bar lady set the chilled glass down on the towel in front of me. 'He's in the back room.' The sound of male ranting from around the corner percolated through my consciousness. One, a voice I recognized.

'Bloody bitch, coming here with her London ways. She's sacked everyone up at the manor, you know. Couldn't care less that they'd worked their balls off for the countess all those years. Sacks them all on the first day, she does, including me. God knows how she thinks she's going to run the place. She'll just strip it and bugger off back to London. And where does that leave all of us? She's ruined my business.'

Someone yelled a sentence I didn't catch to which Fentiman replied: 'You'll laugh on the other side of your face when I give you your cards on Friday.'

'Who shall I say's asking for him?' asked the bar lady.

'Synnove McKenna. From Sanderling. I have some work for him.'

The bar lady's expression didn't change and she disappeared behind the central partition. All sound in the other bar ceased abruptly, replaced by a low-level hissing like a swarm of wasps, which I assumed to be whispering.

I carried my drink outside and sat at a wooden bench. Five minutes later I was debating whether to beard Smithson in the public bar when a lanky tousle-haired man in collar and tie, grey flannels and worn sports jacket, dipped his head under the lintel and blinked in the sunlight. Remaining seated, I extended a hand. 'Mr Smithson?' He took it limply.

'I'm Synnove McKenna and I've taken over at Sanderling. Won't you sit down?'

At that moment a familiar figure emerged from a side door, patted the horse and, presumably not seeing me at the table, yelled: 'Roy, if you want a lift make it snappy, will you?'

Smithson's mouth twisted. 'Can't stop, cricket club lunch. Never miss.' He disappeared through the archway. Seconds later a diesel engine started up and Jolyon St Clair drove up the road, Smithson beside him. As out of place as an Arab at a bar mitzvah, I continued to sit there while a convoy of vehicles exited the car park, among them, Fentiman in his Ferrari.

I'd been avoiding the subject of finance. Since all else followed, normally it would have been the first thing I'd have attended to, but I suppose I'd wanted to enjoy the fantasy just a little longer. If someone gives you a beautiful rose you don't immediately dig it up to see how it grows – even if you suspect its roots may lack robustness. You enjoy it while you can.

I threw the remnants of the wine down my throat and stood up. Marching back to the car, I slid behind the wheel and trickled down the street to Poulson's office as a Jaguar emerged backwards from the sideway. I drove the Bentley across its path, got out and walked briskly to the driver's window.

'Mr Poulson. I'm so glad I caught you; I need some information.'

'Have to wait, I'm in a hurry.'

'I'm sure they'll keep your lunch hot; though, admittedly, everyone else went ten minutes ago,' I smiled sweetly.

Presumably realizing he couldn't shift the Bentley on his own, Poulson alighted and followed me into his office.

Unbidden, I sat down. 'I want to know about the trust; the inheritance tax; how the money works.'

'That'll take hours.'

I put down my bag, crossed my legs.

Poulson swayed from foot to foot before extracting a bunch of keys from his pocket and leaving the room. His footsteps moved about upstairs. Presently he reappeared with several files under his arm and dumped them on the table by my chair. 'Help yourself.' I couldn't have planned it better; unpressed for time I'm sure he'd have been far more reluctant to let me loose on the Hampden papers – at least would have vetted them first.

I patted the files. 'Thank you. But first I need to know about this trust.'

He continued standing, brought the pipe out of his pocket then replaced it. 'Set up in the late eighteen hundreds. All the assets – there were several other houses which the countess sold – are vested in a company called Hampden Estates. The trustees of that company control Sanderling.'

'And they are?'

'Directors of Gold and Weinstein, private bankers; based in Zurich.'

'So these gentlemen agreed to the countess's scheme – about me, her successor?'

'No choice,' he shrugged. 'Eventually if it doesn't work out – if that detective woman fails to find a suitable candidate over the years, or if anything happens to her – the trustees can sell the property.'

I didn't miss the implication that the right person had yet to be found. So their bets were hedged; Russell would like that. 'You mean, what they can't do is appoint a successor.'

'Never was their role. They're simply there to safeguard the financing of the Sanderling Estate. The Hampden family and their heirs are responsible for its operation.'

'So if the countess had run it into the ground...?'

'Nothing they could have done about it.'

No wonder Poulson felt at liberty to do as he pleased. I hesitated. 'And inheritance tax?'

'Paid from a special fund set up abroad when the trust was created. That way the fund itself can't be counted as part of the estate and its purpose become self-defeating.' And thank God, Poulson couldn't get his podgy little hands on it.

Who had that sort of money these days? 'So Revenue and Customs have already been paid?'

'Well, we've still got to assess the exact value of assets....

I stared at Poulson with disgust. 'You mean you were hoping to filch more treasures before the audit is complete.' Scooping up the files I sashayed out of there like a countess. Dream it may be, idiot I might be, but so far it kept getting better and better.

Chapter 12

Abandoning the Bentley in the drive at Sanderling, I struggled in through the front door. John, the last remaining gardener, was using the telephone. 'Yes, Sir, just thought you should know,' was all I caught before he whirled and dropped the receiver.

Carefully replacing the handset on its receiver with both hands, John touched a forelock. 'Beggin' your pardon, Ma'am.'

'Who were you talking to?'

'Lord Dan, Ma'am.' I frowned. 'Lord Danhanbury, Ma'am.'

'The man who lives the other side of the lake?' Were my servants in the habit of calling him for a chat ... behind my back? I handed John the files. 'Put them on the terrace for me, please.'

I fought as much with my curiosity as anything else. At the office I could have demanded to know; here I should pretend not to wonder. 'What about?' I asked nonchalantly.

'The trout, Ma'am.'

'Ah.' It wasn't the first time I'd overheard staff on the phone. Last week Susan had been talking to someone about barley. Said her brother had rung her. I'd forgotten about it because it was down in the pantry and anyway, Travers, the temporary butler, had been with me. I'd left him to deal with any misdemeanour. I shrugged. They'd been three years without supervision, I couldn't be too harsh.

I sat on the west terrace and opened the first of the files Poulson had practically thrown at me: listing after listing of neatly typed property register; summaries of land holdings and inches long reference numbers – presumably to deeds held elsewhere. I'd glanced into the strong room which Charles Poulson had mentioned and right enough it was filled floor to ceiling with musty old documents ranging from scrolls to hardback casings.

The second file was more recent. It recorded changes of ownership of land and property. I sat back, suddenly hot. What had Fentiman said that first afternoon, when I'd asked if there was an estate manager? He'd muttered about the farms looking after themselves and then: '*Charlie's been selling the stuff that didn't.*' Enraged, I stood up, determined to go and drag Poulson out of the cricket club, wherever that was; show him up as a fraudster in front of his pals.

Yet, since Poulson had given me the paperwork he must consider himself fireproof. He'd say the farms were making a loss or something. That it was impractical to abide by the countess's wishes and keep everything absolutely as it was. He'd already said that, actually. And even if I traced the money from the sale to Poulson's account, wasn't that standard practice for a solicitor engaged in land transactions on behalf of a client?

I riffled through the papers. Four or five separate holdings had been sold off ... all to the same man: Bertram Fanshawe-Parker – Lord Danhanbury. He and Poulson – give or take Fentiman – were in this together, then. I looked at the sums but had no way of knowing if the price was fair or not; though I could guess.

Poulson would have had little difficulty in persuading absent bankers, who knew nothing of farming, that these parcels lacked adequate management and that such management couldn't be found. Therefore, it would be in the best interests of the estate at the present time to dispense with these holdings rather than allow them to decay further. Poulson had then sold five Sanderling farms to this Lord Danhanbury for a fraction of their true value and been suitably rewarded by the noble lord for his trouble. Everyone won – except the Sanderling Estate; for which I was ultimately responsible.

I stared into the distance, willing the man to appear. Occasionally I'd sighted a tiny figure in a boat on the horizon and wondered who it was. I looked at the time; four o'clock. I went back inside, summoned the chauffeur and went up to my room to change.

*

The Bentley swept through the Elizabethan clock arch and pulled up in the courtyard of the classic E-shaped tudor manor, its tall twisted chimneys and mellowed brick fine testament to the builder's craft. A magnificent mulberry wept on the centre lawn and espaliered figs clambered across the front elevation.

Swishing a walking stick from side to side as if habitually surrounded by tall grass, a dapper gentleman emerged to greet me; in his late seventies I'd have said though I'd heard he was older. For a second I thought he'd frozen, his every movement arrested, cane and all, like a marionette in mid step. Then, undeterred, he resumed his advance, smiling. Bowing very low over my hand in a gentle rumble he said: 'My dear Miss McKenna, you don't know what a pleasure this is.' What tom-tom had not only supplied my name but the moment of my arrival?

Something about the silk afternoon dress, the strapped sandals and the broad brimmed hat I'd selected, subdued my customary candour. If I'd dressed the part then I must play it. Fearing failure, I only smiled in return.

Lord Danhanbury led the way across an oak panelled entrance hall and out of the doors on the far side, to the terrace; which enjoyed my own view of the lake only in reverse. We sat at a large table laid with a starched cloth, porcelain tea service, plates of sandwiches with the crusts cut off, a two storey cake-stand laden with madelaines and butterfly tarts and a Victoria sponge.

'I always have tea about this time.' He took his eyes off me long enough to pour. He was a handsome old boy, fit too by the way he moved. Fit to steal.

'This isn't a social call, Lord Danhanbury.'

'Bertie, everyone calls me Bertie.' Should I have referred to him as Sir Fanshawe-Parker? I certainly couldn't call him anything as friendly as he was suggesting. 'That's a pity. It's such a glorious afternoon – made all the more so by your company, my dear. I would have called to welcome you earlier but I wasn't sure if you were ready for visitors....' Why not? He seemed well up on everything else I did.

'Didn't my staff tell you? Or do they confine their intelligence to matters of barley and trout?'

Teacup and saucer poised, he studied me for quite thirty seconds before handing them over. I think he had been about to answer when the overlapped folds of the tablecloth beside him moved and a familiar shape insinuated itself between us.

'Snatched the cat as well, have you?' I put down the tea and stood. That he'd stolen the only thing I had which showed me any warmth, pushed me over the edge. 'First the farms, then my staff and now the cat. Is there anything else you'd like while you're at it?'

He was on his feet in an instant. 'Hildegard adopted me after her mistress died,' he bent to stroke her tail. 'Now she has returned home. This is the first I've seen of her since you arrived at Sanderlin'.' He smiled. 'I expect she knew you'd be visitin' me today, and decided to tag along.'

'You mean she came here when—'

'And very welcome she was. I miss her,' he indicated my chair. Reluctantly, I sat down again. So did he.

'Fancy you remembering her name.' I took a sip of tea. This wasn't working out how I'd planned. If I wasn't careful I'd end up liking the man.

'Ever since her parents died the countess called her cats Hildegard. Reminded me of Agatha Christie's childhood home where the maid was always Susan ... regardless of her Christian name. Saves havin' to remember.' He too drank his tea, offered the sandwiches. I wasn't going that far. With a pout of reluctance he replaced the plate, sat back in his seat and looked out across the lake. I stole a look at his face, the lines turned down, eyes shrouded – ineffably sad.

He twiddled the knob on his cane as he spoke. 'Your staff have been in the habit of ringin' me if they think I can help, especially the tenants. That was the conversation about barley. Susan Pritchard's brother took over in May after their father died. He's a carpenter, knows little of farmin'. He was unsure when the barley would ripen. I've sent Jenkins over to help him.' He turned to look at me. 'And John found a brace of dead trout on your land. He suspects one of Barry Fentiman's layabouts has been poachin' but he daren't tell you in case you thought it was him. I said I'd deal with it.'

'Why come to you?' Aware of half the answer, I felt ashamed. They either found me hard to approach or, worse, judged me incompetent.

'Lady Foxhill was a dear friend.'

He said it so sincerely that if I hadn't known about him buying up the farms I could easily have fallen for that one. Luckily I now had a good idea what he was up to – using the staff to gain inside information on which parts of my property could be annexed next. 'Sanderling is none of your business.'

'Sadly ... not.'

At least that was honest. And it made me suspicious. 'When Lady Foxhill packed up her valuables – furniture, jewellery, much of the china and pictures – in preparation for the rewiring ... do you know where she stored them?'

Pointedly I looked back at the manor, mellow and all-knowing in the late afternoon. What more likely place. Sullivan could have transported the smaller packing cases over here a bit at a time. That way no one else need know where they'd gone. Then the countess had died, shortly followed into the next life by her butler. What was to stop Danhanbury from simply keeping quiet? Why share with Poulson and Fentiman if he didn't have to?

'These old places are the very devil, you know. Too many treasures, that's the problem.'

'I don't understand why she moved them out of Sanderling. The workmen wouldn't need every room at once.'

'My dear, the countess was a shrewd woman. Maybe she felt they'd be safer elsewhere.'

What was that supposed to mean? That she'd foreseen what might happen after she'd gone – and sought to thwart Fentiman from his tricks? I struggled against Danhanbury's clutches, his plausibility. 'Couldn't protect her land from you and Poulson though, could she?'

Lord Danhanbury blanched, rose slowly from his chair and taking the cane moved away from the table, standing half turned from me. 'Have you noticed how good the roses are this year? Isabel loved roses,' he gave a little lop-sided smile.

'I want those farms back.'

He came and sat down, gazing at Hildegard who was rolling back and forth in the sun, enjoying herself. 'I hear you've been renovatin' the west terrace. Don't be afraid to replant the roses, will you. I know it's not supposed to be a good idea, plantin' new roses in old rose beds, but the countess's weren't diseased.'

Was he deaf? 'Lord Danhanbury, I'm talking about the farms; I know Charles Poulson has been selling them off and you've been buying them.'

'Trade, my dear – buyin' and sellin', never could fathom it myself. Don't hold with talkin' about it to a beautiful lady on a nice afternoon like this, neither. Vulgar subject don't you think?' he proffered the cake tray. 'And if you don't help me eat cook's tea I shall get into the most frightful row.'

I could cope with the Fentimans and Poulsons but how did you tackle a Lord Danhanbury ... without being born to it? I'd been blunt to the point of rudeness – as good as accused him of stealing – yet failed to penetrate the veneer of the dutiful host. What would the countess have done?

'Lady Foxhill and I often sat here of an evenin', breathin' in the musk, watchin' the swallows; discussin' this and that.' His face lit up. 'Come on Saturday. I dine at seven sharp. So we can get to know one another better. Maybe I can offer a little advice now and then; while you're findin' your feet.'

Having insufficient evidence to call in the police, along with a nagging conviction I may have missed something, I allowed myself to be deflected. I could hardly blame him for treating me with a good deal of introspection. After all, here was I, a complete stranger, a nobody of unknown family and proclivity, usurping the neighbouring estate. And since the straightforward approach had failed, perhaps I could learn by adopting his more circuitous route.

That same evening I received a phone message from Russell. Due back in England for a few days, he was coming to Sanderling on the weekend. I demanded the west terrace be planted by Friday, even if they had to work overnight, and the billiard room restored to order in case he wished to play. I desperately wanted Russell to like Sanderling; it wasn't too late for us both to enjoy the place.

I asked my assistant to telephone Lord Danhanbury and explain why I couldn't come to dinner. She returned saying Lord Dan was insisting I bring Russell too; would brook no argument. Once I'd let the idea sink in I was pleased.

On Friday I took the chauffeur and the Sedanca de Ville to meet Russell off the train. What had worked for the countess might also work for me. But other than a mumbled: 'What's this thing worth then?' he made no comment, opening his laptop and cursing about the poor connection through his phone the minute we sat down. At the fountain, as we made that memorable turn to face the house, we might as well have been approaching King's Cross for all the notice he took. And apart from a cursory hug when we met on the station concourse, we hadn't as much as touched since.

I'd expected a bronzed, athletic Russell from his sojourn in Africa but instead he was far paler than I remembered, his features drawn and gaunt. Hungover from his journey, at dinner he appeared preoccupied. 'Are you in England for something specific?'

'If you call rescuing my company, specific ... then I guess so, yeah,' without so much as glancing at me he wolfed his chateaubriand as though he hadn't eaten in weeks.

'I imagine this recession is bound to have a ripple effect on everyone.'

'It's the tossers who lose their nerve who're the problem. Our investments were sound, and balanced with alternative stakes.'

'So what happened?'

'The lenders. Wanted their money back before the bets have a chance to pay off.'

'And Africa?'

'Hit by the same events so they're losing confidence.'

'Why don't you stay here for a few weeks, take a holiday, wait for things to settle down?'

He stared at me, rose, and with a muttered: 'I've got work to do,' picked up his wine glass, relieved the footman of the bottle and left.

I'd shown him where my suite was but I gathered from Susan he spent the night in my sitting room poring over his computer. I felt awkward when she told me this. In London, when Russell failed to show up or slept on the couch only he and I had been affected. Living my life in the glare of below stairs spotlights wasn't something I was used to.

I found him still chained to his machine, an untouched breakfast tray beside him; two days worth of stubble on his chin. 'Do you allow any Tom, Dick or Harry to ride around here whenever they like?'

I followed his eyes but saw only John the gardener trundling his barrow around the side. 'Probably Jolyon St Clair; lives at the lodge; been looking after the aviary.'

'Jolyon St.Clair? Anything to do with Steadman & St Clair?'

'I've no idea, but it's a fairly unusual name.'

'What's he doing at the lodge?'

'I don't know. The countess left it to him. Why? Do you know him?'

'Of him. His wife was a Steadman. He ran their family property business which had a bad name, shoddy workmanship. Wife divorced him when the bloody fool sold his own house, everything, and used the money to recompense the customers. It was in all the papers.'

Russell tapped a few keys then looked up again. 'Small world though. The other day he joined the same online gambling syndicate as me and straightaway put in a request for another new member – guy named Fentiman.'

I was surprised. True, the village brotherhood was a closeknit band of beer-swilling mysoginists but I still wouldn't have taken St Clair for a Fentiman fan.

'Don't touch that creep whatever you do. His company was supposed to be caretaking Sanderling. I threw him out. The man's a crook.'

I relaxed into a sofa. At least Russell was talking at last. 'We've been invited to Lord Danhanbury's for dinner, he lives across the lake.'

'Danhanbury?'

I nodded.

'Don't know of him. How big's his estate?'

'Hallingham? About the same size as this.' I leaned forward. 'Actually, he's bought five of the Sanderling farms since the countess died. I think the solicitor sold them off cheap and Danhanbury rewarded him. I accused him of it, told him I wanted them back.'

'I should bloody well think so, if they were sold below street price. The man sounds a sharp operator.'

'That's why I'm pleased you're here,' I smiled. 'Today I thought we might—'

'No chance. I've got five trades going down between now and seven.' He went back to his screen as I crept from the room. At least he would be there to help tonight.

I selected my costume carefully. It was a warm summer's evening, I could indulge my desire for something floaty. I chose a mid-calf length orange silk cut on the bias which swirled as I walked, along with a mink stole for later. The chauffeur took us in the Bentley.

I took Russell's hand as we bowled along. 'I'm glad you're here.'

Russell grunted. Against my pleadings he was dressed in slacks and an open-necked shirt, though I had successfully prevailed upon him to wear a jacket. I was sure our host would be formally dressed if not, heaven forbid, in black tie.

Lord Danhanbury came out to receive us ... wearing a lounge suit. Again he suffered that same strange gap in transmission I'd witnessed the first time I met him. Advancing with hand outstretched he abruptly halted in mid-stride like a TV programme when the signal goes. I could see his mouth working but no words issued forth. Then the power clicked back on, normal working was resumed and the strange interval went unacknowledged.

'My dear, you look simply divine,' Lord Danhanbury kissed my hand while I again reminded myself to be careful. Oozing the kind of charm I wished Russell would exhibit, Danhanbury made me feel very unsafe; in danger of being drawn in. He turned to Russell who was staring at the house with a valuer's attention. 'And Mr Prince, delighted,' he took Russell's hand in both of his.

We were ushered on to the terrace for pre-dinner drinks. Lord Danhanbury made small talk while Russell continued to survey the property. As we went in to dinner Lord Dan asked: 'Are you interested in architecture, Mr Prince?'

'I'm interested in money, Hanbury.'

Over an excellent dinner the talk revolved around the state of the nation's finances and what the government was doing about it. Before pudding was served Russell plunged in. 'I hear you've been buying up the Sanderling farms.'

Lord Danhanbury turned an inscrutable face in my direction, then back to Russell. 'I hear North Tamin is goin' through a tough time since the coup. How are you gettin' on out there?' I gasped and covered it with a cough. I had mentioned neither Russell nor his whereabouts when last Danhanbury and I last met. Though Russell wouldn't know that.

'Bloody fools. Can't understand the markets to save their lives. Don't see you have to invest in order to gain; they think you can just steal the reward.'

'Which is what you're accusin' me of?'

'Did I say that, Bertie? Don't get me wrong, I admire what you've done.' If this was Russell's way of softsoaping Danhanbury I doubted the astute lord would be taken in.

'Why is that?' Lord Danhanbury signalled to the waiters to put the dessert and the cheese on the table. 'We'll help ourselves to coffee, thank you.' The three men, one for each of us, trooped out and closed the door ever so softly behind them. 'You were sayin'?'

'You had an eye for an opportunity. Good for you.'

'I don't follow.' Lord Danhanbury blotted his lips with his napkin and laid it aside.

I hadn't seen Russell so alive in ages. He leaned forward. 'What I'm saying is I think you and I could do business together. I'm starting up a new fund, looking for just three or four people with access to large amounts of capital to go on a buying spree while the market's depressed. What do you say?'

'What has that to do with the farms – unless you want Lord Danhanbury to invest those?' I asked.

'Stay out of things you don't understand, woman,' Russell turned to me, the first time he'd acknowledged my presence since we'd arrived. 'Shouldn't you retire to your knitting or something at this juncture?'

Lord Danhanbury rose quietly, pulled the cord by the fireplace. A butler appeared in seconds. 'Mr Prince is unwell, Morgans. Please see if you can find his chauffeur and have him taken home, will you? Ask the man to return for Miss McKenna.'

I didn't know what to do. Reason, loyalty, codes of normal behaviour ... all told me to go back with Russell. So, the evening had ended badly. Russell had had too much to drink and caused offence. It had happened before. Mind you, this time it was me he'd been rude to, not so much Bertie.

'Oh, for heaven's sake....' Russell rose, threw his napkin on the table and glowered at Bertie. 'Don't know why you're suddenly so uppity, Hanbury.' He gripped my arm above the elbow. 'Come on, Synnove.'

Out of the corner of my eye I saw Lord Dan pick up his cane. Shocked at this abrupt hiatus and still undecided on the best course of action, I hesitated. 'We can't....'

'Make your own way home, then.' Before I could decide what to do he had stalked to the door like a petulant schoolboy and was ushered through by an expressionless butler.

'Won't you sit down, my dear. I do hate an interrupted meal, don't you?'

Mesmerized, I did as requested. He topped up my wine glass and looked at me. 'You are so like Isabel. Sometimes I find myself forgettin'.... There aren't many women can wear tangerine, you know.'

Had he recognized the dress? Was that why he halted so abruptly each time he set eyes on me in another of the countess's outfits – overcome by memories?

He went on: 'Before you condemn me, let me explain one thin'....' I waited, motionless. 'I bought the farms to prevent anyone else from doin' so. You can have 'em back whenever you want – provided you keep the existin' tenants.'

'But why...?'

'I saw what young Poulson was doin' and knew Isabel wouldn't have countenanced it. Went and told him so.' Bertie pushed his chair back from the table, raised both arms over his left shoulder and without standing up, mimicked his golf swing. 'No principles my dear, that's what's happened, no principles.' He looked up at me. 'They think class is about what car they drive, what wristwatch they sport. It's not, you know.' He swung again, this time so vehemently I feared for the china. 'So I bought 'em. Seemed the simplest option.'

'You don't want them then?'

'What would I want with more land – at my age.' There was no question mark. 'Tell you what though....' a mischievous glint appeared in those kind eyes, 'be grateful if you didn't tell your friend. I rather liked throwin' him out. Dashed impertinent to you, I thought. Can't be havin' that.'

I beamed at the old boy. No wonder my staff came here with their troubles – given half a chance, so would I.

Chapter 13

Russell departed for the station before breakfast leaving me a brief and uninformative note. I wasn't sorry.

I was pleased about the farms. To have them back, the estate restored to wholeness as the countess had bequeathed it, was uplifting; as was thwarting Poulson. More particularly, Bertie Fanshawe-Parker had proved to be that rarest of people – a genuinely good man; and I was now free to follow my instinct and embrace this amazing character.

More and more, though, I floundered over the estate workers. Whilst I missed the camaraderie, the closeness I'd enjoyed with all my staff in London, a sixth sense, together with Travers's not infrequent raised eyebrows whenever I crossed that invisible line between them and me, left me feeling isolated. Unlike with my London colleagues, I was responsible for these people. Their lives, their welfare – to a large extent, their happiness – was down to me. If I allowed myself to befriend them, become one of them, heaven knew where we'd be.

I had my place mapped out and so did they. Apart from any other consideration, upending that status quo now, when I barely understood the rules, would reveal my ignorance of this unwritten code. I daren't do that.

After a memorably fraught encounter with one farmer who kept pushing for his brother to take over his tenancy, Bertie called me. 'My dear Synnove. Just wonderin' how you're gettin' on. If there's anythin' I can do to help?'

'Should there be, Bertie?' I'd had a busy day and I guessed he had something specific in mind.

'We-ell,' I could hear him tapping the cane against the side of his foot. 'I'm thinkin' of the Singleton family.'

I groaned. 'Look, I'll decide who has the tenancies on my estate.' That was aimed at the Singletons, not Bertie, but if he took it personally, then tough. 'Wilf Singleton must take his chances alongside other applicants. That seems eminently fair to me. I'm not against him having the farm but he must earn the privilege, not assume it's his by right.'

'You don't believe in inheritance then, things being handed down from generation to generation?'

'Not necessarily....' I was on dangerous ground, my own position being far more tenuous than Wilf Singleton's. I could strangle Bertie. Before this call I'd been so convinced I was right.

'How about a trial? Think of it as a car race. Through dint of his family's hard work – and they've been good tenants – Wilf has earned a place at the front of the grid. Give him a chance; two years say. If he does well, capitalizes on that position, then let him have his reward. That way you've admitted tradition as well as protected your own interests.

'And if I don't?'

'Why's it worth any of those men toiling in all weathers to put money in your pocket if they aren't at the same time safeguardin' their family's security? You'll have welched on the deal.'

'But I'll be giving in to pressure.'

'You caused the pressure.' For all his lovely manner, Bertie didn't balk at fences. I needed a master class in being lady of the manor.

Particularly regarding the Singleton issue, Bertie had impressed upon me the importance – duty even – of employing the local work-force. The estate and the villages had historically enjoyed a symbiotic relationship which I would rupture at my peril. But if the locals refused my offers, what could I do?

Bringing in outside labour would only exacerbate the situation so I hung on as long as I could. One lunchtime I thought I'd have a word with the local landlord, introduce myself, see if he could suggest an answer; I'd nothing to lose. In an effort to at least appear more normal, instead of the Sedanca I took my own Mercedes. I caught myself – weren't they all mine?

I ducked my head under the beam leading into the comfortably furnished saloon bar. The room fell silent. The landlord appeared from the other bar – presumably drawn by the worrying suspension of sound. I glanced behind and twenty pairs of eyes stared back. I gave a half smile before turning and ordering a drink.

Fentiman's voice issued from the next room. 'What's that bitch doing in here? She'll be after your business next, Tony, you see.'

'Actually, landlord, I wondered if you could help me?' Suddenly hard of hearing, the landlord laid my change on the bar mat and without meeting my gaze, slid back around the corner to be greeted with ribald laughter.

As I picked up my wine, the connecting door from the public bar was pushed open. Fentiman come to hurl more insults? A cheery baritone called: 'Afternoon everyone,' and the tension was severed; mumbling good afternoon in response, paralyzed tongues were released to pursue their accustomed discourse. A hum of conversation resumed. 'Miss McKenna, mind if I join you? I wanted a word about your aviary.' He could have been riding his white charger for the effect he had on my spirits at that moment.

Jolyon carried my drink to a table in the corner along with the beer he'd brought with him and we sat down. 'The aviary, yes of course. You've been so kind, Mr St Clair, I can only repay you by making it my first restoration project. I will have the birdhouse rebuilt – better than the original.'

He leaned forward, an amused half smile on his lips. 'What a splendid idea,' he sipped his beer with obvious relish, 'but I'm sure you've more urgent tasks.'

'Like recruiting some permanent staff ... yes I have.' I surveyed the room but now no one wanted to look at me. 'Everyone's way too prosperous to be interested it seems.' Much as I longed to offload my concerns, I couldn't forget this was the man of whom the countess had been so fond she'd left him the gatehouse ... but not Sanderling. How could he not be envious? And Russell had mentioned St Clair's application to that gambling syndicate for his friend Fentiman. I daren't trust him.

'It used to be very different here. Folk went out of their way to help; made it their mission – a matter of pride.'

His tone was so wistful I felt guilty. 'You're saying it's my fault.' St Clair was probably right; never had I felt so inadequate.

He regarded me for a second or two. 'How could it be?' He took a sip of his beer and replaced the mug on the table, staring into its amber depths. 'I guess it was inevitable. The countess held back change more successfully than Canute. Her passing was bound to engender a tsunami. If you'd stood in its way at the time, you might well have been drowned in the onrush.'

'I don't follow....'

'With the old lady gone, along with others of that generation who'd enjoyed her patrimony – old man Poulson, Sullivan and some of the other village stalwarts – and at a time when our country was riding a crest of opportunity, there was nothing to stop this whole area breaking out. Folk had never had the possibilities before. Suddenly Nirvana beckoned from all directions and there was hardly anyone left to stop it. People here discovered greed, aggression and competition; for the first time fearing their neighbour might get more than they did. What can you expect if you take the stopper out of a bottle as influential as Sanderling.'

'You make it sound like some third world backwater where the natives were content with their subsistence level existence – happy even – until they were introduced to western ways.' I hadn't expected a lecture on philosophy.

'That's not a bad analogy.'

'The countess may have preserved the beneficial parts of a bygone age but I'm sure she didn't keep people in the Dark Ages.'

'Let's say the countess had a rather traditional attitude to the lower classes. She felt sorry for them, would do all she could – educate a bright child, pay someone's hospital bills, provide transport to ailing relatives – but she'd been brought up to believe that if you did, as you so charmingly put it, introduce them to western ways, they would not appreciate the changes; that they were genetically incapable of improvement on any significant scale. Individuals perhaps, but as a class, no.' He sipped his beer. 'A cynic might say events since her death are proving her right.'

I drank my wine, studying him. He had a strong, attractive face. 'Are you teasing me, Mr St Clair?'

'About this place? No.' He eyed the withdrawn diners. 'People were so much happier when they had less.'

'I take it they won't want to work on the estate any more, then?'

'Give them time. They'll come round,' he smiled.

Still dangerously close to letting down my guard, I rose. 'I meant what I said about the aviary.' I walked back outside, feeling his eyes following me; more alone than ever.

Chapter 14

Pondering the coming upheaval of the indoor restoration my mind moved on to the Sanderling artefacts, the china and paintings, the books. Since they'd been missing well before the advent of Fentiman, I didn't doubt they'd turn up but then I'd need—

I flung the pad and pen on to the desk and stood up, striding across to the window, aglow with an idea. What I needed was a friend. Someone I could talk to without fear of letting myself down, giving too much away, being undignified, behaving in a manner unbefitting the mistress of Sanderling ... and all those other constraints I was stretched to even recall yet alone abide by. I needed someone I dare trust.

I drove the Sedanca to Warwick Parkway like an excited schoolgirl and waited in the foyer while the train rattled in overhead.

Convinced she must have missed the train I was turning to go when the lift clanked to a stop, the door jerked open and, 'Sy-nn-ov-e Daa-rr-ling,' boomeranged around the hallway, every syllable elongated. Henrietta Winkleton-Beckett waddled out of the metal cage deliberately jamming a suitcase across its perimeter to prevent the contraption from reascending before she was ready. We embraced.

'Mind the specs,' she said, hauling on a velvet ribbon around her neck to retrieve a lornette from her ample bosom. She raised the glasses on their single stalk. 'Wow, look at you, pon my soul duckie. What 'ave yer got yerself into?' And this before she'd set eyes on the motor.

Wink delighted in mixing lower class phraseology with her upper class accent. To tell the truth her family weren't particularly well-to-do, just aspired to be. In fact I'd known times when Wink had been pretty hard pressed.

We retrieved her multiple carrier bags, carpet bags and the luggable suitcase from the station. 'Gadzooks my dear. Is this thing really yours? She looked around, employing the eye-piece with dramatic effect. 'Where's the chauffeur?'

I'd known a driver, and a footman or two, would impress Wink but there'd be plenty of time for that later. 'I'm sorry, but it's such a relief not to have to watch what I say, I left him at home.' By the grimace which greeted this confession I could tell she disbelieved me and was wincing at my excuse.

We spun through the lanes like a couple of 17-year-olds out in Daddy's car, shrieking with laughter at nothing, intoxicated with the fun of shared adventure.

'I say, darling, any moment one of those old-fashioned policemen with domed helmets is going to wheel his push-bike out in front of you and accuse you of speeding,' Wink yelled. More squeals. The lanes smelled of grass and in the distance a harvester relentlessly plodded its way up and down a corn field, at this distance its clanking operations no louder than a bee's hum; industry far removed. Wink leaned out of the window, dribbling her fingers through the long grass as we rushed past.

'You'll catch a stinging nettle if you're not careful.'

Wink leaned her head back. 'It's all right, Ratty. I know what I'm doing. Splash!' More hoots. Showing off, I wheeled the Sedanca in through the gates of Sanderling a little too fast and encountered Jolyon St Clair coming the other way on Rainbow. Startled, the horse reared.

'Oh my dear, the Lone Ranger too. Dreamy,' Wink commented dryly as Jolyon effortlessly controlled his horse, saluting as we swept past. 'You've kept him quiet. Where's Russell?'

'Abroad.' Once across the meadows and into the shrubbery I pulled into the side. 'Now I'm going to make you walk.'

'Oh cripes; and all because I asked about Russell. What about my stuff?'

'Don't worry about that.'

I led the way through the hydrangeas, their heavy pink and blue blooms waving like drunks on inadequate legs, not unlike Wink. She tottered behind me muttering curses, threatening to return to Pimlico by the first available train and keeping up a constant barrage of complaint.

'If I'd known I'd have to commune with countryside I would never have agreed to this. Don't tell me, you never got over me failing my camper's badge and you're forcing me to take it again. Any moment we're going to emerge from this benighted thicket into a clearing of perfectly ordered blue tents – you striding ahead, me staggering behind carrying the rations. I'm experiencing this unpleasant feeling of déjà vu. Hang on a minute while I—

'Jumping Jehosophat.'

'Déjà vu? I don't think so.' I enjoyed doing that to people; so far Wink's reaction was by far the most rewarding. In my letter I'd said only that I'd inherited an old pile and that should she feel like a change I could do with some company – would even pay her to catalogue the house contents. Amongst other things, Wink was a qualified curator.

'I'll have to sit down,' she lowered herself on to the parapet of the fountain and proceeded to raise and lower the lornette. 'I'm trying to find the point at which it disappears,' she explained, rubbing unmade-up eyes.

The Sedanca crawled around the corner, this time with my temporary chauffeur at the wheel. 'You can get back in now, I just wanted you to experience that first impression.'

She flopped into the seat behind the driver. I followed her and we set off at a stately pace towards the house. Wink said not another word until we reached my sitting room and ordered tea. The lornette hung disconsolate to her waist, animated hands stilled. She was beginning to worry me. 'What's the matter?'

'Well I didn't realize … thought you meant an ancient rambling place with one or two interesting books,' she perched on the sofa and remained there, stiff with shock, while Susan delivered the tea, smiled and withdrew.

'Now you know why I need you – imagine what it's been like on my own. Please don't treat me differently, Wink. You're the one person I thought could cope with all this.'

I tackled Poulson on the phone. 'Look, I want to get cracking here and the first thing I'm going to do is restore the birdhouse. And the wall around the estate badly needs repairing; someone has carted off large amounts of antique brick.' Bertie was always citing that as priority otherwise between the deer and the rabbits, my tenants would have no crops left.

'I can't see why you have to do anything,' puff, puff on the pipe as though we were discussing England's batting prowess.

'You don't need to. Now, do I find the trustees myself, or are you going to advance my money?'

'You're going to import the workmen, then?'

'Oh, I see. The local embargo was meant to stop me, was it? I can hear the cries now. How unfair of me to bring people in. How dare I deprive local artisans of work they have refused to do? Mr Poulson, life will be much simpler for you if you just cough up the necessary and mind your own business.' I slammed down the phone.

Emboldened by Wink's presence and feeling much more my old self, I had workmen started on the aviary within the week and finished in just under a month.

Whilst I saw the repair of the aviary as an obligation, and of course, a pleasure, the restoration of the perimeter wall was symbolic. I was convinced Fentiman and God knew who else, had helped themselves to three quarters of a mile of bricks. More than that, though, their breaching of the manor walls was an act of gross contempt, for the countess, the estate and ultimately … for me. They had dared to demolish Sanderling's defences and it was these I must resurrect – and quickly.

Had I been ignorant of her preference, from the time Wink spent with Jolyon St Clair I might have suspected her of becoming rather too fond of him. Relieved of his feeding duties, Jolyon and she still contrived to meet most afternoons to discuss the feathered inmates.

'I wish I could keep him away,' Wink snapped when I commented on it. With all but one cage now fully inhabited, the chorus of birdsong could be heard from the house. Darts of phosphorescent greens and blues, orange cockades and neon wing tips lit up their tropical forests like lightning strikes as the birds swooped and called in their make-believe jungle. 'It's you he comes to see.'

'Nonsense,' I feigned exaggerated interest in a pair of yellow throated laughing thrushes from China, *critically endangered* according to the information sheet. Wink had probably just made it up to tease me, as friends do; but the puzzle as to why St Clair kept coming over, remained. 'More likely he's keeping an eye on me; imagines he has some proprietorial interest in the place.' I turned. 'Don't imagine he isn't just as dangerous as Fentiman, Poulson and the rest – more so, considering his charm.'

One September morning after church, when the chauffeur had deposited Wink back at Sanderling, she galloped down the hall to the sitting room. Hat awry, lornette swinging she pulled the door to and leaned against it, gasping. 'Rejoice my dear, tidings of good news.'

'Gabriel doesn't suit you, Wink.'

'Ah, but you're the blessed one,' she beamed. 'Barry Fentiman's gone bust.' She removed the offending headgear and spun it, frisbee fashion, across the room.

'Are you sure? When? How come people know?'

She lowered her bulk into a feather armchair, the release of weight from her feet engendering a sigh of relief like the air from a squashed cushion. 'Ah, that's the not-so-good bit. He's going round blaming you. Seems nothing's gone right for him since you threw him out of here.'

Chapter 15

Bertie rang. 'I wondered if you'd heard the news, my dear,' he paused, 'you recall that Channin' chap? Car dealer?' The cane tapped the oak planks by his phone table.

'The one who rented out the Sanderling collection for the benefit of himself and Mr Fentiman? How could I forget.' Something in Bertie's tone worried me. 'What's he done?'

'Oh, nothin' as far as I know,' drawled Bertie, 'rather, what's someone done to him. His entire stock of used cars has been stolen – every last one of 'em. Vanished from his compound overnight.'

I felt sorry for him. Yes, he was a chancer, as Russell would put it, but his love of the Sedanca endeared him to me. 'I imagine he was insured.' I wouldn't have put it past Channing to have had the cars half-inched so he could claim.

'Apparently not. And it was a professional job by all accounts.' Thank God for that then, this was one crime they couldn't lay at my door.... Feverishly gesticulating to my PA with my free hand, I hissed: 'Get Travers to check the garages, immediately.' I returned to Bertie, 'Sorry, I just wanted to—'

'I know, good idea. Not that they're likely to take vintage cars – far too easy to trace,' he hesitated. 'No, it's not that....'

'What's the matter Bertie?'

'Put it down to the shiverings of an old man, my dear but ... I think you should be careful; have that butler of yours make sure your doors are locked at night.'

I'd never heard a cat growl before. In the half light, Hildegard stood astride me, ears flat, teeth bared, emitting a grating noise from deep in her stomach that definitely wasn't a purr.

Switching on the lamp, I listened, ears stretched like trumpets to compensate for the inferiority of my auditory equipment compared with hers; straining to pick up what had so disturbed her. Suddenly, outside and to the right came a loud crash like a building being demolished followed by the sound of a heavy engine retreating at speed. What the...?

Would I hear the noise from here if someone brought in a low loader and smashed down the garage doors? The engine grew fainter as I struggled into a dressing gown. Making do with the sash pull which would eventually summon Travers or Susan, I regretted the lack of alarm by my bed so I could wake the whole house at once. But since they all slept in the stables building, above the garages, they could hardly have missed the row.

The cat shot ahead of me down the stairs and jinxed to and fro frantically as I fumbled with the heavy bolts on the front door. As soon as I hauled half of it ajar, she bolted and seconds later unearthly screeching issued from the direction of the birdhouse. In the dawn, owls, buzzards, even a red kite hovered and dropped behind the rise. Drawn by bloodcurdling squawks and with bare feet bleeding from the gravel, I tore across the lawn, around the hill and along the path.

The centre of the restored aviary had been ripped away, slicing the tops off most of the cages and propelling my beautiful rare songsters into instant breakfast for the neighbourhood's predators. I rushed forward clapping and yelling but the monsters swirled away only to reform and charge again; wings outspread, talons unsheathed.

Presumably woken by the noise, Wink appeared by my side, mouth open in horror, pointing at Hildegard. Hackles raised, tail swinging, the cat had just beaten a kestrel to one of my yellow throated thrushes. Beset on all sides I screamed at her to stop but instead she whisked it up, raced back to my side and placed it gently at my feet, apparently unharmed. One of the pens was still intact so I lifted the thrush gently, opened a grille and slipped it inside.

Ignoring the sharp claws which ripped at her fur in fury, Hildegard fought for and won four more of our birds, which Wink deposited in the one good cage. 'They're all the originals, the ones which were here when you arrived,' Wink cried. Slipping off my dressing gown and grasping it sideways with both hands I flapped the material like a sheet to ward off the birds of prey while Hildegard continued her stalwart effort as by far the best catcher among us.

More killers appeared and I feared we'd done all we could when, like that first afternoon, the ground began to shake beneath us and this time a gunshot rang out. Twelve bore in one hand, reins in the other Jolyon raced bareback up the hill towards us. Frightened by the noise, the predators dispersed, though Jolyon fired twice more into the air to make sure before leaping from the horse to help Wink corner a Touraco.

'I'll lay a trail of food into the cage. Before the buzzards return we might just manage to entice some of those who made it to the trees.' He stopped, 'You all right?'

Clad only in a revealing silk nightdress I turned away from him and slipped back into my wrap as nonchalantly as I could. 'Fine. Will they recover do you think?' I pointed at the birds Hildegard had saved.

'Not if that damned cat's still around, they won't.'

'It was she who saved those too frightened to fly.' Having had about as much as I could take, I left Wink and Jolyon to cope with the birds and turned towards the house. Travers and a handful of other staff were straggling across the drive, dressing as they came.

'Ask Mr St Clair if he'd care to join us for breakfast later on.' The least I could do by way of thank you was feed the man.

'Before you go, Ma'am,' Travers detained me, 'there's more bad news I'm afraid. The new wall's been bulldozed.'

'I woke only when I heard this rumbling go out through the gate – heavy equipment. I couldn't figure out why I hadn't heard it go in.' Jolyon sat back from the table.

'Because it breached the wall, two miles away, and tanked across the fields to the aviary. That's what Hildegard's antenna must have picked up. If only I'd stirred that bit quicker….' Not hungry, I pushed my plate away. 'Frank Channing's cars, now this. What's going on?'

'Don't waste your sympathy on Channing. He sold Susan's brother a dud pickup truck, and when he complained, just grinned and refused to do anything about it,' Jolyon remarked, finishing his coffee.

'That's happened to people here too.' Wink added, spreading her marmalade with the precision of a master plasterer.

'You don't think Channing is behind this, thinking I stole his cars? Wreaking revenge?'

'More likely to be Fentiman's work,' Jolyon said, very softly.

'Because I fired him from Sanderling?'

'He was a two-bit trader before the countess died, dabbled in this and that, usually shady. Out for a quick buck. Then, bonanza struck. His mucker, Poulson Junior, gets to wield the power at Sanderling and Fentiman suddenly reinvents himself as chief executive of a property maintenance company. Watching the countess grow old with no heir in sight and Poulson Senior fading fast, they'd probably been cooking it up between them for years,' Jolyon stood up.

'I'm sorry, Miss McKenna, but you must have guessed that neither Poulson nor Fentiman were ecstatic about an heir being appointed.' He strolled across to the window, glanced out and then at me, as if debating whether or not to say more. 'They thought the idea of selecting someone by criteria was a joke and that even if any such person could be found, she would never stay. They'd see to that, one way or another.' He looked out again. 'Which is I suspect why they're becoming a tad impatient.'

'You seem to know a lot about it, Mr St Clair?' Good old Wink. Was Jolyon St Clair also aware that after much prodding by my London solicitors, the probate registry had finally issued the grant of representation? Poulson's power was dwindling by the day as his executorship was dragged, inch by painful inch, towards a close.

'Fentiman made no secret of his plans, any one of the Coach and Horses clientele could tell you the same ... if they'd a mind to.' He looked at his watch as the clock in the hall chimed nine. 'Please excuse me, I have to go.'

'Won't you come back for dinner ... eight o'clock?' I said. 'We've only just started this conversation.' I wasn't about to let a source of information this good go without a grilling – even if he was reeling me in just as surely as a trout from the lake.

When he'd gone, Wink crept into the chair he'd vacated. I turned to face her. 'Jolyon St Clair is in the same gambling syndicate as Russell and apparently requested admission for Fentiman a few weeks ago.'

Wink's mouth fell open.

'Exactly. They're all as thick as thieves – ironic isn't it, seeing that's what they are.'

'You know he was brought up by Lord Dan, don't you; came as a child?'

'So why isn't he living there then?'

'Had a big falling out apparently,' Wink had that mischievous look she always adopted when about to say something she shouldn't. 'I bet it was about Hallingham, Danhanbury's estate. Lord Dan has a couple of nephews apparently but that mightn't stop his nibs feeling entitled....'

Chapter 16

I grieved for the end of peace and the overt declaration of war. What would the countess have done? From all I'd heard, she would have brazened it out.

So I dressed in one of her costliest cocktail dresses and released Travers from his butlering to play the Steinway. The air was heady with scent from the basketfuls of roses heaped down the centre of the dining table. And since Jolyon St Clair was more likely to open up with only one person listening, Wink invented a pressing engagement leaving Jolyon and I to dine alone.

He arrived on Rainbow – in evening dress. Any less stylish a man and I'd have laughed aloud at his presumption but he carried it off superbly. Was he so sympathetic to my feelings that he'd guessed how I wanted to stage the event – understood my need to revert to those better times, retreat back to when Sanderling commanded respect? Or had someone simply tipped him off? Either way I appreciated his willingness to enter into the spirit of the evening.

Neither did the inverse comparison escape me. In the nineteen thirties, the wearing of evening dress had been as Vita Sackville-West once put it: 'a formula, a safeguard, like good manners.' Only those truly comfortable with their position would dare flout the convention. Now everyone dressed down; yet still only the truly confident dare go against the accepted standard.

Seated at the enormous dining table, Jolyon grinned at me. 'What a splendid idea of yours after such a gruesome morning.'

I studied his face as he negotiated helping sizes with the footman. Genial, open, no sign of sarcasm or self-congratulatory cleverness ... and all the more dangerous because of it.

When we had finished the game pie, he put down his cutlery, leaned back and waited until the footmen had left. 'Did you know, that egged on by Barry Fentiman, Charles Poulson saw a way to keep hold of Sanderling – at least for the foreseeable future?'

Listening to Jolyon anybody'd think he despised Fentiman. I wondered why he'd not taken up the stage as a calling.

'Poulson got in touch with one of the other candidates – said he could ensure she won Sanderling in return for allowing them to continue running the estate.'

Nonplussed, I rang to have pudding brought in, which breathing space only increased my anger. Waiting for the footman to refill the glasses and again retire was excruciating. 'So you think that's what I've done? Made a deal with the Devil?'

He raised his head, stared at me and relinquished his spoon. 'You'd have told those creeps to get lost. A woman who could make such a deal is not the person the countess would have chosen to inherit Sanderling.'

He was good. I'd give him that.

'Which brings us back to last night,' he stood and leaned over the back of the tapestried chair; few men were tall enough for that. 'As I tried to tell you that day in the pub, you have to understand what happened here after the countess died.' With Jolyon St Clair overseeing things from the gatehouse, nothing he wasn't aware of, I was certain.

He went on. 'You're talking about a feudal estate. Cherished though they were, the staff, the tenants, the surrounding villages, even the vicar, were all dependent on Sanderling. Protected, as were their crafts. The estate was succoured by enlightened ownership. Life was good.'

'You make it sound idyllic,' if I sounded sarcastic, well, perhaps I meant to be. I took in those heady bouquets on the table, our costumes, the sonata wafting through from Travers in the salon and privately admitted my hypocrisy.

He looked at me a second longer than is usual before replying. 'It was,' he said quietly. 'But as with all strong leaderships, once they go, the structure they built and maintained implodes and the undesirables rise to the top of the pile – largely because they're the pushy ones and the populace haven't learned mistrust.'

'What are you trying to say?'

'That after the countess died, trained to follow, folk around here transferred their allegiance to the first person who came preaching a different gospel – Barry Fentiman,' Jolyon resumed his seat, leaned towards me earnestly, fingering the stem of his glass. 'Unused to thinking for themselves, they were outlooking an unbelievable upheaval in their lives, needing someone to fill the vacuum ... when along comes Barry, officially appointed interim lord of the manor. It's hardly surprising they adopted him as their new provider. In some ways, he was. Nothing happened here without his say-so. Carpenters, brickies, plumbers, electricians, architects, suppliers of all manner of goods and services, upholsterers, cleaners, you name it – all made their living from Sanderling.'

'And now they don't,' my turn to stand. He offered to rise too but I waved him back into his seat. I set off along the table. 'Well, it's not through lack of trying on my part. The only two people I fired were Fentiman himself and that Channing man. Both were robbing the estate.' Needing the distance, I sat down several chairs away. 'After that I couldn't get anyone local to work here. Look at the adverts I placed. I even talked to you about it that day in the pub. "Give them time," you said.'

Memories of that meeting gave me an unwelcome warmth about this man. I'd been so relieved when he appeared – as I had again this morning. I couldn't afford to feel like that. 'Fentiman threatened them with the rack if they dared to work for me – then blamed me when his business failed and everyone ended up out of work. How can that be my fault?'

'They made a wrong call.' The poker reference brought me up with a jolt. 'Suddenly all these artisans and professionals have lost their jobs with Barry ... because of you,' he viewed the room. 'Think of it from their side – now you have everything.'

'But it's Fentiman who was the false god,' this was so unfair.

'I know that,' he studied his highly polished black evening pumps. 'You probably won't credit this but the villagers dislike Barry intensely. Think he's a conceited "johnny cum lately" puffed up by his own success.'

'So how could he incite them to commit the damage here?'

'Because they hate you more.' Inwardly reeling from his bluntness I was slow to resist when he moved up the three chairs to sit beside me, took my hand. 'I'm sorry, I should have put that more diplomatically. Sometimes I forget you're not a man.' He smiled. 'I want you to succeed, Synnove. And I'll do anything I can to help. But cutting yourself adrift from the community—'

'Huh. Fat chance of that,' I snatched back my hand and stood. So did he. 'To borrow one of your gaming analogies, Mr St Clair, the dice have been loaded from the start. I never stood the remotest chance of being accepted. It was a waste of time trying.' Even as I said it, my mind leapt to picture the consequences – barbed wire on all perimeter walls, twenty-four hour security patrols, dogs, the old gates closed and padlocked. Inherit an estate and become a prisoner.

'I'll see what I can do about that,' he rebuttoned his jacket. 'Meanwhile, with your permission of course, I'll ride around the grounds at unpredictable hours of the night. Just in case.'

Chapter 17

Wink burst in without knocking; hair in curlers, voluminous padded dressing gown over her nightdress, fake ocelot fur slippers as big as snow shoes. 'My dear, I could contain myself no longer. Do tell all.' Flinging herself into a nearby armchair, she leaned across and pinched a slice of buttered toast off my tray. 'That man has been on guard duty out there all night. I'll swear I saw his white horse on the horizon when I woke at four. Serves him right.

'By the way, I forgot to tell you in all the excitement yesterday ... that architect chappie who cut you dead, Smithson is it?' I nodded. 'His cleaning woman was telling Sheila in the shop that she hasn't been paid. Gone to the wall I hear.'

'Not another one. That's three in almost as many weeks. Fentiman, not that he didn't deserve it; Channing, the car dealer, must be in deep trouble since he wasn't insured and can no longer use the Sanderling motors ... and now Smithson. What's going on?'

'Divine retribution, dear. They'll be burning you at the stake soon,' she chomped thoughtfully. 'By all accounts he's bone idle. That can't have helped. Leaned back on one plaster laurel too many if you ask me.'

Russell called from Africa. 'Why don't you answer your bloody e-mail? If you knew how difficult it is ... hell, I just dropped—' a sound of scrabbling. 'Bloody mosquitoes and bats the size of monkeys eyeing me up for lunch. Everything wants to eat me. Put me in a pot and stew me til I'm done; that's the way.'

'Russell?' I felt immediately guilty; had hardly touched a computer in weeks. My PA dealt with the business correspondence and as for my personal life, any I had didn't revolve around e-mail. So no, I hadn't logged on for days.

'Out of sight, out of the country, I know,' he rattled on. 'Don't worry about me, Synna, ensconced in your green and airy mountain where the bluebirds are buzzing.'

'Russell, what's the matter? Stop rambling and tell me.'

'Go on, tell me off. Just like the rest. It's all Russ's fault.'

We had something in common after all. 'What is?'

'Up and down, up and down. 'Cept its down, down, down, but that's ok. That's business. It'll turn, turn, turn, turn. Got to go, feeling diiii ... zzy—' the connection was cut.

Business had obviously taken a turn for the worse. Russell's winner mentality couldn't take failure. I shrugged. I could do nothing from here. A nagging little voice said: 'Go out there. You haven't been to see him in all this time; he came to see you. What if he's ill?'

'He wouldn't want me out there, under his feet. And he's never suggested it.' Actually that wasn't true, hadn't he asked me to go with him when I first learned about Sanderling? 'Yes, well, not since.'

By tea-time the next day, there was no further word from him. I'd tried telephoning the hotel where he'd told me he was staying but they denied any knowledge of him. I tried his mobile several times during the evening but from his comments about the signal there, didn't seriously expect it to function.

Travers appeared proferring a silver tray. I glanced at a visiting card I'd seen before: *Frank Channing, Motor Dealer*. 'What does he want?'

'I couldn't say, Madam. Asked most politely if you were at home.'

'Are all the cars where they're meant to be?'

'They were this morning, Madam.'

'I'll come out,' I didn't want Channing contaminating my personal space.

Channing snatched a cap off his head as I approached. 'Wondered if you needed a chauffeur, Ma'am,' he blurted without looking at me. What would the countess have done? Left it to her butler I imagine – seeing as how she'd had eight chauffeurs, was it?

'Why should I entertain that idea?'

His eyes changed from the crinkled cockiness of our first encounter to watery and fearful. Not of me, I was sure, but of not having a job, I daresay. 'My granddad was head chauffeur for the countess. Taught me all about the cars here. I'd love them as though they were me own.'

'The last time we spoke about my cars you thought they *were* yours.'

He didn't reply. 'How can I trust you?' Again, no reply. Was I being taken for a dupe? Giving him access to the garage would be like putting an alcoholic in charge of a bar. 'I don't need to consider you at all.' If I had any sense I wouldn't and yet.... It would please Jolyon. Besides, Channing's undoubted mechanical skill wasn't easily found these days. I could just imagine what sort of a mess any modern garage would make of those beauties.

'You can service the fleet?'

'Absolutely I can. You been drivin' the Sedanca haven't you?' Did I detect respect there? 'Well she'll be needing a decoke if I know Sybil.'

'And you won't do anything ... anything at all with any of the cars without my written permission?' I had to find some way of impressing on him a new attitude towards my property.

'Absolutely not, Ma'am.'

I took him on a month's trial, and after Wink had tired of the subject over dinner, spent a sleepless night interrogating an unresponsive Hildegard as to the wisdom of my action. Over the next few days Channing turned out to be the first of several. Which surprised me; that having rejected previous advances, they should all present themselves at much the same time.

I put it down to the loss of jobs with a major employer like Fentiman taking a week or two to bite – for the cheques to stop. Until, that is, not meeting my eye, one of them mumbled: 'Mr Jolyon thought you might need a plumber.'

I resented being manipulated but clearly something had changed. From would-be destroyers, they were suddenly inquiring after work. Wasn't that what I'd wanted? And what choice did I have? Jolyon was right. If the estate stood apart from its environment, an island separated by mutual animosity from its locale – then I wouldn't be carrying out the countess's wishes. I had to give these people a chance – in the hope they might just reciprocate.

One autumn afternoon a few days later, I set out across the fields to blow the cobwebs away. Occasionally I'd done that in London, only then I'd had to make do with the bustle of the South Bank and garrishly painted designer cows rather than the verdant paradise which now surrounded me. Ever since I'd stepped into this other world of Sanderling, McKenna Associates had become a distant concept although I still depended on it for my income. I took comfort from having a quite separate source of earnings ... just in case Sanderling didn't work out. I was independent – could walk away.

Besides, McKenna's allowed me to use all my gifts and knowledge and training to make the most of myself. Whereas, trying to run Sanderling as the countess and countless generations before her had done, was a continual reminder of my inadequacy. Might it be better if I admitted defeat and let the detective woman find a more suitable candidate? Instead of Fentiman, was I the cuckoo in the nest, blocking a far better person from doing the job?

Preoccupied, I failed to realize how far I'd strayed. In front of me lay the lodge gates. To the left, the brick and timber gatehouse sat foursquare within its acre or so of garden. A sudden discordant honking shattered the peace.

Chapter 18

What the hell was Fentiman doing here? Come to see his pal Jolyon? Still driving the flash car I see.... As I moved across the path, like an impatient horse pulling at the bit the red Ferrari jerked forward, shifting the light on the windscreen.

'Russell,' I gulped. 'Goodness.'

I pushed back the right hand gate and the car came to rest beside me. 'Pleased to see me?' his tone was downbeat, his face drawn, even thinner than last time. Walking around to the passenger side, I slid into the seat and he accelerated up the track across the field.

'I thought you sold this when you went to Africa.'

'Borrowed it back.' Spinning the wheels unnecessarily, he manoeuvred around the fountain and roared down the drive to the door, finishing this schoolboy demonstration with a handbrake turn in a hail of gravel.

Travers bustled out, consternation creasing his usually benign countenance. 'Are you all right, Madam?'

'Yes thank you, Travers,' I replied, grateful for his steadying hand helping me out while my legs shook unreliably. Russell tossed him the keys, an action I found demeaning. Travers caught them deftly with one hand and a slight bow, outwardly unperturbed.

Russell took my arm and marched me inside. 'Nothing like having a few servants around is there? That's what I've been missing.'

'How long are you here for?'

'Why? Trying to get rid of me already?' he swept me into his arms and planted a long kiss on my lips, something he hadn't found time for on his last visit. Had he realized how distant he'd become and wanted to make amends? Was he missing me, out in that unfriendly land?

I pushed him to arm's length. 'How are you? I was afraid you'd picked up one of those horrible bugs, you sounded poorly.'

'Mmm,' he wandered off down the hall towards my sitting room. 'Got any scotch?' I followed him in and rang for the footman who appeared very quickly, the scotch soon after.

'Have you come to stay or is this a quick hello before you rush off back to Africa?' I sipped my scotch not really wanting it at four in the afternoon. 'You didn't answer my e-mail.'

Having knocked back a good mouthful or more, Russell topped up his glass from the tantalus and flung himself on to a couch, nearly sloshing the liquid down his shirtfront. With his other arm splayed across the back of the seat Russell surveyed the room expansively. 'Decided to come in person,' he grinned, showing a hint of the old Russell, his colour returning. He leaned forward. 'How's it going then?'

'Sanderling? One forward, two back ... but I think we're making progress at last.' It was the sort of answer you give someone you think is inquiring out of politeness. 'The wiring and plumbing need replacing and we no longer comply with fire regulations so all the floors have to come up and be lined with fire retardant stuff. You don't want to know.'

'And McKenna Associates?'

'Doing well,' convinced he wasn't really interested in my concerns I rose only to change the subject, but he held out an empty glass so I duly topped it up. I attempted to place it on the table beside him but he insisted on holding it. 'Tell me about North Tamin. What's it like?'

Slumped into his seat, Russell stared into his drink, the flesh on his face downcast, 'They don't understand how much money it takes to make the sort of return they expect. And while the country is still in turmoil, the International Monetary Fund isn't keen to lend. So it means I have to find it. "You hedgies", they say,' he mimicked an African speaking English and jabbed the air with a vicious forefinger, ' "you hedgies, ain't that what you do. You do eet," ' he shuddered.

'I hate to suggest this, but wouldn't it be better to just draw a line under this – walk away.' Intensely competitive, he'd no more give in than stop drinking ... especially if he thought I'd succeeded in my venture where he'd failed.

'When I've invested hundreds of millions of their money and can't pay it back yet? Fat chance of that,' he suddenly stood up. 'I feel like a walk. How about showing me round this heap. I missed out on the guided tour last time I was here.'

We set off upstairs. 'So does this all interconnect? What's down this passage here?'

I answered his questions as best I could then left him with the plans from the library. 'Wink knows the layout better than me. In her quest for the missing—' Wink had been searching Sanderling for the treasures Sullivan had packed away; but some indefinable caution stopped me mentioning those. Russell was too buried in the plans to notice. But at dinner, he did quiz Wink on the structure of the building.

Wink left us after the pudding, taking her coffee up with her to watch TV. Russell and I strolled outside. The early scotch plus claret with the meal had left me less tolerant of his whims. 'Why the sudden interest in Sanderling, Russell?'

'What do you do for capital?'

'Trustees look after that.'

'But they give you what you want.'

'Well, I have to make a case ... for a new barn for one of the farms say.'

'All I need is sixty million, Syn.'

I chuckled, 'Developed a sense of humour, I see.'

He spoke softly, intent on his shoes. 'I'm serious. It's just about enough for a new issue of derivatives I know will come good. You'll have it back in under a year.'

'Wouldn't that be throwing good money after bad?'

Brows knit together in a scowl, hands thrust deep into his pockets, he stood in front of me, manoeuvring a selected pebble around on the path with the toe of his shoe. 'I've got to have sixty million – within the month.'

Gone nine, it was growing dark. I shivered. As Russell turned to follow me in he caught sight of the figure I'd been watching over his shoulder for some time. 'Who the hell's that?' To the right of the lake a ghostly horse followed the bank, its hoofs airbrushed by the mist. 'Bloody man's spying on us.'

'It's only a security guard,' I answered, taking Russell's arm to usher him back inside. I'd not seen Jolyon patrolling so close to the house before but I found his presence comforting; and justified my lie on the grounds that, otherwise, Russell might draw an embarrassingly erroneous conclusion.

Helping himself from the decanter refilled since this afternoon, Russell threw himself on to the sofa. 'Fix a meeting for me to speak to these guys,' he looked at his watch. 'Now would be good.'

'Don't be ridiculous. That's not their role.'

He leaned forward, eyes cold. 'I didn't ask your opinion. Look at you, you're sitting here on a fortune,' he waved a hand expansively, 'and you think you're going to keep it all to yourself. You ungrateful bitch. I gave you money when you needed it.'

As he stood, I unconsciously backed towards the french windows. 'Yes, when I founded McKenna Associates – but not because you believed in me. You just saw McKenna as a way of making a quick buck.'

He moved towards me, hand outstretched. 'Synnove, listen to me. Invest in this new fund of mine and you could make a lot of money.'

'Even if I thought you could recoup your losses by keeping on gambling – I still don't have sixty million, Russell. And from what you say of the markets, I can't borrow it any more than you can.'

'Stop backing away from me. What do you think I am?' If he advanced any further I'd be outside. 'You'll just have to sell McKenna.'

Chapter 19

Hadn't I already done that? First to him for a chance to build my own business and now to a dead countess. 'What do you mean, sell McKenna?' I had my back to the glass.

'McKenna Associates, sell the company.'

'In the middle of a recession?' My high-pitched reply shocked me; lighting as it did on the timing rather than dismissing the very idea as preposterous. The wine must have gone to my head more than I'd realized.

Admittedly I'd had little involvement with McKenna's lately but subconsciously I now realized I'd been treating my absence as a sabbatical; a break in which to taste Sanderling.

'It's easily worth sixty million, even in this downturn. And anyway, I can get some punter to write me a cheque for that much on the basis that, if it's not, you'll pay the difference back in, say, two years' time. That way I get the cash now and he gets McKenna's at the lowest possible cost.' Less than a foot away from me, Russell took a swig from his whisky, a lascivious sneer on his features. Even in my hazy state I picked up on the pronouns.

'You want me to sell all I've worked the last ten years for, at a knock-down price, with the possibility of me personally owing the buyer several million at the end of it – without seeing a penny back.'

'So what? You landed in a bed of roses through no effort of your own – why shouldn't I? It's about time you learned that responsibility goes with the perks.' As he lunged towards me, I shoved him as hard as I could with both hands. He tottered across the room and collapsed back on the chesterfield.

I caught a flash of white outside the window as I ran out of the room waiting only for Hildegard to back out behind me, hackles on end, before I could shut the door. Anywhere else I'd have slammed it but at Sanderling the sheer weight of the wood prevented me.

Wink would be fast asleep by now. And because I still disliked having footmen eavesdropping on my conversations, the rest of the staff had been instructed to retire to their quarters in the stable block after dinner had been cleared, including Travers. With Hildegarde running ahead I moved swiftly up the stairs, nervously glancing behind me at every turn. With relief at having made it unpursued, I rushed through the door of my suite, locking it behind me.

Far from the romantic reunion I might have imagined, I was, if anything, afraid of Russell. Previously subdued by the City environment, his aggression channelled into vehement keyboarding, vitriolic notes and punishing gym sessions, his African experience had released the latent animal in him. The roughness which made him such a ruthless trader, had surfaced. I no longer trusted him – with anything.

But for Jolyon St Clair patrolling the grounds, I'd have felt extremely vulnerable; alone in this massive house with a man turned wild by greed and circumstance. Far from sleepy, I crossed into my bedroom and drew back the curtains.

Reflected in the old panes was a woman I no longer recognized. Who was I now? Who did I want to be ... and was that even relevant? Russell's demands, whilst unreasonable and unexpected, had dredged up a much deeper question. Given the choice – a hand that chance had dealt me and anyone would envy – why should I find it hard to cast off my former self? Was it because I still doubted the reality of Sanderling? It felt substantive, appeared reliable – indeed its very lack of frivolity of late bore testament to that solidity. An idyllic situation without problems would have been truly unbelievable.

So was it failure I feared? I had run Mckenna Associates successfully, I possessed no such proof about Sanderling. Some of the locals had crawled back through necessity. The country was going through a bad patch. What would happen when the sun shone again? I had no faith I could engender the loyalty the countess had enjoyed. Equally, could I risk Sanderling falling into the wrong hands?

Now and again my feet cramped and I had to shift Hildegard and pace the room for relief but otherwise I sat in my eyrie, batting the subject back and forth.

If what disturbed me was my lost love affair then its ending was not before time. Only when apart from Russell did I nurture feelings of love for him. I had clung to the dream of him and me as a couple, way beyond its practicality, inventing feelings for him to give my life a lift; an injection of warmth like a drug or an adrenalin high. And for fear of being an old maid. I'd told myself every relationship has ups and downs so to assume mine would read like a second rate romantic novel was juvenile. Hence I'd stuck with it. So, no. I didn't regret the inevitability of a break with Russell; we'd both been suffering the death spasms for too long. But I did owe him. By selling McKenna Associates ... and even the apartment, I could discharge that debt.

I don't know if I dozed off, or dived so far down in thought my conscious brain had switched to standby. There were no preceding shouts, no doors opening and closing, no galloping horse ... only the shot.

Chapter 20

Hildegard sprang two feet in the air. Paralyzed, I listened intently for several seconds until footsteps sounded in the hallway outside.

'Synnove, are you all right?' Jolyon's voice. He rattled the handle but I had locked the outer door.

Squashed for hours by the cat, my feet wouldn't work properly. I staggered to the door and flung it open. Jolyon had backed to the other side of the landing. I'd left the lights on when I came up so I could see him clearly. He had one hand behind his back. 'The shot…? Where's Russell?' Had Jolyon shot him? I was too bemused to question my feelings, but my calmness was incriminating.

'It's OK, he's phoning the police.'

Readjusting the fur blanket over my crumpled evening dress, I followed Jolyon down the stairs without sighting the weapon I was sure he carried. At the bottom he stood aside and I headed across the ill-lit hall to my sitting room.

Head in hands, Russell was sitting more or less where I'd left him, the carpet in front of him was splattered with blood and a knife lay on the floor. The decanter had been smashed into a thousand fragments and what was left of the whisky dripped in nauseous yellow globs off the side table.

Russell looked up as I came in. 'I told you. Bloody bastards. I warned you.'

He didn't appear hurt. I sat on the edge of a chair and looked from one to the other. 'Well? Is anyone going to tell me?'

Jolyon waited, but when Russell remained silent he ran tanned fingers through his hair and said, 'Ever since they destroyed the aviary I've been alert to the slightest noise. About three o'clock I heard the gate rattle – as though someone were scaling it. I rushed out but could see no one.

'So I took Rainbow across the bottom meadow and skirted the north wing where whoever it was would neither see nor hear me. Leaving the horse on the far side I crept back here in time to see a figure about to stab your friend. I was too far away to stop him; all I could do was shoot. The light was still on in here which made it easier.

'The man fled into the hall, escaped through the unbolted front door and into the darkness before I could catch him. It's hopeless trying to find him out there in the dark but the police can follow the trail of blood; I shot the knife out of his hand.'

'Who was he, Russell?' I asked.

Russell glanced at Jolyon and shrugged. Beyond the sitting room, the sound of police sirens and flashing lights ricocheted around the cavernous great hall like arc lights at a son et lumière. 'Someone hired to get me … or frighten me. I told you, these people don't play games. Either I deliver or….'

Russell had led these African thugs to my house, my home – albeit unwittingly … if I believed that. Thinking back through the evening I could be persuaded he'd been expecting someone – and that his clumsy lurch in my direction had been designed to hasten my departure to bed without him. That he had remained in the sitting room with the french windows open because he was too drunk to move, and the front door had been left unbolted by Travers in a misunderstanding as to who would lock up … were feasible explanations I didn't entirely swallow.

And what had Jolyon's part really been in this? Had he overheard the intruder and Russell? Was he trying to spare my feelings … or Russell from my wrath?

Frank Channing ran me to Heathrow. I could have driven to the continent in style, taken one of my 1930s Tourers and called in at Paris, Geneva and Lausanne on the way. But apart from the fact that appearing at their offices in a chauffeur driven Sanderling limousine would have been making an unnecessary statement, I was in a hurry. This was a business trip, not an indulgence.

I'd no doubt my old team would want to buy McKenna and I owed them that opportunity. After all, my success had been built on their sweat too. But that would take months, even if it were feasible in the prevailing climate ... and Russell couldn't wait. If I delayed by so much as a week he would sell his shares for what he could get on the open market and McKenna would be controlled by God knew who. The only reason Russell hadn't done that was he couldn't sell without my knowledge and he also needed what my share would fetch ... as well as the proceeds from the apartment we jointly owned; I had already instructed agents.

I took a taxi from Zurich airport to the Gold & Weinstein offices in a discreet glass-fronted building on the corner of a tree-lined boulevard overlooking the lake.

They had told my PA I needn't come over; that they would be happy to consider any proposition I may have in the usual way, as they had with the countess, and get back to me. But I needed no lessons in the importance of face to face contact in selling. I also understood their apparent courtesy to be a euphemism for they'd rather I didn't visit. They were Swiss bankers, comfortable with their faceless anonymity ... and mine; unlikely to welcome the substantiation of an otherwise shadowy character towards whom they felt no obligation. Once I became flesh ... I'd be much harder to refuse.

Travelling skywards in a spotless lift, I was conscious of this being the most important sale I'd ever negotiated. As usual, it was on someone else's behalf, or so I told myself; but never had it felt so personal.

Conditioned by Hollywood, I'd pictured an oak panelled sanctuary where morning-suited minions trod noiselessly through marble-floored halls wearing white gloves and carrying gold inlaid deposit boxes. The modernity of Gold & Weinstein's offices therefore surprised me, but not the soullessness.

Ferdinand Weinstein the seventh awaited me in the upstairs lobby. Tall, spare, sixtyish, with iron-grey hair, a hooked nose and the personna of a benign heron, he conducted me wordlessly along the wide corridors of my imagination and into a startlingly light board-room. An elliptical maple table, doubtless a priceless work of art, was ringed with Picassos and Hockneys hung on white walls and surrounded by sumptuous tan leather chairs in art deco shapes; as stylish as the films had depicted, just updated.

The twenty or so seats were all occupied; by Ferdinand's brothers and cousins if their similarity gave any clue. They rose as one as I entered and was ushered to a place of honour at the far end. I put the vast turnout down to curiosity and a desire to be reassured en masse that an heir selected by lottery – which is how it must seem to them – could be in any way suitable.

Ferdinand remained by my side and formally introduced the various Weinsteins and Golds by name. They each gave a polite bow. Coffee was poured and little sweetmeats handed around in silence.

I stood, indicating with a gesture that they should remain seated. 'Gentlemen, I am honoured and grateful that you should agree to meet me today. I know you're busy so I'll come straight to the point.'

Uncomfortable in one spot, I set off around the table, talking as I went. As I progressed, those with their backs to me twisted their necks in synchronized formation. 'You all know who I am and the extraordinary events which led to my appointment at Sanderling.' Although inscrutable expressions were obviously part of the heritage they nodded deferentially making me feel I was indeed the next countess, treating me as I'm sure they would have done her.

What were they thinking I'd come for? A free hand at Sanderling? Removal of them as trustees? 'Well, first, I thought it was high time we met anyway,' I gave them my best smile, 'and I've come to ask for your help.'

'Go on,' Ferdinand said, when I paused in case they wanted to say anything.

This was the part I was largely unprepared for. Normally I'd have known something about each of these men – how they thought, their past history and, most crucially, who they followed and what would be his likely reaction. Here, I knew none of these things – was pitching cold; whilst they all had my inside leg measurement committed to memory.

'I need to sell my sales outsourcing business, McKenna Associates, in order to give my complete attention to Sanderling ... and pay off my former partner.' Desperate to control my shaking, I hurried on. 'I don't need to tell you gentlemen that now is not an ideal time to contemplate such a transaction as the price I receive will be at its lowest. However, due to my partner's circumstances, that can't be helped.' No one stirred. 'But I believe the team I have left behind at McKenna's would be the very best group to take the firm forward.'

'You're advocating a management buy-out, Miss McKenna?' I was warming to Ferdinand.

'I am, and that's why I'm here,' I scanned those stoney faces. 'I would like Gold & Weinstein to fund the buy-out.'

'Have you prepared an estimate?'

'Sixty million pounds, payable immediately, in cash.' I handed out the brief prospectus I'd prepared showing McKenna's turnover, pipeline of work and projections for the next three years along with the profiles and success rates of the key staff.

Still only Ferdinand addressed me, although a low murmuring which I wanted to interpret as relief, emanated from a number of stations around the table. 'And what do you offer as security, Miss McKenna?'

'Me ... my ability to make a success of Sanderling.'

I travelled back via our old flat, finding it even more lacking in atmosphere than I'd previously felt. The contrast with the manor was stark. I wandered through its rooms, looking for memories and found none; searched its cupboards for keepsakes and pocketed few. Like a hobo vacating a temporary lodging, I took only a handkerchief's worth of possessions and left a sign to say I'd moved on.

In retrospect I think the trustees had been pleased to meet me, to put a face to the person whose enterprise they were charged with protecting and yet had so little say in. Sanderling must always have been an incredibly difficult proposition for them to grapple with, none more so than now; yet not one of them had challenged my credentials or behaved less than charmingly.

Putting myself forward as security had been accepted in the spirit with which it was intended. They understood a whole lot more about me than I did about them but I had banked on them viewing my withdrawal from McKenna's as a positive step, a committal – and therefore worthy of their assistance.

I caught the 2.15 from Marylebone and sped back home to the crackle of burning wood as the bridges collapsed behind me. Raised off the ground I lost contact for the duration of my journey, felt a break – a discontinuation – while the soporific clickety-clack lulled me into a trance and the scenery whizzed past like a Victorian peep show, transporting me to a different place.

Up to this point I could, theoretically at least, have returned to my former life; stepped back through the mirror, picked up those familiar reins and written off Sanderling and my time there as little more than an interesting interlude.

Instead, like much of South Warwickshire, I now had no other job, no other source of income. I relied entirely on Sanderling for my existence.

Chapter 21

By the time the king walked away, in December 1936, the shock had at least been dissipated by its growing inevitability. Nevertheless England stood divided on whether or not he should simply have stuck it out – defied the establishment and married Wallis Simpson regardless – or followed the path of his ancestors and kept her as his mistress.

At twenty, Isabel was too caught up in her own private whirlwind, too elated by a newly bright and shining universe to be dismayed by the king's problems. She too had stolen licence from the changing times.

Ted Arrowsmith, estate manager at Sanderling and highly regarded by Isabel's father, had lost his first wife in the influenza pandemic of 1919. In 1934 he remarried; a distant cousin, herself a widow with a grown-up son who had recently won a scholarship to Cambridge. In 1936 at the age of 42, she died in childbirth.

An intelligent woman, dogged with ill-luck, Molly Arrowsmith and Isabel had shared a passion for roses. The evening before her funeral, Isabel ordered the gardeners to ransack the terrace for blooms and took them to the chapel herself. Propping open the west door to admit what few rays still had the strength to pierce the nave, she was busy with her task, when the building darkened. Tutting with impatience that the door should have swung to, she let drop the stems in her hand and was turning when a figure loomed in the doorway.

'Come in or go out but don't just stand there blocking my light.'

The man advanced towards her, young, broad-shouldered, wearing a three piece serge of the sort the estate workers wore on

Sundays. He clutched a small suitcase in one hand and removed a battered brown trilby with the other.

'I was on my way from the station,' he said in a rich voice.

Arrowsmith had said Molly's son would be coming down. Apparently he'd visited his mother here often, though Isabel had never met him. He had the bluest eyes, literally like sapphires. The little church was a two mile detour from the route which ran from the station to Arrowsmith's house – itself a three mile trudge.

'Didn't your stepfather send a car for you?'

'I wanted to walk.'

Isabel knelt back at her task, fearful her legs would buckle.

'Do you mind if I just sit here for a minute, I'd like to just—'

Isabel jumped up. 'Look, I'll come back later.'

'No, no, please don't go,' he put out a hand to detain her. She'd never experienced a sensation like it. Hurriedly he released her. 'I'm Jim Tennyson, by the way.'

'I'd guessed. I'm … Isabel. How do you do,' she gathered up the debris around her work, desperate to stay but afraid she'd embarrass him if she did and he realized who she was. 'Honestly, I'll leave you to it.'

Walking back along the lane she lambasted herself for her reaction. Thank goodness he couldn't have known what she was thinking. Isabel ran for home, dashing the tears from her eyes, disproportionately upset … without knowing why.

Following the service, refreshments had been organized at Arrowsmith's house. Isabel arrived alone. Jim Tennyson nodded politely to the stream of folk in front of her, then drew her to one side. 'I'm dreadfully sorry about last night, barging in on you like that. I had no idea who you were.' Evidently he'd since found out. Those incredible eyes still held sadness but the rawness had softened.

'Does it matter?' Why on earth did she have to say that in her hoity toity way. 'I mean, I liked your mother very much; I miss her.'

'Thank you.'

When the others had left, they walked for miles across the Sanderling parkland, Jim in his shirtsleeves, Isabel without her hat.

After that, every weekend Jim would cadge a lift from someone at the college or catch the train and Isabel would pick him up from the station. He had two more years to do until he won his degree in engineering and could look for a job.

One Sunday in January 1937, after the biennial Hallingham ball at Bertie's, which Isabel had been forced to attend and from which Jim had been excluded, Isabel's parents called her into the morning room.

'Shut the door, Isabel, your father and I have something to say to you.'

Impatient to be with Jim who would have to return to college that afternoon, Isabel perched on the edge of a chair dreading what was coming.

'Wasn't it a wonderful evening, darling? You in your orange organza ... dancing with Bertie on the terrace. I remember thinking: This is the future. When I'm long gone, there they will be, Bertie and Isabel, upholding all we've worked for, us and the Danhanburys. The two estates conjoined, as we've always planned.'

So they didn't suspect. Isabel stood up, clutching in front of her the newspapers she'd brought from the dining room. Unchecked, her mother could go on like this for half an hour or more.

'It was a lovely evening. I shall be writing my thank you card this afternoon. I'll get Sullivan to go over with it.' Bertie would be out on the lake anyway, or thumping around his estate on his Douglas motorcycle like the ill-fated Lawrence he so admired.

Her mother wound a silk handkerchief around the thumb of her right hand, pulled it taut. 'We have humoured these modern ideas of yours long enough, Isabel, allowed you to do as you please, go to Oxford, learn about the estate. Now it's high time you accepted Bertie Danhanbury's proposal. You'll be practically an old maid soon, people will begin to wonder. I always think a spring wedding....'

She'd been expecting it. This same conversation, or less urgent versions of it, had taken place at regular intervals since her 18th birthday. Her mother hadn't finished. 'Your father spoke to Bertie last night and has assured him that when he asks again, he will be accepted.'

Breathing deeply, Isabel began to shake. Had they guessed? 'Mother and Father, you know I hold you in the highest possible esteem but ... I cannot marry Bertie.'

'You'll do as we say,' growled her father.

'I can't marry Bertie because ...' she cast around desperately, wishing the moment could be over without ... 'because I'm in love with Jim Tennyson.' Rehearsed so often in her head, she sometimes convinced herself she'd already played the scene.

Her father muttered: 'Is that all,' and retreated behind his newspaper. Isabel stared at the black and white print as if seeing her own obituary.

'Tennyson? Arrowsmith's stepson?' Overcome, her mother dabbed at her brow with the handkerchief. 'Quite unsuitable. Why he has no money at all and he's not—'

'In our class, Mother? I'm not marrying Bertie. I've been telling you that for years. Now there's absolutely no doubt.'

'I'm shocked you can even contemplate such a thing. You'd be dropped from society ... as would we all.'

Her father put down the paper, stood up and paced in front of the fireplace. 'Isabel, I never thought I'd have to remind you about duty. Forget this romantic nonsense which'll likely fizzle out anyway. What matters is tradition, responsibility, what we owe the servants, the estate workers, our tenants—'

'Oh, so that's it. You of all people, who've taught me so well, still think I'm incapable of running Sanderling – because I'm a woman. Well I'll show you.' Isabel stormed out of the room.

She walked briskly away from the house and down to the stables, barked at Channing to take the cover off the Lagonda and roared off in it across the track to the gate. She wished she'd had more courage. She may have succeeded in fudging the issue, diverted her parents into thinking this was about her capabilities – but the truth would out soon.

Navigating at speed through the lanes, she sympathized with their erstwhile unhappy king. That had been the problem with Mrs Simpson, not that she was divorced, but that she wasn't of royal blood. Kings must marry their own kind, and so must countesses.

Otherwise the order of things would be upset and they all knew where that led.

Slowing automatically as the crossing lights flashed, Isabel considered her alternatives. Keep driving? She braked, sat strumming her fingers on the wheel while the express raced past – free as air. Not really, even the train must keep to its tracks. She could follow the king and abdicate. Go off somewhere with Jim. Her body diffused with warmth as she envisaged their life together. She could get a job – they wouldn't be destitute. She considered her expensive dress, the car. Trappings weren't important, being with Jim was what mattered.

But what would happen to the estate? Unlike King Edward, she had no sibling to undertake the job. If Isabel abdicated that would be the end of Sanderling – centuries of tradition ended by her selfishness. The train rattled away around the bend, unheedful, glad to be away. Unlike her; she could no more give up Sanderling than cut off her arm.

She let out the clutch, let the motor run forward. Time, she needed time. Time for her parents to come round to the idea. Time for society to change some more, as her contemporaries vowed it would. In ten years she would look back and wonder what all the fuss had been about. But not if she'd already given up her inheritance. Somehow she had to hang on to Sanderling as well as Jim. If that meant they couldn't marry just yet, it was a small price to pay. Just as long as, in the meantime, she wasn't forced into marrying Bertie.

Chapter 22

'Since you arrived, whatshisname Fentiman got the old heave-ho which brought down half the village ... including his playmate Charles Poulson. It didn't help that he then forbade the other half to work for you in the mistaken ruse that this would send you hotfoot back to the bright lights. Then the car chappie has his stock stolen, the architect man stops paying his bills, the shopkeeper loses all but one of her shops and even that's hanging by a thread so I hear.'

I laughed. 'Well you certainly can't pin her troubles on me. Wasn't she done by the food hygiene police? Anyway, from what I saw she's a nasty piece of work.'

'Ah, but it was you who caused the local populace to be out of work—' Wink held up her hand. 'As they see it, Synnove ... as they see it. Perception is everything, don't forget. They therefore have no money to spend in her shop, ergo....'

'Oh, so it's all my doing is it? I can't be responsible for everyone's welfare – especially,' I thought about that, 'yes, especially when I gave everyone several chances.' I whacked the thistles with my stick as I'd seen Bertie do. For the same reason – the release of pent-up anger?

'Don't you understand – it's down to you, whether you like it or not.' Wink was sounding more like Bertie every day. 'The owners of Sanderling have held responsibility for these people for generations. You surely don't think that obligation's going to change just because they're withholding their labour at present.'

Arriving at the aviary, I skimmed pebbles off the hill into the bushes below, startling the rabbits and sending the pigeons flapping like grey paperbags caught by a gust. 'Seems to me they make up the contract to suit themselves. So, what do I get out of it?'

Wink leaned against a birdcage to catch her breath. 'Don't ask me, I didn't invent the system,' she pushed herself upright. 'It's you who signed up to it when you took on the job.'

'Why didn't the countess have this trouble then?' Because she had lawful authority, the locals knew I didn't. It had been easy for her. 'And why did she never marry and have children? Then she wouldn't have left this problem.'

'For the same reason as Elizabeth I? Unwilling to relinquish her power? I'd say a lot of the situation in which you find yourself was her doing.'

I sat down on a fallen log. 'Ha ha very helpful. Of course it is, her and her flaming criteria.' What was I complaining about? I'd chosen freely hadn't I?

Wink joined me. 'I didn't mean that. The countess witnessed momentous social changes in this country and yet refused to embrace them.' Wink turned to look at me directly. 'Do you realize the folk around here consulted her on absolutely everything. If they couldn't get their kid into the right school she pulled unseen wires at County. If anyone was in trouble with the law the local magistrate would discuss the punishment with her before passing sentence. And I daresay most felt they had to seek her permission before they could even marry.... Isabel Foxhill and Bertie Danhanbury ruled this part of South Warwickshire as if nothing had changed since the Domesday census.'

'Trouble is she's still doing it, isn't she? Directing other people's lives.' I wasn't running Sanderling according to my own conviction, I was simply a bad imitation of her; constantly striving to do what she would have done – and failing. 'I'm not her, Wink. Even if I were a proper heir I still couldn't always do things her way.'

'That's why I said it's the countess's fault for refusing to change with the times,' Wink sighed. 'Except she may have deliberately created a gap after her death because she was aware things had to move on.'

I wandered over to watch the birds. 'I'm sorry, but there's one major flaw in your argument.' One of my favourite yellow throats flew on to the netting and serenaded me. 'If the countess wanted to affect the change you say then why not do it herself?'

'Because she hailed from a different era, was brought up in a very distinct way. Has it occurred to you that she did indeed recognize what needed doing but was too entrenched in the past to do it herself?'

Wink was out and Travers had just served my soup when we heard tyres on the drive. When they swiftly drove away again I relaxed. I didn't feel like visitors. Seconds later a footman appeared ... Russell at his heels.

Chapter 23

'Clear out you lot, go on', Russell shouted, waving his arm briskly towards the door like a policeman encouraging slow-moving traffic. I caught Travers's eye and nodded.

I'd not seen him since the night someone had tried to kill him in my sitting room. After the police had gone he'd grabbed my arm and whispered hoarsely: 'Now do you see? Get me that money, Synnove,' and hared off up the drive in the Ferrari. Thanks to the gnomeish brothers, Russell had received his sixty million within the week.

'Hello Russell,' I picked up my spoon and began to eat.

He marched around the table and thumped his fist so hard on the polished oak next to my plate that the leek and potato bounced from its bowl. The unused knives and forks rattled like dismayed maiden aunts. The dining room door clicked open a fraction and silently closed again; Travers making sure I was all right.

'Do sit down; soup's on the sideboard if you want some,' I invited, maliciously pleased that through his own ill manners he was forced to serve himself.

'For God's sake, is that all you've got to say?'

Appetite gone, I stood. 'What do you expect me to say when you bring some crazed killer into my house, demand sixty million pounds – half of which wasn't yours anyway – then vanish without so much as a thank you.' Bertie would have been proud of me. 'I owe you the square root of bugger all, Russell Prince.'

Running grubby fingers through unkempt greasy hair, he collapsed into a chair opposite. Dressed in a linen jacket crumpled enough to have been sat on by an elephant and a once-white shirt which had long since embraced multi-culturalism, his eyes had retreated into mauve sockets, like closed buds in need of dead-heading.

Instead of the excitement Russell's unexpected arrival would once have engendered, I was irritated by the disruption. He was someone I knew well but now could view only objectively, as a stranger. I felt no obligation towards him, no friendliness, no warmth. I had sold my company to pay him off, get him out of my life ... yet here he was again, like bindweed.

Russell glanced furtively over his shoulder as the rumble of the alarm clock sounded in the hall, preparatory to its chiming. 'North Tamin have applied for an extradition order. They want me to stand trial for fraud.'

Visions of African jails bombarded my brain: rotting, fetid flesh; diarrhoea-fuelled gulleys; the stench. I relented and fetched him a bowl of soup which he frowned at before attacking with an urgency only days of not eating could have engendered. I stood looking out of the window while he swilled three bowls only to flee the room abruptly, clutching his stomach.

Travers entered, cleared the debris and served the lamb. Russell returned looking whiter than ever.

I studied him as he ate, like a museum exhibit. Of course, I saw it all now. This renegade government in North Tamin had sought and found exactly what they required – a man already in trouble who would stop at nothing to advance his financial position. A gambler with so many chips on the table he daren't fold his hand. A man who knew how to manipulate the world's markets ... whom they in turn could control.

They must have inquired for someone gullible enough to try and win them a fortune – by dubious means – and lighted on him. How flattered he'd been – headhunted specially.

Fearful I'd start feeling sorry for him, I wandered across to the fireplace leaving him to eat. We had both wanted to escape. He his debts, me a life I'd grown increasingly uncomfortable with. Of course, I'd only realized this fully once I'd come down here but in retrospect I'd disliked many aspects of my existence for a long time. But instead of facing my unhappiness, I'd counted my blessings –

good job, nice flat, rich boyfriend, or so I thought – and told myself to get on with it.

Russell came towards me but he smelled so ripe I rose to tend the fire. 'Couldn't give a toss could you?'

'You say they want you extradited. How long have you been back?'

'A few hours. They thought I was here when they applied but I'd only got as far as Mozambique. Even from there it was touch and go. Took all the spare cash I had.'

'Doesn't it take a long time to get those things through the courts?'

'Not if you can lean on the Foreign Office, threaten to slaughter hundreds more of your own helpless women and children unless Great Britain send you back one measly citizen to answer charges ... swear it will be a properly constituted hearing,' he drew a grubby sleeve across his brow. 'They're desperate. The regime needs a guinea pig to explain away where all that money's gone – and I'm it.'

'So what happened to the sixty million?'

'Wrong timing. I knew it would be but—'

The squeal of brakes on the drive – three, maybe four cars had arrived. Russell threw back the curtains. 'The windows are jammed; we've not sorted them out yet,' I shouted. He rushed towards the main door as it opened to reveal Travers ahead of several policemen cradling automatic weapons.

'Russell Jonathan Prince?' asked a plain clothes man in a nondescript suit.

They marched him out of the manor house between two officers, a lonely bedraggled man, too defeated to put up any resistance. I stood helplessly by, wondering what to say.

Sitting in the window seat of my bedroom talking to Hildegard, who dutifully purred with pleasure at my every utterance, I gazed into the darkness. Although moonless, I sometimes thought I caught the clump of galloping hoofs or a high pitched whinny, or glimpsed a white cloud shimmer across the lawn; but I couldn't be sure.

Russell's sudden appearance and abrupt arrest had upset me. As much for its surreal quality as anything else. He had rushed into my house – leapt on to my stage, forced his way into my drama – an alien creature, out of place and out of context. Unsure what to do, the rest of us players had simply arrested our actions; stopped what we were doing and stood gaping, as still as marionettes in the puppeteer's teabreak. Like Bertie when he lost track of which era he was in.

Then just as suddenly, learning they'd mislaid a character, a handful of equally unexpected extras turn up, scoop Russell off our board and whisk him away so we can carry on as before; nothing altered.

It was late and I was becoming fanciful, yet the main dislocation in my brain wasn't about Russell. Apart from hiring him a good solicitor, which I'd set in train immediately after the police had hauled him away, there was little I could do to help. Doubtless the law would take its course.

My unease had more to do with how well I related to his incongruity. Watching Russell's performance had wedged open a door in my brain I'd been stood with my foot against all these weeks. I didn't belong at Sanderling, had no right to be here. The local people knew it, I knew it.

That's why nothing was gelling; why, as soon as I restored something, it immediately unravelled. A malignant force kept turning the clock back so nothing I did could have any lasting effect. Russell's ill-placement this evening had highlighted my own predicament – that of a stray character tossed into the wrong play.

There must be a blood relation. 'Trouble is, Hilde, how do I find him? After all those generations, some unsuspecting person in the backstreets of Preston or Hull, Edinburgh or Bath ... or in the colonies – America or New Zealand – has far more right to Sanderling than I.'

This conviction had haunted my stay at Sanderling. Initially I'd written off my apprehension as a by-product of the way in which the estate had been thrust upon me. But, admittedly fuelled by the reception I'd received and the difficulties I faced ... my misgivings had multiplied.

Worse still, I had alienated the very society I was sure the countess intended the heir of Sanderling to protect. Despite the social and behavioural signposts she'd put in place: the cars, the clothes – and dear Bertie – if I'd not directly caused, I had at least presided over, the declining prosperity of the whole area. An unwarranted number had lost their livelihoods, their self respect and, let's face it, their anchor; had been cast adrift at the mercy of people like Fentiman. While I sat pampered by possessions I'd played no part in acquiring and didn't deserve.

'The two have to be connected, Hilde,' she looked over her shoulder at me, unblinking. 'Otherwise, I still can't believe that so many businesses would fail at the same time.' Unless I can solve that I'll never be accepted, can't carry on the estate as the countess wished. Which has to be what that unseen hand out there is banking on. Whoever's behind all these failures I'm being blamed for, feels he has a claim to Sanderling. Find him, and maybe I find the rightful heir.' Hildegard stalked out of the room.

At breakfast, after Wink had stopped crowing about Russell's arrest, I told her about my idea.

'Don't look at me, dear one, I can't even locate your blessed buried treasure. Have you considered a visit to Baker Street?' Wink raised the lornette and peered closely at her egg with it.

When I failed to respond she yelled: 'Sherlock Holmes. That's who you need,' as though I were deaf as well as slow.

'That's what I've been thinking.' I'd raised the subject with Wink to check that my all too subjective night-time brooding hadn't completely obscured my judgement. 'Except her name's Jean Edwards and she's the detective the countess hired to find her successor ... me. I'm sure I've mentioned her before.'

Chapter 24

Synnove McKenna had caught Jean by surprise. 'Miss Edwards? I have a job for you.' Keen to keep her plan secret, Synnove had suggested they meet in a pub the other side of Warwick.

They exchanged pleasantries and ordered lunch. She had lost weight, the muscles of her face were tense, shoulders taut.

'How's it been going?'

'You're the only person with any real idea why it was me who ended up at Sanderling. How sure are you that you got it right?'

From the moment of the telephone call, Jean should have expected that. 'We tested you exhaustively. Everything fitted.'

'But those criteria of the countess's, and believe me, I've reread them till I'm cross-eyed, demanded, "the qualities required to run Sanderling as it has been run".'

'Look, Ms McKenna. For whatever reason, the countess chose to dispose of Sanderling as she did and lighted on me to interpret her wishes. Which I can truthfully say I did to the very best of my ability. Obviously the fact that I've no idea what it takes to run Sanderling, and even less about how the countess ran it, is evident. And we both have to live with that – I admit, you rather more than me.' Jean drew breath and resorted to her soup slightly ashamed at her outburst. She'd been so sure Synnove McKenna could hack it....

'I'm sorry. That came across as though I think it's your fault. I only meant....' Synnove screwed up her eyes, 'I'm trying to understand why I got the job when I am so unlike the countess.'

'What makes you say that?'

'Because they despise me.'

Desperate words. Twenty years Synnove's senior, Jean found it hard not to feel maternal towards the woman ... and to some extent responsible for the predicament in which she'd been landed. She put down her spoon, concentrating carefully on her words. 'I don't think the countess was looking for a clone. From what she wrote and what she said she wanted, I believe she sought someone who could and would run the estate in the *spirit* of how it had been run. In other words taking into account honour, responsibility, fairness – those things.'

Jean sat back. 'That's why she found it difficult to spell out. The countess knew she lacked the skills and the mindset to run Sanderling in today's world – yet was equally adamant she didn't want the good things tossed aside. So she concentrated her selection criteria on qualities. So, no, it most definitely wasn't a self description.' Jean waited a moment for the idea to percolate. 'You were chosen for the skills the countess deemed necessary.'

Synnove toyed with her salad for a full three minutes, after which she appeared to park the subject. 'So many local businesses have collapsed, more than makes sense, even in this recession. And I'm being blamed for each and every failure.'

'A variant of *noblesse oblige*?'

'Wink, an old schoolfriend who's keeping me company, suggested something of the sort. Said they need someone to blame other than themselves.'

'I'm sure she's right.' Jean took a bite out of her baguette, chewed.

'I've collated all the details for you,' Synnove reached into her bag and slid a computer memory stick across the table.

Jean sipped her wine. 'You think someone has engineered these disasters and you want me to find out why?'

'Oh, I know why. To get me out of Sanderling. To make life so impossible for me to carry out the countess's wishes that I give up. Someone who thinks they have more right to the estate than I do – which, let's face it, applies to the vast majority of Blakesley and beyond.'

'Isn't that rather a long shot? Now you have tenure why would you worry about what the countess wanted? You could continue to use imported staff and ignore the locals ... if you felt so inclined. Hire a security firm, live in a bubble.'

'But I wouldn't, would I. That's just it. So it's someone who's learned that much about me,' Synnove put down her glass carefully, her fingers remaining wound round the stem as she stared at it. 'I know why. I want you to find out who.'

Back at the office Jean descended to the cellar and dug the files out of storage. As she re-read the list of criteria she lingered over that last one, the one no one understood and which the countess had referred to as a tie-breaker – designed to frustrate.

Jean searched for the earlier notes, the ones on the blood relation ... before she remembered that the countess had burned the entire file. She recalled the furrows in that controlled face when the countess saw the name; stunned, disbelieving ... amazed and horrified that Jean had discovered it at all. And then she had dismissed it – and Jean must honour that decision.

The person Jean had unearthed would be an obvious suspect for sabotaging Synnove's position ... yet without Jean's skill and experience, the relation could never have discovered their own link to the countess. Jean straightened, sighed. At least this time she could start with concrete names and work back, which should be much easier.

Chapter 25

One fateful night in March 1941, recovering from flu, Isabel had remained at Sanderling while her mother and father kept a longstanding dinner engagement at The Café de Paris, off Leicester Square, to mark the 50th birthday of one of their dearest friends, Hugh Rochester.

Her parents had already closed up the house in Mayfair and brought all the staff down to Sanderling. Determined to go ahead, Hugh pooh-poohed the danger. They wouldn't have to stay in town ... and anyway, the fashionable club was billed as the safest restaurant in London on account of its being twenty feet underground.

Home on leave from his ship, Bertie had been riding his motorcycle along the lane from the village when a police car shot past him, taking the turn for Sanderling on two wheels. Knowing the senior Hampdens had gone to the party and concerned something had happened to Isabel he followed it, arriving as Sullivan showed the policemen into the drawing room.

Bertie had held her; put the brandy into her hand, sat with her until daylight, telling her not to worry, that he would get special leave, stay home to help. But much as she'd wanted his company, she couldn't let him do that; not after the way she'd treated him. She would have to stand on her own feet sooner or later and the estate workers were good people – if elderly.

The bomb which had hit the Café de Paris with such devastating finality, killed not only its owner, but many of his staff and, among the guests, both of Isabel's parents. At 24, Lady Isabel Foxhill became the Countess of Hampden, chatelaine of Sanderling.

*

Before her parents' death, Sanderling had been used as a clandestine meeting place for senior politicians and military planners but Isabel wanted to do something more proactive with it; above all to preempt having the place commandeered and herself relegated to the gate house. There was also another reason.

Five years earlier, on the pretext of redecoration, her father had shepherded both the staff and the family into one wing for several weeks. Let back into her customary apartments Isabel found a new half-wing had been erected and her father confided he'd had a secret vault prepared. Over the months which followed, she once or twice caught the sound of trucks moving slowly across the ten acre field at night and on another occasion a couple of gentlemen with East European accents had stayed as guests at Sanderling yet dined apart.

Distracted by her own affairs she hadn't pressed her father as to the exact whereabouts or purpose of this chamber. All he'd said was that friends had need of it. Nevertheless, she now feared the bunker's discovery by the authorities. Invasion by field units, artillery batallions and goodness knew what, would be inconducive to its continued seclusion.

The Hampden money – Sanderling, the Mayfair house and all the other assets – had been put in trust by Isabel's grandfather; for security, the avoidance of death duties and for sundry complex reasons to do with circumventing Victorian marriage and property laws which bore particular consequences for female succession. No ne'er do well would be allowed to seduce a Hampden heiress for her fortune.

Isabel's mother hinted that Isabel's great grandmother had been prevented from marrying the man she loved because he was Jewish. So she had married a homosexual earl for mutual convenience and borne her lover eight children. Thus, Isabel's grandfather had benefited from an army of financially well-connected relations.

The proceeds of the estate were Isabel's to do with as she pleased, and property could be bought and sold with the agreement of the trustees; but the men in Europe handled the underlying finances. Sanderling thrived.

A few months after her parents' tragedy, Isabel received a phone call from the senior trustee. 'Forgive my intrusion, Countess, but these are extraordinary times and we need your help.' He explained that from the mid 1930s the British government had accepted into Britain any children whose lives were in danger. Thousands and thouands of Jewish children had been put on trains out of Germany. Separated from siblings and friends and often very young, they had arrived in an unprepared England and the authorities had struggled to cope with them. Some had been taken in by relatives, but since the outbreak of war, because of their nationality a number of these people had themselves been interned here in the UK, leaving these infants yet again homeless.

Looking back, it had been the happiest time of her life. She was reborn. From a silent, glowering museum, the halls and corridors of Sanderling rang with the sound of children's footsteps, echoed with their laughter, came alive with their joy. Her father would have been horrified but she laughed at the thought. 'You always wanted more than one child, Papa. Now we have hordes.'

As the blitz on England's cities raged, she added hundreds of home-grown orphans to the imported children in need. Transforming corridors into long dormitories, billiards and card rooms into classrooms and using the great entrance hall as a refectory, Isabel housed 630 at the peak.

Outside, the few elderly gardeners delighted in marking out football pitches as a change from tennis courts and the lake was a godsend as a makeshift swimming pool. 'Beggin' your pardon, my Lady,' Sullivan approached her one morning. 'Harry, one of the 4-year-olds, has locked himself in the gun room; refuses to budge.'

If he'd been anywhere else, she'd probably have left him to it. 'Have you got one of those kites handy, Sullivan? Would you mind awfully just trotting along the lawn outside the gun room window with it. In about five minutes' time?'

Isabel went along to the gun room, tried the door. It was her fault, the room was always kept locked but she'd opened it herself for something yesterday, then been distracted. The boy must have moved the key from the outside to the inside, which showed worrying initiative in one so young. The guns were secured in cabinets and the ammunition stowed in the drawers beneath. Even so....

'Harry, this is Lady Isabel ... I need to fetch something. Will you let me in?' No answer.

'Harry? Are you all right?' she rattled the door, trying not to panic. 'Look, look at the kite. Would you like to do that?' From the corridor she could see Sullivan gamely manoeuvring the colourful flyer with its long pigtail, up and down the grass outside.

'You won't be cross?' came a hesitant piping.

'No of course not, now open the door, Harry.'

Footsteps approached, the key turned. Footsteps retreated. She opened the door. The boy stood six or eight feet away holding one of her father's pistols in both hands and aiming it at her. Glancing to her left she saw the smashed glass of the pistol case and the drawer open beneath it. Towed by an oblivious butler, the kite bobbed backwards and forwards outside. She put up her hands. 'I surrender.'

'You have to fall down.'

She crumpled to the floor curled in a ball. Harry walked over, tapped her with his foot. 'You're not groaning.'

She groaned, rolling over and over, making as much noise as possible in the hope someone might hear ... which would endanger them too. She lay still. Without looking up she said: 'Is it my turn now?' No answer.

Very carefully she raised her head. The gun lay on the floor several yards away while the boy stood on a bench looking out of the window.

After that Harry became a favourite. Since both his parents had been killed, his mother in the London bombings and his father in a night time sortie over Germany, he even stayed on at Sanderling for a while after the war; was there when the men came one night to clear out the vault – though it was his turn to be locked in his room that time. In late 1946 the authorities traced a de-mobbed uncle in Colchester who, estranged from his family in the '30s, had been unaware his sister even had a child.

Harry and Isabel kept in touch. Isabel never forgot birthdays and

Christmases; Harry sent little notes and drawings. When he was older he came for a fortnight every summer with a couple of pals. Isabel even attended his wedding to a solicitor's daughter.

Chapter 26

'I only went to Africa because you decided to go off playing lady muck, bugger what I wanted to do.' We perched on wooden seats either side of a deal table in a cavernous hall filled with rows of uniform desks, lined up and numbered. Guards patrolled the perimeter.

'What do you want, Russell?' A fatuous question bearing in mind where we were sitting.

'They've frozen my assets worldwide, so I can't touch my own funds while the administrators figure out what's mine.'

'I didn't realize they could do that. I thought it was just this African business?' What else didn't I know? Had the whole of Russell's empire crumbled?

'Bloody impatient investors brought in the receivers.'

'I am sorry, Russell.'

Russell screwed his features into a sly grimace. 'You speak as though it's got nothing to do with you.'

'Well it hasn't. And I am trying to help.'

'With all those millions at your disposal? It doesn't sound like it.'

'Don't bring the estate into this. Sanderling isn't—'

'Oh no? I bet one of those famous criteria you talked about was proof you could run something as big as Sanderling?' he leaned forward. 'I can tell by your face, I'm right. So you wouldn't have Sanderling if I hadn't backed you in setting up McKenna Associates. You owe me.'

I leaned back, I'd known he'd do it. I just hadn't figured how. He grabbed my hand. Deep sunk, fearful eyes bored into me. 'They want their pound of flesh, Synna. There's only one way I'm going to get out of this mess intact.'

What could I say? As far as I could see there was nothing that would save him that I hadn't already procured – the best legal team in the country.

'They'll take a bribe. The junta in North Tamin. That's what they're after. Otherwise ... once a week until there's nothing left, bits of me will be found strewn across their landscape. I know, they did it to someone else out there.'

Whether or not I still even liked him was a moot point. In despair, Russell had turned to me, his one-time friend. Hadn't I spent the last year learning about obligation? As a consequence, I felt more duty bound than ever to do everything I could. And more especially when I glimpsed the alternative ... the barbarity of which squelched against my closed eyelids each day in those haunted minutes between sleeping and waking.

I could walk away entirely. Away from Sanderling, and thereby, away from Russell's trauma. I had no money left of my own; he'd seen to that. Was it then poetic justice that we both should fail?

I opened the french windows and meandered out on to the west terrace. How could I sit amidst all this wealth while Russell slowly decayed in some filthy foreign flea-pit? Knees tight together I squatted stiffly on the front edge of the damp seat. But those shadowy Swiss brothers would never countenance me selling off Sanderling to free him. And, even if they did, wouldn't that defeat the object of my staying – the protection of the countess's estate?

Head down I wandered towards the water, turning at the edge to wonder at the stunning edifice behind me, its outline fast fading with the light. The Hampden family had understood it wasn't Sanderling as a building which was important but rather what the estate stood for. They'd attempted to preserve a way of life, a set of standards by which life should be lived – *Virtue Alone is True Nobility*. Though, if I sold off a goodly chunk of it, I'd still be demolishing that which I had been specially selected to defend. Was the fate of one man more important?

'Ahoy there; grab the painter, won't you?' Expertly hurled to pay out hemp as it spun, a coil of rope snaked towards the jetty, landing at my feet. I grabbed it, made it fast.

'Much obliged to you,' Bertie nipped ashore like a 40-year old, straightened and considered my face with an extra crease puckering his forehead.

His eyes followed where I'd been looking, towards Sanderling. 'I wouldn't say no to a cup of tea if there's one goin' ... and a tot of rum to go with it,' he proferred his arm and we strode up the lawn together. '... While you tell me what's troublin' you so much you've near frozen to death.' He rubbed my hand between both of his to warm me up. My father had done that when I was a little girl.

We entered the house through the sitting room windows, shutting them behind us. Shivering, I rang for Travers who had already lit the fire and who dispensed our order so fast – along with mouth-watering scones and Swiss roll – I'd have sworn he'd had prior notice of the request.

I leaned against the mantel, toasting myself. 'It's Russell. I told you he's been arrested. North Tamin want him extradited for fraud.' Bertie listened attentively but said nothing while he munched. 'Well, now they want a bribe or else they'll....' I couldn't bring myself to say it.

'How much?' he asked with an almost nonchalant air.

I shrugged. 'Your guess will be better than mine but since I've already given Russell the proceeds from McKenna Associates I've no money of my own – neither has he.' I felt no compunction in telling Bertie the truth. On a personal level, I was penniless and there was little point in pretending otherwise.

'I don't see the problem – unless you intend to marry the man.'

'Oh no,' I said quickly. 'But he sees me with all this.... You can understand it.'

'He wants a loan?'

'Not exactly, but I'm sure—'

'Since you're askin' my advice....' Bertie put down his tea and studied me gravely. 'The man's a bounder. You've given him your life's savin's – and now he wants the countess's. Let him fight his own battles.'

'But how can he, locked away like a criminal? He has no access to the internet or even a phone. He can't possibly help himself.'

Bertie lifted his cup, gesticulated towards me with it. 'Now, tell me, have you decided on a date for the ball yet?'

I stared at him dumbfounded. Conscious my mouth was standing open, I closed it hurriedly. 'What ball?'

'Why, the annual ball, of course. It's held at your place or mine on alternate years in January. And it's way past bein' your turn. You will wear your orange organza and we will dance the veleta til dawn. Tradition must be restored, else what will we use for hooks to hang our lives on?'

Chapter 27

'Most of the skilled artisans who worked exclusively for Fentiman at Sanderling could have quickly recovered ... if only Fentiman had paid their outstanding invoices.' Jean paced the floor in front of the whiteboard.

'So that's the hold he had over them. Do as I say or sing for your money,' Jean explained to the team ranged in her office for the weekly briefing.

'You mean it wasn't his attractive personality which made all these people obey his bidding?' said Sharon, the crew-cut haired field operative.

'On the contrary. Once Fentiman had been handed the maintenance contract for Sanderling, and before the advent of Synnove McKenna, all these people who'd traditionally depended on the countess, found themselves inexorably bound into Fentiman.'

'No wonder they blamed Ms McKenna,' Sharon sympathized. 'These poor people only realized the Aubusson had been pulled from under them when she fired Fentiman and threw him off the estate.'

'Exactly, which occurrence coincided with his refusal to pay them their dues. Of course they associated the two events, considered them cause and effect. So either he explicitly blamed the lack of cash on Synnove, or they assumed she had stopped his payment. Which wasn't true,' Jean continued. 'Most tellingly, her action resulted in his being denied access to the treasures he was auctioning off every week.'

'But what happened to the money he had received from the estate?' Sharon asked.

Jean raised her eyebrows. 'Do you want to enlighten us, Cheryl?'

The much put upon in-house researcher whose earlier career in the army had been thwarted by the onset of MS, wheeled her chair to the front and executed a perfect about-face to address the audience.

'Jean asked me to look into the gambling connection which Ms McKenna said her partner Russell Prince had remarked upon. Apparently Jolyon St Clair has only recently joined an exclusive online gaming outfit – owned by an old Etonian friend of his. That in itself is puzzling, I'll come back to why later. Sticking with friend Fentiman though ... as soon as St Clair gained membership, he put Fentiman up for election. The strangest thing is, I can find not the slightest evidence that Fentiman had ever before gambled in his life.'

'Oh, that's easy then,' Annie a newish recruit, volunteered. 'Fentiman knew he was about to be caught short and was grasping at ace-high flushes or whatever they're called, to pull him out of the abyss opening at his feet.'

Jean nodded at Cheryl to return to her place. 'What Cheryl said she would come to later is the fact that St Clair has never gambled in his life either, still hasn't. We've had people touring the local bookies, frequenting the dog track and nattering to the barmen – asking if they'd seen or knew of St Clair – all to no avail. We've tapped into the better known internet bookmakers, the poker matches and so on ... still nothing. Which facts force us to conclude that St Clair deliberately introduced Fentiman to gambling.'

Jean threw her hands up in the air. 'Who knows? But it's a sure bet that's where Fentiman's money went. We're hacking into the gambling club's computer, but I have no doubt that's what we'll find.'

Sharon scratched her head. 'So St Clair realizes how easy it would be to relieve Fentiman of his money through gambling – the man's ego alone makes him a dead ringer for it. St Clair sets him up and takes a slice of the house winnings. Nice one.'

'No evidence of that,' Jean said, tight-lipped.

'Well they're hardly going to post the divvy-up on Facebook are they? Why else would he go to all that trouble?'

'So all those businesses would collapse and Synnove McKenna would get the blame?' Jean replied.

'Oh come on, I am so not into that idea,' Sharon adopted a droll tone. 'A mite convoluted, don't you think?'

Jean sighed. 'I agree, I dismissed it just like you. But wait.' Jean turned to Cheryl again. 'You don't need to come up to the front, Cheryl, but tell us what else you found out.'

'You asked me who reported Sheila Parsons to the Food Standards Agency. And the answer is....' Cheryl mimed the slitting open of an envelope, extracting an imaginary piece of paper, scanning it, 'Mr Jolyon St Clair of Blakesley in Warwickshire.'

'What?' the others gasped.

'The complaint is logged with his name against it. For obvious reasons of protection, the names of complainants are not given out but one of my—'

'Why should he give his name at all? Won't they act on anonymous tip-offs?' Sharon asked.

Cheryl shrugged. 'Wanted to make sure he was taken seriously? After all, people can die from food poisoning.'

'But someone could have done it pretending to be St Clair ...' Sharon suggested.

'What on earth for – when it's obvious the agency don't name their sources?' Jean said. 'I think it's one of those instances where it's so weird it's probably true.' She faced the whiteboard. 'OK, so we find ourselves amassing a prima facie case for Jolyon St Clair.'

'But why? What's his motive?' Sharon wailed.

'Can we please finish exploring "who" before we get on to "why", Sharon? Annie, you have something else for us, I believe?'

'Yes. About the stolen cars. The police have a pretty good idea who took all those vehicles from Mr Channing's yard, but they can't prove it.'

'Don't tell me that was Jolyon St Clair too. In his spare time,' Sharon sighed.

'Well, it seems it was the work of a ring based in Manchester. They were well organized; brought three car transporters and a specially adapted fork lift, according to forensics. They lifted the cars, clamps and all, and were probably away within twenty minutes. What's more, they knew where to go and when to strike.'

'So they did their homework – so what?' Sharon said, sinking into a chair.

'Well there are two other snippets which are at least intriguing,' Annie continued. 'Circumstantial I admit, could be a coincidence, but in light of what we've already heard.... The car dealer, Mr Channing, was with his wife at a tennis club do when his stock was stolen.' Annie glanced at the tight-lipped Sharon. 'Which, you're thinking, is no big deal except neither of them belong to the tennis club, have never been to anything there before and were invited by – one Jolyon St Clair.'

Sharon shot up. 'So? We know from the way he's always instigating lunches at the cricket club, that he's the social secretary for Blakesley. Take Smithson for example, St Clair's always busy taking him somewhere.'

'Yes, but put that with the fact that members of this same car ring were convicted and jailed for a similar offence against St Clair & Steadman, three years ago ... and you have yet another link to Jolyon St Clair,' Annie finished with a flourish.

'But he was the victim that time,' Sharon wailed.

Jean took a step forward. 'It proves he knew of them, though, doesn't it. I mean, if he wanted a parking lot of cars stolen, who better to approach?'

Sharon stood, walked to the whiteboard, studied it. 'You mean Jolyon St Clair has gone out of his way to ruin all these people? 'She scratched her head, frowned deeply. 'Based on what you've already told us about him – how he never fails to support Synnove McKenna against local bricbats; his work on the aviary; his nighttime patrols to protect the estate – your conclusion seems so at odds....'

Jean perched her bottom on the edge of a nearby desk, grateful to relieve her feet. 'That's why I wanted you all to hear it. If anyone has an alternative explanation for all these ... coincidences, I'm listening.' Eyebrows raised in invitation she surveyed the group. No one spoke.

'And all that's before we get to friend Poulson, the solicitor who stepped into Daddy's shoes soon after the countess died. His is an interesting case because not many solicitors go bust.

'The key to this one turns out to be one of the few local businesses who did not go under – the estate agent. He had a tip-off from a man in Blakesley that Poulson encourages his clients to drop their offer the night before exchange. After that the estate agencies refused to deal with him. The identity of this whistle-blower? From the description – Jolyon St Clair; without a doubt.'

Jean went on: 'And it's not as though these things happened by accident, is it? St Clair has methodically hoisted each of his victims by their own shortcomings; hired a car thief, knowing Channing was too mean to insure his property; inveigled Fentiman into gambling by playing to his ego; deliberately warned estate agents off Poulson; welched on Sheila Parsons to the Food Agency – and laced the alley to alcoholism for Roy Smithson,' she ran tired fingers through her cropped hair. 'I daren't even look for more examples for fear of what we might find.'

'These people aren't exactly saints though, are they?' Sharon mused.

'Hardly the point, is it – when you think how all this has rebounded on Synnove McKenna and Sanderling; whether intentionally or not.'

Jean turned the whiteboard through a hundred and eighty degrees to its clean side and grabbed a marker pen. 'OK. Why is St Clair doing what he's doing?'

'Envy? His own business failed so he's set out to make those around him fail too. With nothing to do all day, he sits there thinking what useless tossers people like Fentiman are and decides to wreak revenge on them for his own misfortune.'

'How about jealousy, hatred of a rival, a man scorned?' Sharon turned to Jean. 'We know he was a favourite with the countess – hell, enough to be left the gatehouse. Can't say I'd turn my nose up at that sort of legacy. But maybe he felt he should have had Sanderling. An obvious reason I know, but....'

Jean considered this. 'I've no problem with the motive per se. As you say, it would be very understandable. It's the method I have a problem with. There must be easier ways to drive her out without ruining the locals in the process. Apart from being unfair, how could he be sure it would work – even now?

'And if he'd really wanted Sanderling why not embrace the plan he told Synnove about where Poulson aimed to pick someone they could manipulate, do a deal with?' Jean went on, 'And how do you reconcile your idea with the fact that he loses sleep every night patrolling the grounds – protecting Synnove and her property?'

'His property as he sees it?' Sharon replied.

'It could be seen as controlling behaviour,' Cheryl added.

'And we know he likes the birds,' Sharon said. 'Whoever attacked the aviary picked the wrong target if they wanted St Clair on their side.'

'So you reckon there's more than one person or persons who want Synnove out?' Cheryl queried.

'Undoubtedly,' Jean answered, 'but let's not get sidetracked.'

Sharon tugged at a fingernail with her teeth, like a terrier with a shoe. 'What do we know about his background?'

Annie flipped open her file. 'Appeared in the area as a youngster of five or six when Lord Danhanbury took him in and paid for his education: Eton, Cambridge and the Guards.'

'But who were his family?' Sharon persisted. 'How come Lord Dan knew him – a byblow of his, perhaps? They don't look much alike.'

'I take your point and you're right. We must follow it up,' Jean signalled to Cheryl who dutifully scribbled in her notebook. 'Who knows? Discover Mr St Clair's identity and we might have this thing solved.'

Chapter 28

Summer 1943 – the Soviets had decimated the German Sixth Army, Axis forces in North Africa had surrendered, Eisenhower had landed in Sicily ... and the world had changed. Out after curfew for a breath of fresh air, Isabel glanced up to where a new moon lit the front of Sanderling. *Sola Nobilitas Virtus* – Virtue Alone is True Nobility.

Hardly daring to breathe she stared at the motto her grandfather had chiselled into their existence. Having failed to confront the question for over two years the answer had been here all along yet only tonight had the war's unremitting reality broken through. All sorts of people were dying – rich and poor, noble and ignoble, titled ... and otherwise. Those she knew and loved, as well as strangers. Could she at last emerge from this purdah and embrace a life which was hers to do with as she pleased?

Later, on the west terrace, the countess looked out over the moon-bathed lake, wondering where he was now. Was he, too, watching the night, thinking of this garden? Could he smell the scent of musk, feel the dew on his skin, hear the foxes call? After he'd been sent down he had joined the air force – before war broke out; that's all she knew. Isabel shuddered. She'd devoured every newspaper listing of casualties since the fighting began ... just out of interest, worrying about the estate men. His name had not appeared. He was alive, somewhere. All she had to do was find him.

Why on earth had she waited so long? Who could it possibly harm? The old order? Maybe, and she did care about that but Jim was even more of a traditionalist than she was. Besides, who knew what the world was going to look like after this – other than very different.

First thing the following morning the countess phoned an old university friend in the War Office. 'Betty, it's me, Isabel Foxhill. How are you?'

'Spiffing. Lost two more merchant ships and four aircraft last night.'

'I'm sorry, silly question,' the line was very crackly. 'Hey, I wondered if you might look someone up for me.'

''Gainst the rules, Bel.'

Like the countess, Betty Courtenay hailed from a large country estate. 'Really? The trouble is my head dairywoman has lost touch with her son and is so distracted it's affecting the cows. Our milk's coming out as cheese.'

Betty laughed. 'I could lose my job.'

'They wouldn't dare. One man, Betty: Jim Tennyson. Joined the RAF in 1937.'

'Leave it with me.'

She felt bad abusing Betty's trust but the euphoria of release she felt from the sweeping away of those long dark years of guilt and remorse and hopelessness – the fetters of position, the cage of propriety – was a torrent which gouged through any other considerations. At last she could marry the man she loved.

Betty rang back two days later. 'He's been in London on leave, with the rest of his unit. That's why it took me forty-eight hours. Due back to his squadron in East Anglia tonight. The train leaves Liverpool Street at seven o'clock so if you're lucky you can catch him there. Civilians aren't allowed at the base as I'm sure you realize.'

He was alive – and obviously well. 'Thank you a thousand times Betty ... his mother will be so pleased.'

'Mrs Tennyson died in 1936, Isabel. Toodlepip.'

Could he ever forgive her? Would he even recognize her? Had he transferred his affections elsewhere? To think he'd still feel as he had was ludicrous. Did he know her parents had died? It had been in all the papers. She sat on the low sofa in her dressing room and wept into Hildegard's fur for fear the maid would hear her.

Why pretend any more? She'd waited over two years for him to make contact and he hadn't. He knew where to find her. It couldn't be through respect for her parents ... or her grief; not after this length of time. The strictest Victorians would have been through black, grey and out of mauve by now – and Jim hadn't been remotely Victorian. Besides, it was then that she'd needed comforting most. He'd have known that too.

He'd been destroyed; joined the forces to end it all. She sniffed. 'Maybe it's that death wish that's kept him alive, eh Hildegard? But it's up to me, isn't it. He's not going to risk that happening again, is he? How could he know I've changed? I know him, he wouldn't dare believe....' She sat up. 'It's me who has to make the first move. Why on earth didn't I see that sooner.' Isabel wrung her damp handkerchief in anguish. 'I've waited two years and not even got in touch. That must have quashed any glimmer of hope he might have had. Two years, Hilde. How could I have been so stupid.'

Isabel rang for the maid and spent the next two hours refusing every one of the woman's suggestions on her outfit. It was late morning before she remembered to instruct the chauffeur.

'Alfred, we're going to Liverpool Street. I must be there before half past six this evening.' It would be pitifully little time to have together but she'd no way of finding Jim in the chaos of London today even if she'd been able to get up to town earlier.

'Very good, Ma'am; I'll prepare the Austin.'

'I'm not going to London in that ... that runabout.'

'I was thinking of fuel, Ma'am. The Delage drinks a goodly amount and the Sedanca even more.'

'I'm sure you'll cope, Alfred. We'll take the other Bentley.'

'Ma'am, there's not enough fuel on the entire estate to get the Bentley to London.'

'Then we'll find some, Alfred. Don't fret.' Honestly, what would these people do without her to do their thinking for them? Alfred Channing, fifty next March, who'd learned his craft on horse drawn carriages, was unused to driving beyond Maidenhead; for him Central London was as remote as Land's End. She couldn't be doing with these minor irritations. It was high time her staff earned their keep.

'No Emily, not that way. I look like Mother.' She tugged the pins out of her upswept curls and threw them on the dressing table. The one day it mattered, her hair resembled the home-making efforts of a wood pigeon.

Wound as tight as a blackout fixing, Isabel finally set off from Sanderling at one o'clock in the afternoon with Channing behind the wheel, a footman and her maid beside him. Their route lay through the Cotswolds to Oxford, the Chilterns, and picked up the main London Road at Maidenhead. The weather was fine, dry underfoot with a light breeze, nothing to slow them down.

Although Channing maintained a stately pace, the scenery rolled unseen past Isabel's window. Jerky trees and meadows, streams and byways, towns and villages all blurred into a mesmerizing backcloth as the car carried her forward, too fast for second thoughts. She rode on a crest of expectation all the higher for its years of suppression.

Approaching Eton, the Bentley's throaty engine coughed its way into the kerb. While the footman alighted and poured more fuel into the tank, Channing came to her door, removed his peaked cap. She inclined her head. Now what? 'Begging your pardon, Ma'am, but that's the last of the petrol going in now. We must stop at the next filling station.'

Isabel consulted her watch; half past five. 'Very well, Alfred, just as long as we're at Liverpool Street by half past six.'

They set off again, and after a mile or so pulled into the forecourt of a garage. The owner came out and shook his head gravely, pointing to a makeshift sign which read, *No Petrol*. On they drove, slower now. All the sign posts and street names had been removed to confuse the enemy – if they landed. Further on they stopped at a police station to inquire after fuel only to find the recommended establishment closed.

At Chiswick they managed to purchase a gallon but that was unlikely to get them as far as the City. From whizzing past, now the scenery was being carried; might it be quicker to go on foot the rest of the way? Except, even the countess's rudimentary knowledge of London told her it must be a good few miles still to Liverpool Street and she without walking shoes.

From garage to garage they crawled their way into London, past the museums, and on through Knightsbridge as the minutes ticked by. Quarter past six. Gaggles of servicemen and headscarfed women hurried along fast-darkening pavements. She could imagine the station, steam billowing over massed soldiers, sailors and airmen, their muted uniforms mingling in shades of earth, sea and sky, kit bags barricading the platform. Three at a time, Jim was taking the stairs down to the concourse, the route back to hell, exchanging banter with a couple of friends, hiding his fear. He was bound to have lost weight, not that he'd any to lose, and she dared say these last years would have etched deep lines in his forehead.

An atmosphere of overwhelming tension had pervaded the car, when a rare sight presented itself – a taxi batting past Sussex Gardens. 'Stop the car. Peters, get me that conveyance.' Channing pulled the Bentley smartly under the canopy of a large hotel just as the cab was pulling away.

Peters sprinted to apprehend the vehicle and Isabel could see the driver's arm gesticulating; witnessed a hurried exchange of five pound notes. Helped by Channing she alighted from the Bentley, instructing the maid to remain where she was. Peters removed his hat. 'Beggin' pardon, Ma'am; cabbie says he can't wait for us at Liverpool Street.'

'Never mind, Peters. You stay here, with the others.' Peters opened his mouth to remonstrate but she glared at him. She'd wondered how she was going to manage the meeting in full view of her staff. This was the silver lining. And she'd not be alone for long, not once she found Jim.

Her watch said it was ten minutes to seven but at least the cabbie would know the way. Paid well by Peters, he sped along wide thoroughfares and darted up narrow inlets, weaving through the traffic in Oxford Street just as Jim would be shouldering his way through those hundreds of soldiers, peering at smudged blackboards, searching for his platform.

Did he know how close she was? Could he feel it? Like Isabel, had he too spent those intervening centuries half expecting to catch a glimpse of her on a street corner or in a box at the theatre, getting into her car or talking with a friend at church? Now, across a crowded concourse....

They were held up by police at Holborn while a cavalcade of jeeps and military paraphernalia took precedence; she couldn't bear to look at her watch.

'Which platform yer want?' the cab driver asked.

She shrugged, unable to answer. Anyway, it was none of this man's business.

'Where yer goin'?' Damn his impertinence. 'I can drive yer right on to the platform if yer want.'

'Ah,' she didn't know you could do that. 'Er ... East Anglia somewhere, Cambridgeshire? Norfolk?'

The man glanced around at her. It must be unusual not to know one's destination.

'Far end then. Hold on, Duchess.' The car took an abrupt right, lurched over potholes and rubble and dived down a partly hidden alleyway between two bombed outbuildings.

Headlights dimmed by regulation, the car groped its way along a subterranean passageway then shot up into the light like a clay from a trap, amid the bustle and belching smoke of the station. Next to the noise it was the enormity of the cavern which struck her. Massive Corinthian columns soared hundreds of feet into the darkness where the angles of metal gridirons hovered like ill-nourished bats against a hazy night sky, the structure dwarfing her and the thousands of other souls scrabbling in murk below.

'Next platform along, I shouldn't wonder,' said the driver, holding the door open for her. 'One minute to seven. You'll be all right. They're never on time,' he gave a little bow and was gone.

She swirled, frantic and lost, among gleaming military cars depositing senior officers and their entourages – the way she was wont to travel; not left here on the kerbside to fend for herself, looking on at the important ones with servants and position, out of her metier.

With less than a minute to go, she stumbled into the crowd and tried to run. She tripped over baggage, was sent flying by sprinting aircrew and would have fallen had it not been for the crush keeping her upright. A shrill whistle sounded in her ear, carriage doors slammed and a train just in front of her began its increasing chug to a chorus of goodbyes and arm-waving, forced smiles and hidden tears.

'Train to East Anglia?' she gasped to the ticket collector.

He pointed along the platform at receding dull red tail lights.

The station began to revolve, suddenly nothing mattered any more, it was all going away, like the train, hurtling into the night, clickety-clack, clickety-clack. She felt suffocated, her head was spinning....

A strong hand came under her elbow. 'Isabel? What on earth...?'

Chapter 29

She was lying on a couch in the Great Eastern Hotel. A handsome naval officer crouched beside her.

'Bertie! I.... Where am I?'

'I couldn't believe it was you. What are you doing here? Where's your maid; where's Peters?'

Feeling foolish and embarrassed she struggled to sit upright, swung her legs to the floor, numb but physically unharmed.

'Look here, shouldn't you rest?'

'They're waiting in Knightsbridge. I wanted to see off a friend.'

'A railway station is no place for a lady on her own. What were you thinking about?' Bertie sounded like her old governess.

Had she engineered the hold-ups and obstacles deliberately? She'd been so fearful Jim would not even acknowledge her that one part of her had balked at the meeting; deferred the inevitable rejection, delayed having to face him.

Even when she'd been tearing along that platform, desperate to catch a glimpse of him, strong claws had gripped her shoulders, pulling her back, telling her it was best not to succeed, he wouldn't want to know her. And anyway, how undignified it had been to go haring after a serviceman on a train, hat askew, stockings lacerated by all the luggage she'd encountered, red-faced with anxiety.

Then to be rescued by dear Bertie, who'd sprung out of nowhere. She'd have hated anyone else to have seen her like that. Risking court martial for abandoning his naval duties, he'd insisted on accompanying her to Knightsbridge and the care of her staff.

Back in the comparative serenity of Sanderling, even a Sanderling overrun by hundreds of boisterous children, Isabel considered it had been for the best. Yes, she was disappointed she hadn't seen Jim but that would teach her to be impetuous. Now she could work towards a reconciliation in a more becoming fashion.

She knew where he was, she could write to him. Lots of women corresponded with servicemen – it was encouraged to boost morale. Under that guise she could rekindle their relationship lightly, find out about his life, discover how he felt before upsetting him with inappropriate displays of emotion; especially when his and millions of other lives depended on him keeping his concentration.

She lit two bonfires on the pretext of turning out private estate papers when all she was burning were her draft attempts to communicate with Jim Tennyson. Still, as she'd learned to her cost, better to get it right than rush things.

Meanwhile, the Luftwaffe were stepping up their bombing raids and the reports of heroic airmen's exploits in retaliation were daily in the newspapers. Any pertinent local news was swapped between Bertie's staff and the countess's in the village ... and his stepfather had gone to work for Bertie after the trouble. So it wasn't long before the sad tidings reached Sanderling.

A week after Isabel's abortive mission to London, Jim Tennyson's plane was shot down over Germany ... with no survivors.

Chapter 30

According to a caretaker still living at the boarding school, though long since retired, a big posh car with a chauffeur came to take St Clair away: 'An' we never sin him agin.'

Jolyon's father, one Harry St Clair, had been an engineer whose parents had both perished in the war; Jolyon's mother was the daughter of a Norfolk solicitor. Posted to Nigeria, Harry and his wife had placed their only son in an East Anglian boarding school for the duration. Both Harry and his wife had been killed in the uprising.

'Lord Dan sent a car for him,' Jean said when Sharon imparted this gem.

'Well, maybe ... but the caretaker also said, and I quote. "She were an angel. The most beautiful woman I've ever sin. Took young Jolyon, she did." '

'Knowing nothing of children, might Lord Dan have co-opted a woman friend to help him?' Jean wondered aloud.

'The countess?'

Jean nodded. 'But what was the connection between Jolyon St Clair and Lord Danhanbury in the first place? Distant relative? His ward? Knew his grandfather during the war p'raps?'

Sharon shook her head. 'Sorry, boss, we're still working on that. Lord Dan was in the navy is as far as we've got.'

'Well, whatever it was, it seems the countess took a shine to the boy. He became a surrogate grandson. No wonder he might have expected a bigger share of Sanderling.'

Uncomfortable with this outcome Jean sank into her office chair and turned to Sharon who was examining her fingernails like a hungry bird of prey selects a victim.

'I don't like this any more than you do but facts are facts. Bizarre as his behaviour appears, St Clair has a good enough reason for wanting to drive off any newcomer. I think we have our motive.'

The way in which Jean presented her findings could make the difference between Synnove accepting the issue as going with the job, or backing off in favour of a more legitimate heir ... as she saw it.

Anyone more grasping, less upright, would have no problem in asserting their authority, but the qualities that made Synnove unique were the ones which could undermine her. That's what Jolyon St Clair had figured out. How like the countess he was in his ability to understand people ... and manipulate them. Was that why she'd stipulated a female – precisely so Jolyon couldn't succeed? Had she mistrusted him?

Jean opened her eyes and sat up, recalling the final criteria. 'Why be so bloody convoluted about it?' she mouthed to herself. It was almost as though, unsure of the correct course, the countess had thrown the ingredients together in the alchemic belief that right would out – or at least she'd given it a chance to without preordaining the outcome. A tie-braker the old lady had said. Would 'decider' have been a better choice of words? And what on earth did it mean, anyway? '*Seek the very holy one westwards.*' Was Jean meant to have searched the States ... or Ireland?

'Come down tomorrow,' Synnove had said when Jean rang. 'If you know who's responsible, your being spotted won't matter now. And I want you to look into something else while you're here anyway.'

She was grateful when Channing the chauffeur greeted her and offered Synnove's apologies for not coming to the station in person. The journey gave Jean that bit longer to think. She needed something else to offer, some other avenue of inquiry to stave off any knee-jerk impulse of Synnove's. Given time to calm down, consider the subject rationally, realize how inevitable Jolyon's reaction was – and indeed how unfair the countess had been in throwing them both into this untenable juxtaposition – Jean hoped she could persuade her to stay on.

As they pulled up outside the front entrance, a portly figure in mid-calf tweeds and a crimson bobble hat emerged from the porch. 'Just orf to see the birds. You must be Jean. How de do. I'm Henrietta but everyone calls me Wink,' she gave a warm smile, extending a Fair Isle-mittened hand.

Jean shook it. 'Notably barmy but otherwise spotless,' had been the report returned from Jean's brief check on Henrietta last week. 'Can I tag along? I've heard so much about this aviary.' Jean ran to catch up the striding Wink. 'How's it been since the attack?'

'You've heard about that, then. Poor dear, she won't admit it but her nerves are hanging by a thread. What with Russell and the nastiness around here – Synnove's had about as much as she can take.'

'I'm sure it makes a big difference having you here.' Jean wished she'd suggested a companion earlier.

'Thank goodness that damned St Clair man isn't here today, always popping up,' Wink said as the aviary came in sight.

'You don't like Mr St Clair?'

'Would you? Always muscling in, insinuating himself into Synnove's good books.'

'Ms McKenna tells me he fed the birds the whole time Fentiman had control of the estate ... and helped with the re-stocking.'

Wink straightened from filling the water bowls. 'Oh you can't fault him, my dear. Beware those dressed in lambskin, is what I've found.' She finished her jobs and they wandered back towards the house.

'You're saying he has an ulterior motive?'

'He's after Synnove.' If Sharon or Cheryl had said that, the words would have been edged with scepticism or a, 'you mark my words' surety ... even sympathy. Whereas Wink's mouth tightened, her eyes dulled and the phrase rang with heartbreaking disappointment.

Did Synnove know about Wink? Not that it made any difference per se ... other than rendering the woman's opinion of her perceived rival inadmissible.

Chapter 31

'I'll come straight to the point, Jean. The man I used to live with, Russell Prince.... I don't think you ever met. Well, he's in a remand prison facing extradition to a renegade African republic. I've hired Crombie and Nashe to defend him but they're running out of gambits. However, this African state would accept a large sum of money instead.'

'How much?' Jean asked automatically.

Wink paused her knitting pins, took up her lornette and peered at Jean. 'By the way, she's already handed him her share of McKenna's – a cool thirty million, plus their London flat, for him to throw on to this same pyre; a typical Prince bid to gamble his way out of trouble. Which, need I say, failed.'

Synnove shrugged. 'What's the going rate for a white body on the dark continent? Russell will be into them for tens of millions – has to be.'

Jean gulped. 'But you can't ...' her gaze swept the room. What had she done? Prince had always worried her. Leaving him behind when she came to Sanderling was the wisest thing Synnove had done.

'What choice do I have? He perceptively pointed out that I could not have evinced sufficient management experience to be chosen by you without having run McKenna's ... which he enabled me to start. Which means you'd never have chosen me but for him. Ergo....'

Jean's body slumped as though someone had withdrawn the needle and released all the stitches. 'Well I....' What else could they have used to measure her ability? It was true, Synnove's previous work had demonstrated some of the required qualities, but without the evidence of McKenna's they couldn't have been so certain.

'Right. So you see my dilemma.' Synnove cast glazed eyes around the room, then out to the terrace and beyond. 'Either I somehow use Sanderling to buy Russell's life in which case – for even considering selling out – I should go. Or I leave now so I can't betray the inheritance with which I've been entrusted. Either way....'

Jean needed time to come up with a solution. Visions of an empty Sanderling and that man Fentiman marching back through the door with a jaunty swagger flashed across her internal screen.

Synnove turned back. 'A lot of the things the countess and her family had collected, paintings, silver, china, most of the antique furniture and her jewellery, were packed up and stored in preparation for the internal restoration.'

'And in case someone disreputable came and half-inched them before you arrived. The countess was some sharp cookie,' Wink added. 'I know what's there from her own records. For instance, she had this favourite picture of Theseus being given the ball of thread so he could deploy it to find his way out of the Minotaur's cave. Find that, and we'll have found our way in, I reckon,' Wink sat up straight, taking a deep contemplative breath. 'But I've plenty to be getting on with and seeing as how all the internal work still remains to be carried out – well, I don't see any hurry.'

Jean understood. 'You mean they're probably safer left where they are for the present.'

'Thank goodness someone's thinking straight,' Wink stared hard at Synnove.

'Wink's right. Apparently Fentiman spent a lot of time and effort turning everything upside down looking for this cache, but as far as we know, failed. He's not the sort to have kept quiet if he had located it.'

'You want me to find Aladdin's Cave so you can pawn its contents to save Russell Prince? Against the countess's wishes.' Though would it be, if it meant keeping Synnove at Sanderling? She was also aware that if Synnove mounted a serious search for the stuff or hired another bloodhound, she would likely find it anyway, without Jean's help. In the circumstances it was better to stay involved, maybe even ensure the treasure was not, in fact, located. Which was underhand

and deceitful, but might be justified. 'I trust you and Fentiman have searched the house and the stable block pretty thoroughly, so what do the old staff say?'

'Other than Mary and John, who've no idea where it all went, the old staff are either dead, gaga or won't work here now on principle. And with relationships as they are, I hesitate to ask them in case it jolts their memory and they come and steal the hoard behind my back.'

'How about a storage company? That's what I'd do if I needed to empty my place for a while?' Jean asked.

'Tried them all,' Wink raised her lornette in Jean's direction. 'We're not entirely without a wit or two, y'know. Why d'you think we called you?'

Jean looked out across the lake. 'And Lord Dan?'

'Says he's no idea. I all but accused him of harbouring it in his cellars; delighting in the countess's death because now he could keep it without anyone being any the wiser,' Synnove said.

'And is he?'

'Now I know him better? Categorically not.'

'Didn't he bring up Jolyon St Clair?' Jean watched for reaction.

Synnove raised an eyebrow. 'Yes, but they fell out.' Wink's concentration remained on her work. 'Why, we've no idea.'

Surprised, Jean struggled to assimilate the implications. 'When did this break-up happen? Recently?'

'Oh, no. Before the countess died.' Synnove sat down on the fender seat. 'We reckon that's why she left Jolyon the gatehouse – to give him a roof over his head. He'd sold his other property to pay off the people his wife's family swindled.'

Wink straightened abruptly, dropping a needle. Synnove spoke with animation for the first time. 'We can't understand why those two should be at loggerheads, not after all those years.'

Hoping something would occur to change her mind, Jean had delayed as long as she could. She stood, as did Synnove. 'You told me you felt that the scale of business collapse in the vicinity could not be accidental – that a person or persons was deliberately causing the failures – and asked me to discover their identity.' Synnove nodded. 'Well, you were right.'

Jean traced the pattern of the carpet with her feet, eyes cast down, concentrating. 'We've examined at least five of the more notable situations plus a number of artisans who ostensibly went down with Fentiman but who, bearing in mind the demand for their skills, should have had no trouble in surviving his demise.'

'So it is Fentiman?' Synnove and Wink chorused.

'That much was, yes. But not all his businesses were unprofitable. Their contribution along with his significant plundering of Sanderling should have kept him afloat far longer.' Jean met Synnove's eyes. 'It was the gambling which really did for him.'

Jean took a deep breath. 'Examining Poulson, Fentiman, the lady with the shops, that wholesale theft Channing sustained and the countess's erstwhile architect ... we were surprised to find that there is considerable circumstantial evidence linking one man with many of the critical events which led to each of these people's ruin.'

Synnove sat down as if felled by a heavy object.

'We haven't finished our investigation so we cannot as yet prove these allegations, nor confirm a motive—'

'It's Jolyon, isn't it?' Synnove whispered, staring at her hands.

'He certainly seems to have been the catalyst in many of them, yes.' Jean still felt driven to defend the indefensible, or at least soften the blow. 'But there's no evidence of his blaming you – quite the contrary.'

'Ha, doesn't need to, does he? He's got everyone else doing that,' Wink screeched.

'I bet that's why they fell out then, he and Lord Dan. Because Jolyon coveted Sanderling and Lord Dan suspected his overtures to the countess were simply mercenary and didn't like— Oh, goodness.' Its approach unobserved, a long-haired tortoiseshell cat leapt on to Synnove's shoulder as she spoke, swaying to keep its balance, eyes wild, body tensed, aggressive. Synnove unhooked its claws from her jacket and lifted it gently on to her lap.

'Goodness, that's the cat which was on the countess's bed the morning she died.' Jean could see the elderly lady soundlessly beckoning her, the files spilling their contents on to the bedside table, the cat curled on her mistress's counterpane, keeping her company.

'Hildegard? Yes, she went to Lord Dan afterwards but came home when I arrived.' Synnove moved towards the door.

Jean followed her, concerned at the shock she must have had. Synnove had buttoned up her reaction, just as the countess would have done. For all her sangfroid there was a danger Synnove would feel that if an otherwise upright man like St Clair had gone to such lengths to dislodge her, it could only be because he had more right to the place. She put her hand on Synnove's arm. 'I'll get to the bottom of St Clair's purpose—'

Chapter 32

Isabel could no longer hide her burgeoning figure. If she waited for her mother to notice, the revelation, when it came, would be even worse.

When the servants had departed she rose and stood at the farthest end of the long dining table – the limit of range for polite conversation without shouting; subconsciously distancing herself, blurring vision to lessen the sharpness of the message. 'I know this will come as a shock, and I've thought very carefully about how to tell you both but, well …' Isabel drew her fringed wrap tight across her belly, clinging to it as to a comfort blanket. For a few seconds longer she was still their beloved daughter, their rose-clad little girl, their doted-on only child … only a few seconds.

'I'm going to have Jim Tennyson's child. We are to be married.'

Had the words come out? She strained to hear the echo playing back to her but there was no resonance, only a silence so complete that a log shifting in the fireplace made her start.

As if in a slow motion film, with great deliberation her father replaced his napkin on the table, pushed back his chair and unfurled his length to an upright position. Isabel could almost hear the reel of tape rattling in its holder as the picture unwound. 'What …' it was neither question nor expostulation, simply an uncertain start as if her father had something stuck in his throat. 'What an absurd notion. You'll do no such thing, young lady.' He offered his arm to her mother who, trance-like and holding her head ridiculously high, allowed herself to be conducted with great dignity from the room.

At twenty-one years old and heir to Sanderling, the following morning Isabel was summoned to the library to stand on the spot where poachers and backsliding estate-workers stood to be dismissed ... or worse.

'This regrettable mistake on your part must not be allowed to interfere with Sanderling's destiny. I have spoken with Lord Danhanbury and apprised him of the situation.'

Isabel gasped, staring open-mouthed at her father. She'd never dreamt he'd do that. Poor Bertie, she'd wanted to tell him herself, explain how she felt about Jim, convince her childhood friend he'd find someone far more suitable than she. Now he'd never understand.

'And he says he's prepared to bring up the child as his own.'

They were all ganging up on her. Couldn't they see how she felt?

Her father stood, but remained behind his desk. 'This isn't an offer, Isabel, it's a command. If you continue to defy us, at your mother's death Sanderling will be sold because we can no longer trust you not to sully the Hampden name. In that event on your conscience for ever must lie the destruction of the Hampden lands and all they stand for. You will have betrayed your family, your ancestors and the people of the estate.'

Isabel fainted.

She had almost come to terms with thinking her love for Jim and her unborn child were worth the giving up of Sanderling when her father, probably intuiting the dangerous direction of her thoughts, tried one more time to persuade her.

'Is Bertie so bad? I always thought you were good friends. We're hardly condemning you to life with an ogre.'

'You might as well be.'

'Isabel, this is not a matter of sentiment or feelings. It is a matter of honour.'

'No it's not. It's a matter of expedience, of face.' She whirled out of the room, wishing those huge solid doors would slam. Regarded as the eighth deadly sin, not only was emotion banned at Sanderling but even her surroundings with their immoveable oak barriers had been designed to enforce its continued exile. Wrapped in chunky winter woollens to conceal her expanding waistline, time was running out. Soon her parents must give in. Three days later her mother sent for her.

'Isabel, if you persist in this foolishness there's only one thing to be done. You must go away. We'll say you've gone abroad to continue your studies. I've been making inquiries and I understand there's a convent in Essex called St Hildegard's where the nuns take in unmarried women. They will arrange for the child to be adopted the minute it's born. No one need ever know.' A capitulation of sorts.

In her long walks around the estate, wondering what to do, Isabel had herself considered this option as a temporary compromise – a way of giving her parents longer to become accustomed to the bombshell she'd dropped in their midst. She had placed her hands on her now rounded abdomen, marvelling at its inexorable growth, pleased the new life couldn't be stalled or put off. But deciding its future – and hers – could. Certainly for the moment.

Accepting her mother's scheme would avoid the forced marriage to Bertie. As a plan it was the best she could hope for; with one important alteration. She would arrange for the child to be fostered by a family she would personally vet so that when her parents had had more time to get used to the idea of her marrying Jim, and he was established in his career, then they could be reunited with the child. The world was changing fast. Why should she have to choose?

She and Jim discussed it endlessly. He wanted to wed now – they were both of age, officially neither needed permission to marry. It would mean Jim giving up his studies in order to earn money for them to live on, but once the baby was at school, Isabel could get work too and that way they could all be together.

Like Egyptian torture, her limbs were tied to separate horses driven in opposite directions. She so desperately wanted to be with Jim and their child, could envisage no other life, yet was petrified any further act of defiance would push her parents beyond their powers of toleration and alienate them completely. As things stood, she felt sure her mother and father would relent once they saw their grandchild. If Isabel and Jim could be a little less impetuous, follow convention as best they were able, they might still have each other, their child ... and Sanderling.

'It's your inheritance, Bel ... and your child. I can't insist,' Jim whispered, the catch in his voice audible.

The forbidding stone abbey hovered over the Essex marshes like a malevolent vulture. Home to curlews and cormorants and miles from the nearest human habitation, it could be reached only via a causeway at low tide – an isolation ideal for purpose.

Reluctant to trust any of the chauffeurs with the knowledge of Isabel's destination, her parents had allowed Isabel to take the new open-top Morris Eight they'd just purchased. Which also meant she could motor to Cambridge on weekends to be with Jim.

Whilst an unostentatious and unremarkable model, having a car of any sort marked Isabel out from the start; her clothes and cut-glass accent did the rest. Expected to perform her share of the chores as well as attend at least four of the eight daily services in the convent's chapel, Isabel felt about as cut off as the convent itself from the life to which she was used.

'Miss Nose in the Air's on washing up tonight. Sure you know which way round to hold a tea towel, dearie?'

'La-de da toff – should have kept yer legs shut, shouldn't ya.'

Like schoolchildren they whispered behind her back and giggled. 'Was it the gamekeeper then?'

On the whole the nuns said nothing but by the looks on their enclosed faces Isabel suspected their sympathies lay elsewhere. Except for Sister Agnes ... who loved everybody. It was Agnes who suggested Isabel might like to drive her into the village to collect the mail and essentials. 'To be cheering up the poor unfortunates ...' she confided to Isabel – who quickly picked up the bill insisting no one be told. After a while they'd take one or two of the others with them on the outing. Gradually, with Agnes's help, and by sharing what she had, Isabel became more accepted ... her fellow internees, less hostile.

Religion apart, she and Agnes had much in common; a love of literature, a fascination for crossword puzzles, anagrams and word-games – for Isabel a way of passing the time in this cultural wilderness – and, though Agnes would have vehemently denied it for fear of being in thrall to the Devil ... a penchant for motor cars. So it was to Sister Agnes that Isabel entrusted the mission of finding suitable foster parents for her baby.

'But hasn't Mother Superior agreed wit' your own mother that the baby's to be adopted?' Sister Agnes gasped, hand to her mouth, eyes popping, when Isabel first approached her about it. Finding a willing ear, Isabel had already unburdened herself of the real reason she was here when, discipline and fortitude thwarted by rampaging hormones, Agnes had one day found her dripping tears into the milk churn.

'Yes but Mother won't know the difference. And all she really cares about is that no one should discover its existence. So you see, there's no harm.'

Two months after her ordeal, still no one would say a word. They kept Agnes from her and whenever she asked for the young nun, Isabel had the impression Agnes was in trouble over something, doing penance. 'What's happened to my baby?'

Mother Superior arrived. 'You're to calm down, young lady. Your body's had a lot to cope with and getting worked up will do no good.' She was right there, the aching and tenderness in her insides stung whenever she moved; stretching or lifting the lightest weight was excruciating. Her knowledge of childbirth was scant but this couldn't be normal.

A few days later, around mid morning, Isabel's door was pushed open gingerly. Agnes snaked around the opening, putting her finger to her lips to stop Isabel exclaiming. 'Hush there, I can't stop long; I'm forbidden to see you but I didn't want you to think....' Kneeling beside the bed, she grasped Isabel's hand and burst into tears.

Isabel struggled to prop herself on one elbow, comfort the girl. 'What's the matter? Where's my baby?'

More sobs. 'I knew they hadn't told you. Your mother came.'

'What? What for?'

'Because Mother Superior sent to say you were dying.'

'Is my baby dead? Is that it?' Isabel held her breath.

Sister Agnes shook her head vehemently. 'But your mother was adamant so her and Mother Superior ...' Agnes's words were jumbled in haste and anguish. Isabel fell back on her pillows. She'd been telling herself the baby was safe, was desperate to hold it, see who it resembled, watch it smile and clutch at her with its tiny fingers.

'He came too.'

'My father?'

'No, Mr Tennyson. But Mother Superior refused to admit him. I slipped out to tell him what had happened but your mother caught me.'

Isabel's only sensation was one of sinking, falling down a deep dark well with no way of stopping – and no desire to. 'How will he ever forgive me? I've let them give our child away. I should have listened but oh no, too selfish wasn't I.' Sister Agnes wiped her brow. Isabel brightened. 'I'll make it up to him. We'll have lots more children.'

Something in Agnes's eyes echoed her own emptiness and looking down at her ravaged body, she finally realized why she was still lying here and what had taken so long.

'Doctor had to do it. You'd 'a died otherwise.'

Isabel turned her face to the wall and wept so dangerously and for so many days that, again concerned for her life, Mother Superior allowed Sister Agnes to sit with her through the nights.

Long months in that austere atmosphere of divine retribution eventually convinced Isabel that what had happened was God's will – part of the price extracted for transgressing His commandments. She also discovered that having taken a vow of silence on the subject, the nuns would rather have faced Tourquemada's Inquisition than reveal where her baby had been taken – including Sister Agnes.

Why hadn't they let her die? She had betrayed the man she loved and lost her only child; she'd no wish to face the world again, not now, not ever. And but for Sister Agnes she may have had her way. With the young nun's dogged help, despite herself Isabel began to recover; accepting that having sacrificed so much she must now fulfil her destiny – else what had it all been for?

Chapter 33

Jean Edwards returned to London with an enigmatic: 'We'll need to tackle this from the other end,' whatever that meant. Prey to those cognitive deficits they say come with stress ... or grief, I was in such a daze I could concentrate for less than two seconds at a time and was incapable of applying a sensible perspective to anything important. Some of it was pride. I'd not only liked the man, I'd trusted him.

''Bout time you realized you're hopeless at picking men,' Wink said that evening. 'I'd have thought you'd have learned your lesson and given them up as congenitally unsuitable long ago.'

I smiled at her wanly. I'd known Wink a long time.

Had it really all been a charade? The charm, the concern, the manners – picked up from Bertie, no doubt, as a means of getting what he wanted? All a stylish facade beneath which slid a scheming nature? Alone and vulnerable and shocked by the sheer enormity of a task for which I was completely unprepared, I'd attached myself emotionally to one of the few people who'd welcomed me. And how he'd played that to his advantage.

The day after Jean Edwards's visit, in the briefest of phone calls I checked that St Clair would be at home. Feeling that self-sufficiency was important, I took my own Mercedes as far as the gatehouse. The last thing I wanted was to be caught there in a thunderstorm or with a twisted ankle, dependent yet again on his succour. Neither did I wish to hide behind others, need servants to get me around or undertake my unpleasant jobs for me. This morning I wanted to be plain Synnove McKenna, not a surrogate countess. He'd attacked me personally, not my role.

'You sounded very formal,' he said with that sardonic smile of his as he stood aside to allow me through into the kitchen.

I quickly realized my mistake. I should have done this on my territory, not his. 'I imagine you know why I'm here.'

He pulled out a chair for me which I ignored. 'Should I?'

'Oh for heaven's sake, stop playing games. I know what you've been doing and I don't want you trespassing on Sanderling property any more. You deliberately set out to destroy people's businesses so they would all blame me.'

The light went from his eyes as if the mains switch had been thrown. Dragging out a second chair he sat down, ran a hand through his hair. A crease appeared between his brows as he tilted his head, now very serious. 'Not true ... at least, not the last part.'

His eyes downcast, shoulders slumped, even with what I now knew, I feared he could still sway me. I marched to the door. 'Keep off my land, Mr St Clair. From now on, I don't need your kind of help. If you thought you had a genuine grievance about who should have what, then you should have come and aired it, not concocted this charade to force me out. You thought you could exploit my weaknesses behind my back, all the while pretending to be Mr Nice to my face so I didn't suspect you. Well you picked the wrong one this time. I'll thank you to stay away from Sanderling in future.'

Roaring back across the meadows, the car bucked on the uneven track as I pressed the accelerator to the floor and gripped the wheel in anger – my sense of loss so strong I wanted to howl. Accepting that any genuine feeling we'd shared had all been in my imagination; that he was nothing more than a smooth version of Fentiman, had never cared about me or for me and that his bird feeding and patrolling of the grounds had all been part of his elaborate play acting ... only turned the knife in the wound. For all I knew he'd instigated the destruction of the wall and the aviary himself – just so's he could perform his saviour scene; give himself a platform on which to base his act.

I felt revolted that anyone – least of all a man as tender as he'd appeared to be – could turn out to be so cruel. And that attack on

Russell; had it, too, been staged? Were they in this together to part me from the Sanderling cash?

I braked and slew the car round on the grass, roaring diagonally across the meadow to bounce and pitch up Drover's Hill to the top. I got out and let the wind tug at my head, pulling me nearer the edge. Below, the Cotswolds lay mapped in three hundred and sixty degree glory. I lighted on Sanderling glowing beside the lake and laughed out loud to think I'd once thought it Camelot; complete with my own knight. Now what had I left?

'Done enough grieving for your own folly, have you? Thrown enough of a tantrum to last for a day or two? At least you've learnt to do it in private.' I whirled but only the buzzards kept me company, wheeling high above in their incessant circles, watchful, waiting. That insistent voice was right, though. If I carried on like this he'd have won. Behaving like a spoilt child was no way to restore confidence in the neighbourhood.

I descended the hill much slower and, hopefully, wiser than I'd gone up it. The impulse to throw things diminished, perspective restored, if not spirit.

'Nice drive?' Wink asked at dinner.

'I just feel empty ... the fight's not worth it.'

'It's a good thing your detective friend can't hear you or she really would be questioning her judgement.' In danger of pointing her spoon at me, Wink replaced it hurriedly in her dish. 'You weren't picked to balk at the first hurdle, dearie. Especially not one of male devising.'

'The whole thing's ludicrous, Wink,' I threw down my napkin and pushed my chair back, delighting in the grating noise it made across the grain. 'I've no idea how to run something like this. Oh I know Bertie's tried to point me in the right direction, bless him, but his interventions only underline my incompetence. I question whether the countess had all her marbles, honestly I do – with that laughable list of criteria.'

Wink glanced at the cat, warming herself by the radiator. 'Hush, you'll upset her,' she beamed. 'On the contrary, remember that chap

Greiner?' I frowned. 'Best known for Greiner's Theory – it was you who told me about it – like all good ideas it's obvious once you know.'

I thought back through my years of business studies. 'Something about the various incarnations of an enterprise and the different styles of management required at each stage. Yes, I remember. He talked about the need for a thrusting entrepreneurial type, full of ideas and chutzpah to start a business, but once it grows you need to set up systems and processes to oversee how things are done – because by then one person can't possibly do everything themselves.'

'Exactly. And because you rarely find a go-getter with a fondness for detailed organization ... at that stage you need a new chief executive.'

'But that's the mistake I keep making – Sanderling isn't like a business. You can't think of it the same way; there are so many non-commercial considerations you have to take into account – as Bertie never ceases to remind me.'

'You don't think it's that Sanderling is more advanced than any business you've come across? Think about it. Early businesses, say in Victorian times, were run by dictators, autocrats – as were estates. I bet the countess's grandfather – the one who built this house – was a right old tartar. And when the world evolved, the estates foundered. I wonder why.'

'Because they failed to change, failed to share their power.' Dragging my chair back to the table where my dessert was cooling rapidly, I scoured the recesses trying to dredge up that curve with the levels of maturity mapped out on it. 'You know, I remember the last stage being irritatingly much less well defined than the others. Few businesses ever survived that far so any research was, by definition, unsound. Though I do recall its needing more of a collective effort than a master–slave approach.' I took a mouthful of cold rice pudding and pushed the dish away. 'What's your point?'

'That you were selected, as we know, very specifically. Not for your knowledge of how things have been done around here for centuries – but precisely because you aren't thus burdened. Don't you think she'd have picked a toff otherwise? County's crawling with 'em.'

As Travers came to clear we left the dining room and wandered out of the front entrance to grab a breath of air before it grew dark. Had Wink got something? Was Greiner the answer not only to why I was here – but to what I should do about it? Bestriding two worlds, on the cusp of change – and before the illustrious American business consultant purloined the idea as his own – had the countess realized that a new way of thinking and a new set of skills would be required to accomplish transformation?

If she was up there somewhere, watching, what a disappointment I must be. She'd left me all those pointers, the wardrobe, the cars, Bertie ... as symbols of a style worthy of study, things I could learn from. But she hadn't intended me to run Sanderling as an anachronism. Hell, she could have let the National Trust do that. I straightened, for the first time daring to believe that maybe, just maybe, I could do this.

I turned my head towards Wink, worried I'd presumed on her good nature for far too long. The estate was paying her handsomely for her cataloguing work and she'd let out her little two up two down in Richmond so she wasn't suffering financially, but when I caught her staring at me longer than was normal, witnessed the sadness in her expression, I wondered whether I was being selfish in asking her to stay. Hands behind her back, head down, she was walking in little circles, confined by invisible barriers from widening her scope; forced to concentrate lest stepping outside engendered immediate forfeit of that she held dear: the loss of my esteem.

The house and its fairy tale architecture still grabbed me every time I saw it. I stared at the motto etched into its portico: *Sola Nobilitas Virtus*. Had they been just impressive words to those Victorian grandees and earlier Hampden worthies? Or, being themselves untitled, had one or two of the consorts favoured the saying for its denigration of social position. Had *Virtue Alone is True Nobility* made them feel more worthy? Allowing my gaze to traverse the rest of the edifice, from east to west, balustrade to below stairs, I imbibed the magnificence, the beauty and the danger of its corrupting influence. Was it as a warning that my ancient predecessor had nailed that homily to the bulkhead – a reminder?

I'd been blind. I wasn't being called upon to be clever, or knowledgeable. It was kindness, generosity and selflessness which was being demanded – for me a much harder proposition. I needed to share my authority in order to gain power; let others in.

I called across to Wink. 'Did you know that John Sedan Lewis handed over ownership of his business to his employees as early as 1929?'

Jolted out of her introspection, Wink retrieved her lornette and surveyed me with it. 'What made you think of that?'she asked warily.

'He created a capitalist-style collective. Up until then the co-operative societies, experiments in Russia, and later the Israeli kibbutz idea, had socialist roots. He was the first to solve the problem of unfairness, the unequal distribution of resources, by capitalist means. The partners, as he called them, shared in the profits, which gave them an incentive – a stake.'

'I knew curry was a mistake. I'll have a word with cook, make sure that new-fangled menu isn't repeated. Go and lie down, dear. You'll be reciting Adam Smith's *Wealth of Nations* next or upbraiding me on the repeal of the Corn Laws.'

I walked across, impatient she should agree with me. 'Jean Edwards said it and so have you, that the countess chose someone like me very deliberately.' I grabbed her arm. 'I misunderstood, interpreting her, "*qualities required to run Sanderling as it has been run*" literally. Whereas she was talking about running Sanderling for the benefit of all its people. That's how she was running it, but it has to be done differently nowadays, the era of paternalism is over.'

I shook Wink gently. 'You were right, she did know Sanderling must change – and that she was too steeped in the old ways to do it. More important, people's expectations of her were so rigid – they wouldn't let her. Now, thanks to St Clair and Fentiman in particular, the estate workers' opinion of me is so low, anything might be seen as an improvement.

'With her they felt secure, therefore would have resisted any sort of change. But having had upheaval thrust upon them, they might now welcome the return of a more solid structure. Except that having tasted freedom and respect and the mores of the outside world, it will have to be an organization in which they share.'

I let go, moved a pace or two away. 'She couldn't have done it if she'd had a son or daughter to inherit the old mantle. The expectations wouldn't have moved on enough on either side. But the countess was in a unique position.'

'Left you in a pretty precarious one, though. If she was so clever why didn't she write all this down instead of leaving you to figure it out. Bit risky don't you think?'

Taking Wink's arm I marched her around the end of the building and on to the west terrace. The wind rippled the grey surface of the lake and apart from a few crows high in the stratosphere, the birds had deserted.

'I'm not sure what's come over me – must have been you reminding me of Greiner. I've been so determined to do everything as she'd have done it that even when people disappeared in droves, blamed me for their business failures and physically attacked the place, I still didn't see.' I leapt up on the bench with a grin as wide as a teenager allowed out at night. 'I'll show the likes of Jolyon St Clair that the countess got it right after all.'

'What about Russell?' Wink asked. 'How are you going to find the money for him if you're going to share things out?'

I came down from bestriding the seat. 'Maybe this new approach solves the problem. The assets and profits of Sanderling aren't mine to give.'

I'd waited long enough. The internal restoration would go ahead even if I had to do it myself. I phoned Smithson that afternoon. Unusually he answered his mobile phone. 'Roy, where the hell are you?' I demanded, tired of being nice.

'Outside the Coach & Horses.'

'Stay there.' I rang off and called Mr Channing in the stables. 'Go and fetch Roy Smithson from the pub. Don't take no for an answer. Bring him back here.'

I went down to the library and fished out the old plans and was poring over them when Smithson shambled in. Without formally acknowledging his arrival I jabbed at the drawings. 'I have no idea where we need to start, whether there are any new regulations to take into consideration or what I need to do.'

He attempted to perch on the arm of a sofa but, almost overbalancing, stood up again, hanging on to the knob at the back for support. I wanted to throttle him.

'They came this morning. Repossessed my house.'

I rang for Mr Travers. 'Get my PA to phone Switzerland, will you. We need to buy a house.' This was one thing I could ask the trustees for – its being vital to the restoration project.

Mr Travers disappeared without a word. Smithson plumped heavily on to a settle, impersonating one of those swinging heads with wide open mouths into which people lob ping-pong balls at fairs. I sat beside him. 'Roy, can you hear me?' He turned, mouth still gaping, eyes searching for focus. 'Mr Travers will find you a room. Go and sleep it off, then come back here. You've work to do.'

A couple of days later, I made the arrangements with the receiver to buy back his house for him and thus bribed Smithson into Sanderling's employ – though, sober, he was a willing professional: competent, knowledgeable, authoritative on his subject.

Smithson, Wink and I discussed the best place to start the work, and although I didn't relish the idea, the countess's private apartments, now mine, topped the list. Which meant me moving.

Wink flung herself on to the low couch in the first dressing room, stroking Hildegard. 'Seems to appear out of nowhere doesn't she?'

'The place is riddled with servants' passages. Who knows, she may even have her own catway. She disappears underneath that seat at the far end is all I know.'

While I flung open wardrobes, to decide what could be packed away, Wink heaved herself up with a sigh and plodded along the dressing room corridor, lornette at the ready. Glancing in that direction I could see her ample floral rump protruding from the ornate bench beneath which Hildegard habitually slinked. The cat was sitting a little to the left, head on one side. 'Hey, come and help me move this thing,' Wink extricated herself backwards from her investigation site. 'You're right, there's a cat flap thing but there might be a low door too.'

Together we managed to swing one end of the baroque curlicued monstrosity away from the wall. Camouflaged by wallcovering, behind it lay a wide door barely three feet high with a ring pull handle recessed into the medallion design of the paper. Wink and I exchanged glances. Averse to both bats and spiders I was in no hurry to explore Hildegard's territory. 'I'll get Mr Travers to have a look at it later.'

More used than I to scrambling about in attics, if less suitably built, Wink exclaimed: 'Oh you great wimp, here let me.' I moved aside so Wink could insert her bulk between the seat and the door. She lifted the ring out of its slot and turned. The door creaked open and, bent double, she crawled through. There must be a window in there because I could see light beyond her. I'd never thought to count the ones on the outside. She stood up, her legs moved across the floor, a door was opened. 'Oh my goodness, come and look.'

I hesitated. Surely it wasn't a crypt or something. I crouched down on all fours and padded through the opening. Surprisingly, Hildegard remained in the dressing room; indignant at the invasion. I stood up in a large room similar to the other dressing rooms. That is if I ignored the odd bird skeleton and mouse carcass which ringed a further cat flap in the corner by the window. We had indeed invaded Hildegard's lair.

Wink waited while I got my bearings, then indicated several cupboards she'd opened. They were stacked with baby-clothes. At one end, in pink: layettes, shawls, bootees, bonnets, smocked silk dresses and satin edged blankets. On the other side of the room the same in blue. I opened the cupboards on the third wall to be confronted by every conceivable soft toy, from fur cats and crimson and grey squirrels to chocolate coloured monkeys and yellow elephants. Everything an infant could desire.

Speechless, we stared at one another. I felt we were trespassing on something very personal and very sad. Else why had the room been blocked off? But for the Achilles heel of Hildegard's escape route –

and the forthcoming rewiring – we'd likely never have known it existed. Was that why the countess had delayed?

Brightening, Wink said: 'My professional opinion would be 1930s vintage or earlier. Look at the long dresses, even for a boy.'

'Left behind after the war, do you think? This place was a children's home for several years.'

'Children ... not babies.' Wink opened the remaining cupboards but aside from stacks of nappies and other essential equipment, revealed nothing suitable for over 1-year-olds.

'If my dressing rooms are anything to go by there might well be further rooms we haven't discovered yet – one for each age of child.'

We both scoured the walls. 'If there are they don't lead off here. This room's a dead end,' Wink sighed, sympathetically. 'P'raps not having children, she hankered after them?'

'Then why not adopt?'

'During the war, that's exactly what she did. Hundreds of 'em.'

Loyalty to the countess prevented my voicing my thoughts – afraid that by actually saying something it could take on a substance it shouldn't have; hang forever on the ether like a Damoclesian possibility. But I did wonder whether in those days if you were expecting, and had plenty of money, you stocked up on both colours.

For days afterwards, and despite telling myself the last person I wanted to think about was Jolyon St Clair, I nevertheless found myself dwelling on the subject. What if he really was her grandson? But if that was the case, why keep it a secret? And why hadn't she left him Sanderling – instead of just the gatehouse; symbolic though that might be? What had he done that was so bad she'd effectively disinherited him?

Chapter 34

Over the next few weeks I recast my life at Sanderling. Physically the house became a cacophony of noise and turmoil as, with a revitalized Smithson in charge, phase one of the restoration got underway. Everywhere I went I tripped over dust sheets, was minded to skirt gaping holes in the floor and suffered numerous bruises. I even packed off Hildegard to Bertie, fearful she'd be nailed under floorboards or behind the panelling; unintentionally more of a fixture than ever. She came straight back – reluctant to miss the fun.

Workmen and women poured in through the gates at eight sharp and extra house staff were hired to keep the place habitable during the upheaval. I promised all a share in the estate revenues ... as long as they undertook to spend their gains with Blakesley area businesses wherever possible.

Rather than prevail upon one of the staff, one afternoon I drove into the village. Passers-by waved and smiled as I parked the car. They'd never done that before. Actually I was pleased the shop still existed. And was swarming with people.

'Busy in here today,' I whispered to the woman in front of me.

'Oh, 't al'ays is now,' she said, glancing at Sheila, busy joking with the customer she was serving. 'Woke 'er up didn't it, 'aving to close them other shops – what 'er dad worked so 'ard to build up. Saw 'e'd it right after all, I reckons,' she sniffed. 'Any road, we didn't want to lose our shop, neither. Bit of give an' take is all us wanted ... bit o' encouragement, like.'

Buoyed by this new atmosphere of optimism I dropped the car off at the stables intending to get some fresh air by walking back to the house. Ever since my first sight of Sanderling, I'd always preferred to walk down the drive – finding even the Bentley's stately pace frustratingly fast for soaking up the view.

Mr Channing came running out in his shirt sleeves, braces over a collarless shirt, wash leather in hand. 'Ms McKenna?' I'd stopped the Ma'am, far too old school and feudal – nice though it had sounded when I'd been intoxicated by life in a fairy tale. But I still believed that the use of people's surnames enforced a degree of respect which I was keen to foster. So now at Sanderling we retained formality for everyone. 'Yes Mr Channing?'

'Would you mind young Mr Palmer and his Missus sleeping over the end garage? They've been turfed out by the mortgage company because Fentiman, their landlord, hasn't kept up the payments and what with a little 'un on the way.... We'd have taken them in but we've already got the Hughes' staying with us until he can find work. Mr Palmer's a good worker, Ms McKenna; I'm teaching him how to look after the old engines.'

'I don't see why not. But you'll need to ask Mr Travers just in case he's promised it to someone else. In which case ask him if he can suggest an alternative will you?' I'd finally managed to get Mr Travers to come off his temporary contract and join the Sanderling team full time, in charge of house staff and all domestic arrangements. No longer servants, curtseying, until now still practised by the few who remembered how to do it, was banned; courtesy to all was the order of the day. Yet my meals were still prepared and served in the dining room and my chores performed by people whose role it was. Just as my job was to run the place.

By summer, the plumbing and wiring and fireproofing were advancing well in the house and the people had regained their exuberance. Every day I heard tales of extraordinary kindnesses being performed around the estate.

Mr Poulson was one of the surprises. Whether because he no longer had anyone to drink with in the Coach & Horses – I understood even Jolyon St Clair was rarely seen out now – or, like Sheila Parsons, had figured out that the way to survive was to cultivate goodwill, I didn't know. Though I had made sure that the quicker he helped the dispossessed for no charge, the more paid commissions came his way. He could endear himself to me and others only by demonstrating compassion for his fellow unfortunates. Folk began to speak highly of him, couple him with his father in their affections.

Whilst in his office one day on an errand, he startled me by announcing: 'I know I said that criteria lark was a daft idea but I have to take it back. What you've done for Sanderling and this village is more than has been accomplished since the war. More than any relation of the countess's would have done.'

'Lucky she didn't have one, otherwise I'm not so sure I'd have passed that test.' The villagers had done most of the work – looked after each other.

'Oh, she had one alright.' My mouth fell open. 'Didn't she tell you, that detective woman?'

'Anyone we know?' I said in a high pitch, vocal chords strangled by shock. My mind was turning somersaults, tearing through possibilities, wondering why no one had said. Why had there been no rumours; how could Wink have missed that particular nugget?

Mr Poulson fished his pipe out of his pocket, looked at it longingly and stowed it away again. 'No idea. I wasn't let in on it. Overheard my old man when he hired the Edwards woman. That was her original task, to find the nearest blood relative.'

I relaxed an inch. 'Oh, so you don't actually know that she found one.'

'There's no paperwork, if that's what you mean. And believe me, I've searched,' he gave a sheepish smile looking up at me through lowered lashes. 'Though I didn't bother initially.' That didn't surprise me, he and Fentiman could do without the heir while they ransacked the estate. 'But once you came on the scene and started throwing your weight around, well, it was a different matter.'

'So what makes you so sure?'

'Dad's reaction when I asked him about it, just before he died. He was a God-awful liar.'

'Well if you're right, and it's a big "if", he or she was either disregarded for some reason – or even more likely, given the countess's age – was an elderly cousin or some such who died before she did.

Whichever it was, the countess was forced to resort to the criteria approach ... an unlikely recourse had a valid heir existed.'

Glancing out of the window I spotted Jolyon St Clair; the first time I'd seen him since I'd banished him from Sanderling. He was supping wine outside the Coach & Horses in earnest conversation with the woman just mentioned – Jean Edwards. I hadn't even known she was up here. Rather than opposite each other they sat side by side like familiar conspirators, heads close together.

I thanked Mr Poulson and left through the yard door. Why should I care if those two indulged in an intimate tête-à-tête in public at this time of day? For heavens' sake she was old enough to be his mother – shouldn't she know better. Edwards was also fully aware of St Clair's treachery and yet she was betraying me for all to see. At that moment I was unsure whom I most disliked – her or him.

Wink greeted me on the doorstep, waving the previous Sunday's colour supplement held open at an article about a woman who'd thrown a Regency ball at her historic mansion complete with: ' "... floaty empire-line dresses, Hussar uniforms, horse drawn carriages and the soft light of candelabra".' She looked up. 'What's the matter with you?'

'Mr Poulson reckons the countess did have a blood relation. Apparently Jean Edwards was originally hired to find one.'

'Hmm. Funny she never mentioned it. I expect the poor soul died before the ink was dry on the will.'

'That's exactly what I said – otherwise Jean would have told me, I'm sure. Knowing her she'd have already conducted an exhaustive search and having ascertained there was just this one, be highly reluctant to revisit it all – which I admit I might have requested.'

We walked through the sitting room and out on to the terrace; flopped into Lloyd Loom armchairs set beside a marble-topped table. I reached across for the article Wink was clutching and scanned it as Mr Travers brought tea. 'Has Bertie been dropping hints again? Anyway, the period doesn't fit Sanderling and it would hardly be conducive to community relations – far too grand.'

'He thinks it's high time we kept up our end of the social calendar.'

Her face lit up. 'Just think, Synnove – a summer ball by the lake; this terrace garlanded in fairy lights, gaily decorated boats bobbing on the water, curtains billowing out of the ballroom, music wafting on the breeze....' Wink executed an old-fashioned waltz across the paving stones.

I had to laugh. 'All right. I can't fight both of you. A ball it is. But I like the way you describe it, something for everyone.'

Wink clapped her hands. 'A theme, we must have a theme.'

'I'd have said that was obvious. It has to be the 1930s. We can have all the cars out on the drive for people to see and we can easily outfit any lady in need of a costume.'

Bertie was right. I did owe the populace a celebration. Ever since my decision to share Sanderling with those whose home it was, the people had responded with immeasurable warmth and sincerity. The air had a vibrancy, workers smiled and whistled. They were toiling for themselves and their families. All this was theirs too. It was far too good to last.

Chapter 35

The morning of the ball, I was helping to carry an immense display of blooms into the ballroom when I registered a shadow and glanced across. It was all I could do to keep a hold of the giant vase. I must have cried out, because Susan said with concern: 'You all right, Ms McKenna?' Alerted by her tone, Mr Travers moved swiftly to relieve me of my charge ... freeing me to face Russell alone.

I walked towards him, halting six feet from the doormat where he stood clutching a ridiculously small overnight bag. Pale skinned, he'd lost a lot more weight and his once manicured five o'clock shadow had sprouted into an unkempt beard. 'You should have rung. I'd have sent a car to the station.'

'You knew I was out.'

'No, I didn't. Have they let you go?' The question sounded stupid. Did I think he'd absconded? What I'd meant to ask was whether they'd dropped the case against him but one glance at those haunted eyes told me not. I felt unbearably guilty. Thinking there was nothing more I could do, I'd been content to leave everything to the team of barristers I'd hired – while he suffered.

'You pulled strings to get me bail.'

'No, I—'

His face downgraded from white to ashen. 'Oh my God. Then it's them,' he swung the big oak door to with a dull thud. 'They've had me released so they can get me.' He flung his bag aside and gripped me by both arms. 'Money, you bitch. I have to have money.'

I stepped back and his arms fell to his side. 'I can't find the collections, Russell. They've got to be here somewhere and with all this upheaval,' I waved a hand ineffectually, 'they're bound to turn up.'

Russell gazed along the hall. 'Where's all the other stuff gone?'

'Oh that's just piled in anterooms.' Guilt, fear, goodness knows what made me explain – I didn't have to. 'But, in planning the restoration before she died, the countess had the family collections stored away for safe keeping. They're the most liquid of Sanderling's assets – if we can find them.' I listened to myself saying anything to mollify him while I tried to work out how to keep him safe. Now was not the time to suggest I had no right to give him anything from here.

He moved towards the ballroom. Wretched, I just turned and watched his pathetic figure. 'What's going on?'

'We're having a ball tonight, to celebrate the progress that's been made, congratulate ourselves.'

His eyes stared out of his head. 'Strangers, people coming in from outside?'

'A few,' we had invited some local friends. 'Not many. Why?'

He walked across and grabbed my arm again before I could avoid him, dug in his fingers. Pushing his jaw in front of my face, his breath foul, he yelled: 'You just don't get it, do you? There are people in England now, who've been paid to amputate my hands, then my feet, then my arms and legs, one at a time with a machette, until I pay up; or squirm on my belly which is all that'll be left of me.' He threw my arm back at me. 'All because lady la-di-da won't cough up a few million.' He whirled, grabbed his bag. 'Liquid assets eh? My arse! I'm going to find somewhere safe to kip so don't have anyone follow me. And when I wake up I want that money, in cash. We'll soon see what's liquid.' He marched down the hall and disappeared through a door to the lower floor. A man naked of pretension, broken back to base level.

I walked to my sitting room and closed the door. The police could arrest him for causing an affray I supposed, then he'd be safe again; but not for long. My hand hovered over the phone, debating whether or not to phone the trustees. And say what? 'My ex-lover's got himself into deep trouble playing games with a lawless African state and wants Sanderling to bail him out?' When I tested the raw truth like that, it would be wrong to give him any part of the place. Then I noticed my hand ... and burst into tears.

A tap at the door, the knob turned. I blew my nose hurriedly. Jean Edwards was standing in the doorway, she who never missed a thing. And judging by their body language, she who'd been sharing secrets with Jolyon. 'I saw you cosying up to St Clair, what are you two hatching?'

'You asked me to discover his motive for encouraging all those business failures.'

'No. That was your idea. It's obvious what he wants. He's the countess's grandson, isn't he? Mr Poulson told me what you did – you've known all along.'

It had been uncommon, but not unheard of, for Jean to be asked to trace a blood relation – though, usually, a specific one. She had started with the normal sources but was unsurprised when the record offices drew a blank. The countess must have already trawled those waters.

But a blood relation by definition encompassed illegitimate offspring ... generally much harder, if not impossible, to trace; their parents having deliberately hidden the truth because of the shame it bestowed on them and the child. Well aware of this, Jean and her team searched the nursing homes and poor houses – those tucked away places where such births occurred – listing every record they could find stretching back into the nineteenth century. If a concealed illegitimacy stemmed from before that, she was never going to find it now.

Then, in a convent run by nuns on the Essex marshes, Jean came across the record of a baby boy born to one Ariadne Tennyson in the summer of 1937. Women seeking to conceal a birth invariably provided false information to the authorities for obvious reasons, but when looking for the proverbial needle in a cornfield, Jean must grasp at anything shiny. Ariadne was not only the countess's middle name, but her mother's name too. Even so, Jean paid the fact scant attention, convinced that any illegitimate issue among the Hampdens was far more likely to be on the male side – not only because in those days men of a certain class had much more opportunity to misbehave than did their womenfolk, but also because the countess was unlikely to have engaged a detective to unearth a carefully buried secret she already knew about.

The next chore had been to churn through the closely written estate journals and account books in the records room at Sanderling ... looking for clues – such as a regular donation. Usually these turned out to be for old family retainers or penniless third cousins who'd sought charity. In this case Jean had found an institution who, amongst a handful of other good causes, benefitted once a year from the countess's largesse. It was called St Hildegard's – a home for unmarried mothers run by white-robed Irish nuns ... in Essex. Coincidence?

Had the countess met the Mother Superior at some function and been so taken with her she'd agreed to become a supporter? Had the countess's family bundled one of the estate girls off there and ever after felt obliged to the place? Or, and this was the most likely, was the patronage somehow linked to the countess's work with children during the war? The donations started in 1941 so that would fit. Jean decided to take a closer look.

On the pretext of seeking peace – these days the establishment served also as a retreat house, open to all – she went back to the marsh and looked up the child again. He'd been adopted at birth by a London couple. Jean made a note of their name. Without the countess's express permission she could go no further for fear of arousing interest.

As part of an inquiry like this, Jean always perused local records. Once before, she had found a man simply by consulting the area telephone directory. Having been adopted, on discovering his true parentage he'd changed his name by deed poll to that of his real father. The electoral roll was another useful source. The one for Blakesley revealed an entry for that less than everyday name. A name identical to the London adopting family.

It made no sense but three coincidences were two too many to ignore. And the only way to find out had been to tackle the countess about it.

At the time the name hadn't resonated with Jean – why should it; she knew nothing of this part of the world. Of course, since ... well, she understood why the countess had reacted as she did.

Jean could see the woman was deeply disturbed by Russell Prince's sudden reappearance. And just when she could have done with a friend to lean on, Jolyon St Clair had been cast as enemy number one. But the huge danger was that in believing Jolyon to be the countess's grandson, Synnove would feel she had to leave.

Jean sighed. 'Look, I was sworn to secrecy by the countess. Nobody else knows, so you have nothing to fear. But I can't just—'

Synnove advanced towards her. 'Very well, if you won't tell me, I'll just have to prove it myself.'

'All right, all right,' Jean held up her hand, conscious only that she had to prevent the truth from coming out. If it did, Sanderling and all it stood for would crash to the floor. She understood that now – and why the countess had burned the evidence. And Mr Poulson couldn't know the details. 'If I find out where Jolyon St Clair sprang from, will that satisfy you?'

Chapter 36

As I'd hoped, Russell failed to appear all evening even though Mr Travers had found him a costume – in case. But Jolyon St Clair did. The estate had issued an open invitation to the whole neighbourhood; boating, beer tents on the front lawns and the ball in the main house – people could pick their fantasy. The whole idea was inclusivity – so I could hardly ban anyone. I just hadn't thought he'd have the gall.

With Wink's help I'd chosen a slinky backless number from the countess's collection, a heavy midnight silk which followed my every move. Not that I'd any intention of dancing. Rather than light relief for me personally, I considered the occasion to be a thank you – to celebrate finding an encouraging formula after such an uncertain twelve months. I was content to watch others enjoy.

With the ball scheduled to begin at nine, Mr Channing, plus a team of drivers hired for the night, began ferrying the first comers in at 8.30. He'd been working on the fleet for days and the gleaming bodywork did him justice. A stream of models from the vintage collection, the four Rolls Royces retrieved from Mr Channing's wedding hire business, two gleaming eight litre Bentleys, plus the Lagonda and my Sedanca de Ville; the American Lincoln, the Delage D8-120 and a 1934 Bugatti followed by the smaller cars, paraded down the flare-lined drive to the entrance, cheered by the crowds. Ladies in their finery and gents in tails were helped into the house by liveried footmen, plied with cocktails and drawn to the ballroom by the strains of a quickstep.

'Will you do me the honour?' asked a deep baritone behind me. I whirled, knocked off balance. He sketched a bow, that infuriating half smile tugging at his lips. Not knowing what else to do I glared at him and strode off across the dance floor. Now I had two things to worry about, that Russell might make a scene, and the possibility of bumping into St Clair at every turn. Knowing what I did, and suspecting the rest, I didn't trust him; yet he possessed a magnetic quality that scared me. I daren't stray into that field.

'Don't let me out of your sight,' I hissed at Wink. 'That man St Clair is here and I don't feel safe.'

'Whom don't you trust? Him or you?'

Accepting the jibe as the price of her company, we toured the ballroom and the supper room together, exchanging greetings and chatting; toasting the assembled company and giving out little mementoes of the evening. At midnight a gong sounded and everyone streamed out to the lakeside. The firework manufacturers had unearthed their pre-war display diagrams and shown John and the under-gardeners how to construct showers and starbursts from a boat on the water so the shooting stars appeared to plummet into the depths as they shot into space. The finale began with the Sanderling classic – a succession of displays imitating a train running around the lake perimeter – and ended with a traditional tirade of earsplitting explosions.

As the last pops and fizzes receded amongst tumultuous applause I turned back towards the house. It took me a second to refocus, realize the flames and shooting sparks issuing from the far end of the west terrace were real. As the crowd recognized it too, amid shouts for forming lines and fetching hoses, Wink and I ran as one along the outside of the building. The fire was coming from my dressing rooms where the men had been about to start flameproofing the floors. Silhouetted in a downstairs window was the unmistakeable shape of Hildegard on hind legs, pawing frantically at the glass. Her tunnels blocked by fire she'd been forced into a dead end. She fell back on to all fours, choking for air.

With no way of breaking the glass we hitched up our skirts and, holding the bunched material in one hand, chased back through the ballroom and darted into the servants' corridor. Above us timber crashed in the distance; the air was thick and hot and smelled of burning rubber. Impelled by horror, we careered along the passage, fending off the walls with our spare hands, ricocheting around corners.

Surely we must be getting close to that room. How would we see the door in this smoke? Which one was it? Other footsteps thundered down a passage to our left; twenty yards away, Jolyon sprinted towards us yelling and gesticulating. 'For God's sake go back, I'll get the cat.'

What was he doing, coming from that direction? Where had he been? I daren't listen to him. We ran on.

'The wing isn't safe, it could collapse any minute. Go back.' Catching up he grabbed my arm and tugged. For all I knew he planned to lock us in here. Terrified, I wrenched myself free, stumbled after Wink and kept running. Suddenly, there came a jingling sound, chains rattling, and an almighty wrenching and twisting of the structure around us which filled the already dense atmosphere with dust. Like a shute, the floorboards dipped perpendicular and, limbs flailing uselessly, Wink and I plummeted into a chasm.

I don't remember screaming, I hadn't the breath. Bile rose up my throat as my teeth rattled inside my head and I catapulted downwards, stomach lurching unrestrained in my body as I dropped the height of a room.

When I opened my eyes, Wink was crawling away from me, intent on a painting propped against a far wall. 'The very holy one,' she whispered, squinting at a Baroque framed picture of Theseus, to the side of me, scrabbling with her hands in the dust for the trusty lornette she must have lost in the fall. Her words were distinct, yet it wasn't a religious painting. A spurt of freezing foreboding spiralled along my spine, pausing at every notch, chilling the marrow. Had someone come to meet her?

Splinters were digging like nails into my flesh, my dress was being ripped away, the skin razed off my shoulders as I was dragged along concrete; a huge bang amid cascades of masonry and soot and pieces of plaster.... I cared no longer – death was so welcome. Hurry – let me go.

We held Wink's funeral at the little church she'd attended on the edge of the estate. It was a beautiful day and the service took place outside because there were so many mourners. 'Ashes to ashes, dust to dust....' I don't remember much else, couldn't look when they lowered that shining personality into a damp hole in the ground and shovelled earth on her; put out the light.

I'd insisted they let me out of hospital though they'd said the headaches could return. Nightmares they meant. I'd killed her – my best friend. Her death was down to me. It was me who'd brought her here in the first place, me who'd begged her to stay ... and me who'd ignored Jolyon when he'd pleaded with us to turn back. And he was still in the General, suffering with the concussion and burns he'd sustained in saving my worthless life. Realizing the rest of the floor would shortly collapse into the underground cellar, Jolyon had apparently leapt through that gaping hole in time to drag me clear before the beams cascaded inwards. Because she'd moved further into the room there'd been no time to reach Wink, who'd been hit when the ceiling fell, died surrounded by the treasure she'd been seeking all those months. That's what she'd recognized – the countess's favourite painting. She'd always said if she found that she'd have found the rest.

That evening, alone in my sitting room, a buzzing outside disturbed me. Fearful it might be in my head I rang for Mr Travers.

'It's Lord Dan, patrolling on his trusty Douglas motorbike. Been doing it since the fire, Ms McKenna. Blames himself for what happened to you and Miss Winkleman.'

'How come?' I said wearily, not up to fathoming what went on in that wise but weird old head.

'For not being sterner with the countess about having the fire retardant work done years ago,' Mr Travers shifted his weight on to his other foot; he still would never sit in my presence. 'And some theory of his about who did it.'

I began to feel uneasy, swung my feet off the couch and sat up straight. 'Wasn't it caused by a spark from the fireworks – a lighted rocket falling down a chimney?'

Mr Travers looked at his feet. 'We let you think that because we didn't want you worrying while you were lying in bed. The authorities believe it was arson.'

I struggled to stand but thought better of it. Not everyone had been won over by the new regime then. 'That explains how the fire got such a hold before anyone noticed. It could have been lit way before the fireworks started. Open the right windows and doors when we're all engrossed in the display and ... I remember there was a stiff breeze that night.'

In the distance the bell sounded. Mr Travers went to answer it, returning with Jean Edwards. Because of what Jolyon had done, I'd revised my view of her since our last conversation but I still felt she'd not been entirely honest with me. Mr Travers backed out.

'I wasn't sure if you'd want to....'

I waved her to a seat.

'How are you?' When I didn't answer she leaned forward, hands together, not meeting my eyes. She too must be remembering the acrimony with which we'd last parted. 'I don't want to add to your woes but I think the news I have for you might actually help ... well, anyway ...' she parted her fingers then rejoined them in a little gesture of indecision.

'Go on.' Although I'd had enough shocks for one week, one more would make little difference. Perhaps they'd made a mistake, I hadn't been destined for Sanderling after all ... and Wink had died because of an error.

'I told you I'd find out about Jolyon St Clair's background. Actually it wasn't hard. We'd already dug up most of it in the work we did for you earlier.'

I didn't want to think about that. It only confused me when I felt so grateful to the man. Again I had that feeling Jean Edwards had been less than forthcoming. She treated everything on a strictly need to know basis where the open sesame depended on knowing which question to ask. I shrugged; it must go with the job.

'We already knew that Jolyon's father, Harry St Clair, was an engineer who married the daughter of a Norfolk solicitor. Posted to Nigeria by his employer, Harry and his wife enrolled young Jolyon, their only child, in an English boarding school but were then tragically killed in an uprising,' Jean paused. 'The next thing we know is that a beautiful lady appeared at the school and took Jolyon away in a big car to live with Lord Danhanbury.'

'But why? What's the connection?' She supposed she could have asked Bertie but so sure their rift must be connected with Jolyon's behaviour she hadn't dared. That and she doubted she'd get any sort of sensible answer. Bertie would likely adopt one of his *Alice in Wonderland* poses, as Wink used to call them; where he'd mimic the Mad Hatter, The Cheshire Cat or the scurrying White Rabbit in order to avoid unwelcome issues.

'That's what we asked. We found the answer by digging back through Harry's past.' Jean shuffled to the edge of her seat. 'Harry's parents were both killed in the second world war, she in the East End bombings and his father in the airforce,' she leaned back. 'I don't know if you've made the same mistake, we shouldn't have because we'd had the clue of who picked him up. All the time we assumed the connection was between Jolyon and Lord Danhanbury or rather, his father Harry, and Lord Danhanbury – distant relation, son of an old retainer, son of a naval friend ... even something more scandalous. But it wasn't. The link is with the countess.'

I gasped involuntarily. Put my hand to my mouth. 'So Jolyon is her...?'

'Harry St Clair was one of the six or seven hundred orphaned children she took in during the war, housed here at Sanderling. He must have been a favourite because he stayed on after the war until claimed by an uncle who took him to live in Colchester. But they kept in touch – I even remember seeing correspondence from a Harry in the countess's archives.'

'So where does Bertie come into this?'

Jean pursed her lips. 'I imagine the countess thought a man would make a more suitable guardian for a boy than she would.'

'So Jolyon has nothing to do with Sanderling?' I said slowly.

'Not as far as we know.'

'Then who's this blood relation Mr Poulson is talking about?'

Chapter 37

The next day Mr Channing drove me over to the hospital. Jolyon was sitting in the garden in a monogrammed silk dressing gown and matching pyjama trousers, reading *The Times*. Even in adversity he effortlessly exuded the *je ne sais quoi* of an aristocratic English gentleman. He had a long cut on his forehead and both hands were encased in plastic bags which was making it difficult for him to manoeuvre the paper. It dropped to the floor as he rose at my approach. That same smile. I sat on the bench beside him but couldn't think what to say.

His brow furrowed. 'Should you be up?'

'I came out of it better than you did,' I indicated his hands.

'Oh, they'll be OK – this is modern science's answer to burns,' he waggled his fingers in demonstration. We both laughed. He sobered. 'I'm sorry about your friend – I couldn't—'

And I couldn't take his injured hand and I desperately wanted to, so I squeezed his arm instead. 'Thank you ... for what you did. I didn't deserve to be saved.' I felt completely wretched. I had not only mistrusted him but that mistrust had led to Wink's death and Jolyon's injuries. It wasn't so much Jean's filling in of his background that had convinced me of his integrity. That in itself didn't stop him from believing he should have Sanderling. But after I'd ignored him, thus causing the disaster in the first place, at huge risk to himself he had saved my life. He could easily have let me die; no one could have blamed him. So it couldn't be Sanderling he wanted.

'Oh, everyone deserves to be saved, don't you think? It's an infuriating hobby of mine.'

It was just like him to be nice when he must loathe the sight of me after I'd treated him so badly; shown what I'd thought of him … repaid his kindness and protection with contempt and arrogance.

He touched my hand with his forearm. 'Can I explain what I was trying to do – about the businesses?'

'You don't have to; I'm sure there's been some misunderstanding.' Heavens, it wasn't for him to apologize. 'I'm so sorry I got the wrong end of things, spoke to you the way I did after all you'd done for me.' I wiped my brow with my sleeve. 'I realize now that if it hadn't been for you I wouldn't have lasted a week at Sanderling. With crumbling empires of their own to worry about, folk were much less likely to be concerned with me. I see that now. So if you did do any of those things, then I know you meant it to help.' The words tumbled out in a blind haste to reassure.

'I did do it deliberately,' he said slowly then stopped, his eyes searching my face.

I froze. How could he? I'd even convinced myself he must be protecting others, that all I lacked was faith, there'd be a rational explanation. Never have I struggled so hard to control my shock. A blink in the wrong place now would kill his trust forever.

'Fentiman was bound to take to gambling as to the manner born … and I knew he'd lose. That was the only case where I indulged in malice. The man's a wrong-un. I wanted to prise folk from his clutches, stand them on their own feet, make them realize they could. So yes, I showed him how to lose the lot – and he obliged, brilliantly. Which probably makes him a very dangerous man now,' Jolyon attempted to run his fingers through his hair in that way he had.

Accepting he couldn't, he sighed instead and went on. 'I digress. After Channing started copying him, diddling the little people, not caring what sort of rubbish he sold them, I arranged for his stock to be stolen; which I knew would ruin him. But I also knew he had roots here and that when he was down people would rally round to help his family – which, if I was right about the basic man, would change his attitude towards them; albeit by force.'

'You really did those things?' So there was a good reason. 'Well, it worked. These days Mr Channing couldn't be a more helpful, kindly individual. He's running free apprenticeship schemes; teaching village youngsters car mechanics.'

Jolyon rose, held out his arm, bent inwards at the elbow. I linked mine through it and we strolled across the lawn. 'In an effort to set people straight, I'm afraid I did a lot more than that,' he braced his shoulders, symbolically glad to be rid of the burden they carried. 'Shelia Parsons was throwing away all the goodwill her father had built up; fast deterring would-be customers so Blakesley soon would have no shop. I had to concentrate her mind, get her to change ... or sell out. So I ratted on her to the Trading Authority. What I said was true. The way she kept stock was dangerous; she'd have poisoned somebody sooner or later. Now look at her. One of the good guys.'

Having started there was no stopping him, he wanted to confess all, be purged. I wished I could be. 'Poulson was easy to sort – he'd already upset you, which meant he'd lose the Sanderling business. All I had to do was make sure the estate agents were wise to his tricks. Very soon no one would use him for conveyancing – his staple business. He's lazy. That's why he teamed up with Fentiman so quickly – bought the idea as a way to rich pickings with no effort. Without lifting a finger, he could take a cut from everything Fentiman made out of your estate.'

We sat on a bench overlooking a valley, watched the jackdaws ride the air currents.

'Same with Roy Smithson – he was jealous of me for being out of work. I ask you. Yes, I confess, I played on his weakness, kept inviting him to lunches, afternoon do's. He would have gone bust anyway; all I did was hasten it. The solution was there in front of him. The man's good, but he has to work. Look what happens when he doesn't.'

'Weren't you afraid you were taking too much on yourself?' The comment slipped out. I didn't want to criticize but what he'd done did seem a bit....

He hung his head. 'Yes, I know, it backfired – on you,' he turned towards me. 'The stupid thing was I never dreamt they'd blame you. How could they? That's where I went wrong. All I wanted was to get the community back to the way it had been before they all started chasing Fentiman style riches; to stop their selfishness by bringing back the concept of shame. They'd been so much happier before … so much more caring.'

We sat in silence for a few minutes. Could he really forgive me? 'We found the countess's collections. Wink forgot the danger in her excitement.'

'That's why I wanted you to stop,' he stood up and we carried on with our walk. 'When I was small my father used to tell a story about how, after the war, some strange-looking men arrived at Sanderling and every night they were there, convoys of lorries would drive around the back of the house but be gone by morning. He thought these men had stashed their fortunes at Sanderling in the 1930s when Hitler started persecuting Jews.'

We sat down on our original bench. 'Bertie told me the countess's father had a special chamber built, kept its location quiet. Though Bertie always reckoned it must have been under that new wing which had been added so quickly. That's why I was worried. The whole structure had been thrown up in a hurry and judging by the speed with which the fire had already spread I doubted its solidity.'

'As usual, Bertie was right, wasn't he.'

Now I knew there was a secret I couldn't let it rest … regardless of the countess's wishes. But hell would freeze over before Jean Edwards would tell me and Mr Poulson didn't know. On my way home from the hospital I leaned forward. 'Take me round the lake please, Mr Channing. I want to see Lord Dan.'

'It's gone tea time, Ms McKenna.'

'I'm not going for tea.'

Finding the Hampden collections was the only good to have come out of the tragedy and most of it had survived intact. Although Russell had left the next morning – according to Mr Travers, too frightened to stay anywhere long – I felt that maybe I could still use them to help him. With Wink gone I hadn't the heart to look at the goods they'd salvaged in my absence but from all accounts they were stunning. Since no one on the estate was any longer in dire need, perhaps now I could pawn them against the day Russell could pay the money back. But only if Sanderling really was mine, to do with as I chose.

Jean Edwards had explained about Jolyon and his father Harry. But why had Harry been the countess's favourite? It was still possible that Jolyon was her grandson and once again, Jean Edwards had sought to deflect me from finding the truth. But she didn't know Wink and I had stumbled upon a hidden room full of baby clothes did she? Only the two of us had done the packing in there.

The famous motorcycle stood propped on its stand by the front door, ready for action. Bertie had ceased to stop in mid stride whenever we met but still greeted me with effusive charm. Today was no exception. 'Is that really Lawrence of Arabia's bike?' I asked, awed.

'No, my dear. I daresay his ended up as what today we'd call a write-off. He was killed ridin' it if you remember; same model though.'

He showed me through into the drawing room furnished with dark oak furniture and festooned with rich red velvet and sent Morgans scuttling off for sherry, which appeared in seconds. Morgans poured and handed me a glass before retiring.

'Is somethin' the matter, my dear?' Bertie inquired when he'd settled me solicitously in his best armchair. 'I'm afraid you've missed tea but I could ask Mrs—' I waved a hand to dismiss the idea. Before I could say why I was there he drew his chair up to mine.

'Been to the hospital, I hear.' That damned bush telegraph. 'I'm glad. I was worried about you two,' he leaned towards me, a twist to his lips which suggested a certain awkwardness. 'Reckons you'll think he's after your money, y'know.'

I was speechless. Not only at Bertie's implication, but at his tone. He and Jolyon didn't get on. 'Oh that's all right,' I said airily, as though I understood what he was talking about. 'Since I'm coming more and more to the opinion I don't have any.'

He got up and started to move around the room awkwardly. 'Eh? How'dya make that out, m'dear?'

I waited, silently forcing him to look at me. 'Because I know there's a blood relation. Charles Poulson told me. And Jean Edwards, the private detective, as much as admitted it; but says she was sworn to secrecy by the countess. Well the countess isn't here and I am. I want to know who it is, Bertie.'

What would he do? Rattle on about Jolyon, not wanting to upset me? Lecture me about pre-war morals and how this must never get out? He sank on to the ottoman at my feet and stared at his gnarled hands, turning them this way and that, examining every vein and contour, every joint. Five minutes must have passed, maybe longer.

Chapter 38

Eventually Bertie stood and pulled the bell cord. 'You're going to need more than sherry,' he said. 'Ah, Morgans. Bring the brandy in, will you?' Bertie watched him go. Afraid now I'd have to wait until Morgans returned and the moment would be lost or hi-jacked, I was about to demand an answer when Bertie suddenly blurted the name 'Fentiman,' out in a rush. 'It's Barry Fentiman.'

My glass shattered on the hearth as I lost control of my fingers. Bertie hurried across and stooped over me, chafing my hands as if they were cold. 'If Poulson and this detective woman know, then it's only right that you should.' Mr Morgans came and went silently. Bertie pressed a brandy goblet into my hand. Of all absurd thoughts, I was surprised he trusted me with another so soon after my having smashed the first.

What sort of cruel joke was this? I had so many questions all vying with one another to get out. Desperate to acquire some perspective, see things in their proper place, I wanted to make sure I had the generations right. 'So, Fentiman's father was the countess's son?'

Presumably satisfied I was no longer on the point of fainting, Bertie retreated to the sofa nursing his own brandy. The flesh hung on his face like great tears of sadness, pulling him down. 'The detective put it together. You can see why Isabel destroyed the file.'

'So who was the father?' Surely not Bertie. A servant?

'Man called Tennyson. Clever devil, a few years older than me. He was at university on a scholarship when he and Isabel met. His stepfather was estate manager at Sanderlin'. After that, I never stood a chance. Even after he was killed during the war she still wouldn't marry me. Said it wasn't fair,' he turned rheumy eyes in my direction.

'She couldn't have any more children, you see – said I deserved children.'

'Why didn't she marry him? Was he already married?'

'Oh, no, nothing like that. You wouldn't understand.'

From the reverence and tenderness with which he always spoke of her I'd often suspected Bertie had entertained more than admiration for the countess. All those years he'd worshipped her, never marrying, not getting on with his life. I suddenly felt enormously selfish. 'I'm sorry Bertie, I didn't mean to rake it all up again.'

He swallowed some brandy, gazed into the middle distance, reliving the scene. 'Isabel left the decision about her successor very late ... for several reasons. When she hired that woman to find a blood relation she never suspected her own child would come to light. She'd hoped somewhere there'd be a distant cousin worthy of the job.' He swirled the amber liquid vehemently around its bowl before downing it in one go.

'When she saw Fentiman's name she said she'd nearly died on the spot from shock,' Bertie looked across. 'He'd been here about three years by then – built that gaudy monstrosity on the outskirts of Blakesley and raced around in his flashy car. No manners, no breedin' and crooked as hell.'

'She didn't doubt it though.'

'The fact that the Edwards woman had discovered there was a child at all was proof of her ability. That's why Isabel then hired her to select her successor.'

In one way it was almost a relief. Especially since the baby clothes discovery I'd been haunted by the notion there was indeed a blood heir. Mr Poulson had reinforced it ... and now, finally, I had the truth from the person I was bound to believe. The man who'd known the countess at the time and who clearly could still be upset by his memory of those bygone happenings.

'Well, at least that settles it, once and for all.' I stood, placed my empty balloon glass carefully on the side table; controlled, distanced. 'Sanderling does indeed belong to Fentiman. Who would have guessed?'

Bertie rose too, but with jerky movements as if his stiff old limbs were rebelling at every instruction. He came across to me, arm outstretched. 'Oh no, you mustn't think that. Isabel was insistent. "Bertie," she said. "You will make sure that only the person fitting the criteria I've laid down, gets Sanderling, won't you? I'm relying on you."'

'But the man has a right, Bertie, the countess was his grandmother.'

'If that's all that mattered we'd have had a few different kings and queens in this country.'

'Fentiman can't know though, can he? Otherwise he'd have broadcast his lineage from the rooftops. Demanded his birthright. Amassed the world's press.'

'There you have it, m'dear ... so there's no need to tell him.'

My temporary bedroom overlooked the drive. The distant fountain shot tinkling raindrops into a not quite dark summer's night and half-asleep I embraced that drifting feeling where I no longer had to confront hard facts and could melt into a floating world of not having to think ... or make decisions. Like a benign bee, the buzzing of Bertie's motorcycle circling the park lent soporific overtones to the scene.

A singed Hildegard sat possessively on my abandoned mules; other than the shearing she'd received in consequence, seemingly none the worse for her experience. I didn't know how she'd escaped but presumed that when the wing collapsed, gaps opened up in the room where we'd seen her trapped. The following morning Mr Travers had found her bewildered and burnt, chunks of fur hanging from bleeding skin, and had carted her off to the vet.

Arson, the fire people thought it was arson. A few months ago, when they'd wrecked the aviary and pulled down the wall, the list of suspects could have included half the village. I sighed. But the main instigator hadn't changed by the look of it. Having lost his criminally lucrative maintenance contract, attempted desecration as a means of forcing me out, and whipped up the surrounding countryside against me, he'd adopted the classic role of dog in the manger. If he couldn't have Sanderling, then neither could I.

If I were being objective – which was impossible – I'd side with Fentiman. No matter how obnoxious the man, and how unjustified his vindictive campaigns, it turned out he did have a moral right to the place after all. Everything might scream his lack of belonging but in fact he did – belong. In my worst moments I caught myself thinking what a pity it was he hadn't succeeded in razing Sanderling to the ground. What a glorious irony that would have been.

'I'm sorry, Russell. I thought we had a solution when Wink finally found the treasure. It cost her her life – the least it could do would be to buy back yours,' I muttered into the dark. But it wasn't to be. Like eating peas off a fork, just when I thought I'd nailed a sizeable sum for Russell's release, it had disappeared between the prongs of a perverse fate. Sanderling and its collections weren't mine to bestow; not even to borrow and pay back.

I don't know when I dropped off or how long I'd been asleep – judging by my frozen fingers, an hour or two – when the sound of galloping hoofs woke me. Hildegard had jumped up, adopting the on guard position – back arched, feet planted firmly, hackles raised, ears flat to her head, eyes staring. A low growl started in her stomach and worked its way up her throat until it erupted into the room as an unearthly yowl.

'What on earth? Not again.' Grabbing a robe, I stuffed unresponsive feet into cat-warmed slippers and leapt for the door, pushing the bell on the way. I ran for the east staircase and, for speed, allowed my smooth soles to surf its entire length, hanging on to the rope banister for balance and miraculously remaining upright. Hildegard turned frantic circles as I threw the bolts on the main door. Registering sounds of stirring elsewhere in the house, I followed her out.

Hildegard vanished around the corner, but I trotted backwards up the drive to examine the front of the house, expecting smoke and leaping flames. In various states of undress, Mr Travers and other staff poured out of the doors and did the same. 'I'm sorry, the cat was so disturbed I thought it was a repeat of....'

'Better safe than sorry,' Mr Travers comforted. 'But there seems to be no sign of any disturbance.' He held a torch.

'Can I borrow that, I'll see if I can find the poor thing.'

'Would you like me to—'

'No, no, you go back to bed.' I felt foolish. Grateful for the light, I wandered on to the west terrace calling softly for Hilde. God, was I going to carry on like this every night now? About to turn in, a glimmer of light caught my eye from a bend in the lake over to the right. Someone night fishing? Poaching even? I wouldn't want to be in their shoes if Bertie caught up with them.

I walked closer to the water, a direction from which the right side of the lake was blocked from view by a stand of trees but then, out of curiosity, I wandered along the perimeter path towards where I'd seen the flicker. Suddenly the ground shook and I leapt aside as galloping hoofs thundered in my ears and Rainbow streaked past me, ears flat to his skull, nostrils flaring. I tried to grab his bridle but failed. Hoofs; I hadn't been dreaming. Surely Jolyon was in the hospital – he'd be in no fit state to ride. Was that what I'd heard earlier? Was he lying injured out here? I was too far away for Mr Travers or the staff to hear me, hidden from the house by the hill on which the aviary stood. All I could do was run towards the sounds coming from the water.

I rounded the bend in the path where an ox-bow of the lake opened up. Offshore a fire was blazing on a sailing raft; figures silhouetted against the flames. Jolyon stood half in and half out of the water, bagged hands hanging useless by his sides, yelling.

'For Christ's sake, Bertie, come back. Let the police deal with it.'

'Can't do that. All my fault y'see.'

As my eyes adjusted to the dazzle I could see piles of what looked like wood stacked high on the raft ... blazing. 'What's he doing?' I waded into the water beside Jolyon who stared at me in anguish, tears streaming down his face.

'I tried to stop him.'

Casting around I caught sight of Bertie's Douglas on the shore, his cane propped against the back wheel. Tearing off my dressing gown I ploughed into the waves the raft was creating. Jolyon was ripping at the bags trying to free his hands, but the pain when the cold air hit skin rendered raw by attempting to ride must have been excruciating because he screamed and fell back.

'Bertie,' I yelled between strokes, struggling to keep my head out of the water so I could see him. 'Come back in. What on earth's the matter?' The heat of the flames was warming up the surrounding lake and I felt its intensity as I raised my face. The reason I'd been unable to make out the figures from the shore was that the wood had been laid around them and set alight. Bertie stood in the middle of this circle, a pistol trained on a man bound to the mast.

'Caught him red-handed havin' another go. Tryin' to destroy Sanderlin'. So I thought the old Vikin' funeral pyre might prove a fittin' end. He likes fires.'

Jolyon was still yelling, attempting to wade forward. 'Leave it to the police, Bertie!'

'What, and watch them bail him? That's what I did, don't you see? Had him let out. All this is my fault. He thought by burnin' Sanderlin', liquifyin' the asset, he could sever your emotional ties to the place, m'dear, and get his hands on the insurance money.'

I trod water, remembering the day Bertie'd tried to persuade me Russell's problems weren't my responsibility, that he should look after himself. How I'd explained that he couldn't because he was locked up. So Bertie had organized his release ... but it was me who was to blame.

Russell started screaming hysterically.

'Bertie, none of this is your fault. Let the police handle it,' I tried to get closer to the boat which was now wreathed in smoke.

'I promised her I'd look after you.' From the raft two shots rang out. Behind me Jolyon bellowed for me to swim clear. Flames shot high into the sky and panic stricken I lashed the water, kicking and retching, clawing the surface against the drag, gasping for air, chest bursting.

Up to his shoulders in water Jolyon stretched out his arm. I clung to him until I could find my feet. He whistled for Rainbow, helped me on to his back and led us both out.

From the shore we watched as, driven by its own momentum the flaming raft drifted out into the middle of the lake. Consumed by a sudden whoosh it disappeared beneath the water in an upshot of ash and smoke ... the end of an era.

*

Russell's family held his funeral without me. I wasn't sorry. I could conjure no remorse for the man who'd chased false gods so unremittingly, only sadness at the waste.

But after Bertie's memorial service and the wake that followed, I couldn't stop crying. I'd really loved that old man – and he'd died so sadly, thinking he'd failed; when in truth he'd saved all our lives.

Jolyon insisted on escorting me home. We settled in my sitting room. 'He wouldn't have wanted to grow weak and infirm, drooling, unable to stand when a lady entered the room. He knew what he was doing. Probably been planning it for years. Then along came Russell Prince and provided the perfect excuse. He wouldn't want your tears.'

Jolyon must have read himself the same lecture, over and over. How much worse that night must have been for him; normally a physically fit, strong, able man, having to watch, impotent, while Bertie killed Russell and then himself.

'Bertie rang me at the hospital. Said he suspected Prince was prowling the grounds and that he would get him; put him where he belonged. And that everything I'd need was in a trunk in the wine cellar,' Jolyon shifted uneasily on his seat. 'I discharged myself, got a taxi home. I couldn't saddle Rainbow so I rode him bareback to the lake.'

I pictured him clutching the stallion's mane with those screaming hands. The horse had bolted when he saw the fire only because Jolyon couldn't hold him.

'So you and Bertie weren't as estranged as people thought?'

Jolyon rose to pace the room. The bags had been removed from his hands but thinly new-skinned he still couldn't put them in his pockets as his frequent attempts at that revealed. His mouth crinkled at one corner. 'We fell out over my marriage. Apparently it was obvious to him and everyone else that Evelyn married me for what her family thought I would inherit – namely Bertie's Hallingham estates.'

Jolyon perched on the edge of my writing desk. 'Bertie was even more furious when I sold my own stuff to compensate those people her family fleeced while I was heading up the company.'

'I know he loved you,' I was guessing, but I'd long thought it.

Jolyon sighed. 'Let's say he knew I was a sucker for a lady's hard luck story and feared I'd repeat my mistake.' Was there a message there for me? Having admitted me into the secret of Fentiman, I didn't doubt Bertie had also told Jolyon.

'So he disinherited you in favour of his nephews?'

'Not really. For a start, the nephews are as rich as Croesus already so don't lose any sleep over them. What Bertie wanted to do was deter the gold-diggers, not cut me out. So he devised a *trompe l'oeil* if you like. Or in his case, more of an illusion.' Jolyon chuckled. 'Bertie liked things like that.'

He came to stand directly in front of me, looking down. 'He only pretended he'd cut me off without a penny. Even got the countess to emphasize the direness of my straits by leaving me the gatehouse. It was all a sham – she knew that perfectly well.'

'You mean Bertie just wanted it to look as though you were enemies – in case anyone else had ideas....'

'That's about it.'

Without warning he leaned down, lifted my chin and kissed me. 'So thank heavens you showed no interest in me – otherwise you'd have been out on your ear.'

He knelt in front of me. 'Synnove McKenna, now I have the wherewithal to keep us, will you marry me?'

He had to be joking ... yet that hint of a smile was missing. 'I get it, Bertie made your inheritance conditional on your adding Sanderling to the bag.' I stood up, turned towards the window, gazing out. 'Well I'm sorry to disoblige but I'm afraid I must hand Sanderling to Barry Fentiman. I've thought and thought about it but—' I turned to see the door closing behind him.

Chapter 39

'Lord Danhanbury told me Barry Fentiman is the blood relation you found.' I waited for Jean Edwards to show surprise at my knowledge. Nothing, not even a flicker, crossed those immobile features. 'What I need to know is how you arrived at that conclusion.'

I'd sent for the detective because if I was to understand this whole thing she was the obvious person to help. She had been very conscientious in her execution of the countess's wishes, but now I too was party to this untenable secret, I hoped she would be more forthcoming. 'In other words, how sure are you? Where's the proof?'

Jean retraced her steps to the door of my sitting room, peered both ways along the hall, withdrew and closed it firmly behind her. The french windows were shut. I indicated a sofa and she sat, knees together, hands loosely folded in her lap, head bowed, presumably marshalling her thoughts. Inhaling deeply, she looked up. 'The first thing we found was in a convent called St Hildegard's.... I thought that would interest you.' She stretched to stroke the cat sitting patiently at her feet. 'It was nothing on its own, just a name – Ariadne Tennyson – who'd had a baby boy there in 1937.

I stifled a gasp. 'The father was a Jim Tennyson.'

'Well, now you're telling me something I didn't know. All I picked up on was the name Ariadne. We don't expect people to register under their real names but they frequently use a permutation rather than indulge in complete fiction.' She moved back in her seat and over the next ten minutes filled in the details of her search.

After which she stood, wandered over to the fireplace and remained there for some seconds gazing into it, as if remembering.

Turning, she went on: 'It was only when I suggested the name to the countess that I was sure. As you'd expect, she hid it well, but it didn't take much experience to realize she was in shock – stunned that I'd found out. She took the file off me and burnt it in this very fireplace. Expunged it. Swore me and Mr Poulson Senior to secrecy.'

Concentrating her gaze on her fingernails, Jean returned to her seat. 'To tell you the truth, I think that's why she left me in charge of selection. Didn't dare risk some other gumshoe finding Fentiman and taking it upon themselves to appoint him after all.'

The comment found its mark and stirred my guilt complex … but it didn't alter how I felt.

'I also think that's why she insisted her successor be female – as yet another barrier against him. And I'm convinced that's why she came up with the criteria idea. The countess wasn't looking for a particular person but for someone who fitted her vision – unlike friend Fentiman.' Jean looked me steadily in the eye. 'You're thinking of giving Sanderling over to him, aren't you? I never took you for the quitting type.'

'Then help me,' I shouted, sitting down abruptly and biting my lip.

Silence for a while, then Jean said: 'That day you saw me talking to Jolyon St Clair….' Yes? what had that been about? 'If you remember, I was trying to determine his motive … though of course I already knew he wasn't related to the countess. Well, when he'd told me all about his modest family, what he remembered of them at any rate, he got on to the subject of Fentiman. Said Fentiman put on airs and graces because his father had always maintained he was the son of landed gentry. Apparently Barry Fentiman became so obsessed with this notion, he researched and targeted manorial estates who lacked an heir, knowing there'd be no one but lawyers left to defend them. Sanderling was by no means the first he'd had a go at.'

'Which only reinforces the fact that Fentiman really is the heir. Since no one's mentioned him I assume his father's dead?'

Jean nodded. 'As you say, I don't think there's any doubt. But that doesn't justify going against the countess.'

'Well of course I understand why she denied him – doesn't fit the motto does he? Singularly missing the virtue bit. And if I cling to

Sanderling knowing what I now know, then I'll be no better than him.' I was desperate. Having reconciled myself to the rightness of my decision, here was Jean Edwards lending persuasive weight to the anti lobby. In a quieter tone, I asked: 'You're sure you've investigated everything?'

Jean didn't reply immediately. 'The only things I didn't see were the countess's family collections. But I hardly think—'

I jumped up. Action. We needed to get out of here, stretch our minds, start from a different angle. 'That's easily remedied.'

We made our way up the wide crimson carpet of the west staircase and into the splendour of the hotel wing as I called it, built to house and impress visitors. I rang for Mr Travers to unlock the doors to the three salons where the treasures were stacked, which he did with alacrity and then melted away. Fittingly, as Wink had always maintained it marked the entrance to the collections, Theseus accepting the ball of twine had been propped just inside the first door.

I stooped to inspect it more closely. 'Wink caught sight of this after we'd fallen through into that makeshift store room; she said something like: "*The very holy one—*"' I sat down abruptly on the bare floor, overcome.

Jean came across. 'I'm sorry, her loss must still be—'

'The very holy one, don't you remember?' I screamed at her. What with the floor falling in, Wink's death, my own narrow escape, followed by the trauma of what had happened to Bertie and Russell and the revealing of Fentiman as heir, I'd been too preoccupied for its significance to permeate before. Jean crouched to view the painting more closely.

'Not this,' I yelled impatiently. 'The final criteria: *Seek the very holy one, westwards*. For God's sake, Jean, you're the detective. What does it mean?'

The countess had said it almost dismissively. '*It's a tiebreaker – in case you can't decide*.' Sitting on her haunches studying the painting of Ariadne giving the ball of thread to Theseus, so he could find his way back out of the Minotaur's labyrinth, Jean was unsurprised it should hold a special significance for the countess. Unlike Miss

Winkleham, who had doubtless been well versed in Cretan goddesses, Jean would have to look it up; but given that lady's profound exclamation, Jean would bet the name Ariadne meant The Very Holy One. And not only was Ariadne the countess's middle name, it was also what she'd chosen to call herself at St Hildegard's.

The countess had possessed little breath for speech; only just managing to whisper '*St Hildegard's*,' in Jean's ear before falling back on her pillows. But it had been the last thing the countess had said, and to Jean's great shame this was the first occasion on which she'd given it serious thought. She sighed, reminded of the sadness.

Since the countess's hand had been buried in the cat's fur, Jean had first supposed she was concerned for her pet's welfare but was then convinced it had been meant as a final reminder – an exhortation. Only Jean knew about St Hildegard's and the countess wanted it kept that way. In other words, on no account must Fentiman inherit Sanderling.

Which was the guiding tenet by which Jean had conducted her mission. And was why she felt so wretched now; powerless to prevent Synnove following her conscience.

Strange though, if you wanted to forget something, would you name your cat after it ... and send a sizeable donation every year? Racked with guilt over what she'd done, had the countess used the name as a hair shirt; the hurt she'd been condemned to wear for the rest of her life? A private mantra to ensure she never forgot ... and, therefore, unsurprising as her final utterance.

But what if she'd wanted Jean to revisit the place. The night before she died the countess had demanded: '*You will make sure, won't you?*' The following morning, with seconds left of life, she chose to spend that precious moment uttering the words '*St Hildegard's*'. Was there something she should have told Jean that with her dying breath she was trying to remedy?

'I don't know what the connection is, but I feel the answer is at St Hildegard's. That name was the last thing the countess uttered.'

Why hadn't she said so before? 'But that's east, not west – Essex, didn't you say?'

Jean got up off the floor, dusted her knees. 'I'll go over there.'

'No.' I still didn't entirely trust Jean Edwards. Doubtless she meant well and was only following the countess's wishes but if there were paths to follow, decisions to take, mistakes to be made ... this time I wanted it to be my doing, not someone else's. I was tired of being manipulated, kept at a distance while others organized my life.

There had always been someone between me and the countess: first Jean Edwards, then Charles Poulson, Bertie of course.... But now I had the strong sense that at last this was between the two of us; if only I could break through this barrier, confront her personally, then I could be certain of what to do. And what better meeting place than the one the countess herself had designated. 'I'll go ... alone.'

Chapter 40

Against Mr Channing's pleadings I took the open top Morris Eight. It would have been crass to bowl up in my Mercedes – or anything even grander. I could have hired a car, I suppose, but that seemed stupid when I had a whole garage from which to choose and besides, I had a soft spot for the little Morris.

Despite his misgivings I was confident it would convey me to Essex and back unharmed. After he made me promise for the nth time not to blame him if it didn't, Mr Channing waved me on the way with a shaking of his head, mouthing the word: 'Women,' when he thought I wasn't looking. Ordinarily I'd have listened to him, but since I was journeying back in time I wanted a car which fitted the period and the circumstances; one that felt right.

The Morris and I made it without incident to that reedy, water wilderness Jean had described in her directions. Bleak didn't do justice to the forbidding stone building rising fifty feet into the sky; blank windowless walls on this side. I couldn't decide whether its original purpose had been to repel or incarcerate visitors. Fanciful, I know, but as we rattled across the wave-licked causeway, I had the overwhelming impression the car had been here before.

Greeted by a white robed nun at the entrance to a walled courtyard, I crawled the car behind her as she led the way on foot, like a funeral director conducting a hearse, until we reached a row of open-fronted lean-tos where she indicated I might park.

'I'm Synnove McKenna. I rang the Mother Superior....'

Her blank face nodded in understanding, but light played through her eyes as I handed her the bagfuls of goodies Jean had suggested I bring; everything from chocolates to cosmetics; bath salts to body cream; along with cushions, slippers and a selection of magazines. Life's little luxuries for the girls the nuns still housed. I felt as though I'd alighted in a jungle clearing, trading beads for information.

'I'm Sister Rachel. I'll show you where the records are.'

What was I looking for? I hadn't a clue … and fleetingly regretted leaving Jean behind.

'I really wanted to talk to someone,' I blurted. Her face remained serenely impassive. 'Ariadne Tennyson, she was here before the war. I just wondered….'

Sister Rachel finally smiled, a lovely warm, enveloping, lightening of her face. Her grey eyes twinkled at me. 'We may look old, tucked away out here—'

Hell, now I'd offended her. 'I'm so sorry. I didn't mean …' but she was way ahead of me, tripping down dark, draughty, corridors. Arriving at a massive door, she turned the handle and ushered me into a room not unlike the record store at Sanderling.

'The ledgers run by date, starting from 1902 when we came here, to the present. The 1930s are over in the far corner. Ring the bell if you need anything.' With a whisk of her habit she was gone.

In the hope that simply immersing myself in the documents would kickstart inspiration, I heaved the tome for 1935–1937 on to a large stand and occupied myself in tracing the record for Ariadne Tennyson which Jean had found. But nothing else sprang out. Despairing, I left the room and, not wanting to disturb Sister Rachel again, found my own way back outside.

Why had the countess directed Jean to St Hildegard's? And what on earth did that weird criteria mean? For lack of a better idea I turned towards the west … to see a nun examining the Morris. As I watched from the porch, she ran her hand lovingly over its bonnet then opened the passenger door and stooping, peered inside. I suppose, even now, they saw few cars.

Not wanting to frighten her I wandered across slowly but noisily, scuffing the gravel, clearing my throat. She withdrew from the interior and turned to face me. In that second her expression changed. Both hands came up to hide her lined face and she gave a strangled scream.

'I'm sorry, I didn't mean to startle you,' I smiled. 'Would you like to go for a spin in her?'

She leaned against the side of the motor, peering through gnarled fingers, hesitant to remove her hands and look at me properly. 'Ariadne? Is it really you?'

Chapter 41

Unable to catch my breath I staggered to the garage wall and leaned against it. We stared at one another, open-mouthed.

'The car, I recognized your car.'

Cold swept through me like an electric current, shaking me rigid. We stood there, she and I, matching ghosts in our whiteness, she from her robes, me from fear. More used to dealing with things spiritual, the wizened little nun appeared the most composed. Approaching me, she reached out her hand and softly touched my face, making sure I was solid.

'Forgive me, my dear. I'm Sister Agnes. You gave me such a fright. You look so like her.'

I had to swallow twice before I could squeeze out the words. 'Like whom?'

Piercing blue eyes in a nut brown face regarded me steadily. 'Why don't we go into the garden, and you can tell me why you're here. Come.' She beckoned me along a path to the side of the building, through an ancient arch and into a lush paradise of rampant roses, overburdened apple trees and long grass. My legs felt forced to comply and my head was too caught up in astonishment to contradict them. I'd have followed her anywhere.

She selected a bench beneath a damson tree and patted the seat beside her. I sat.

'I don't know where to start.' She smiled encouragingly. 'Well, I'm Synnove McKenna.'

'Yvonne's,' she interrupted.

'Whose?'

She patted my knee. 'Sorry dear, can't help myself sometimes.

That'll be ten more Hail Marys I'll have to say tonight; Mother Superior will be so cross with me.' She could see my perplexed frown. 'Your name, it's an anagram of Yvonne's ... I interrupted you.'

Thrown by her interjection I hesitated. My mother hadn't been called Yvonne, she'd just liked the name Synnove. I went on. 'A lady, a countess I never knew, left her estates to the woman whose qualities fitted a long list of criteria she laid down. A private detective was hired to find this person ... and selected me.'

'Oh my,' she clapped her tiny hands. 'Doesn't it just sound like the work of the little people.' For the first time I noticed the Irish inflection. 'So why are y' looking so glum?'

'Because before that, the countess had asked the detective to find out if she had any living blood relation. When the detective came here and by various clever means found out the countess had borne an illegitimate son adopted by a family called Fentiman – and that his son, Barry Fentiman was the last surviving relation – the countess destroyed the file. I can understand why, he's a despicable man, but—'

'That's all right then,' Sister Agnes's wimpoled cheeks went from an O of surprise to a slump of relief.

'Well, no, it's not. Because the estates – Sanderling – are Fentiman's by right. I'm an interloper, I can have no claim to them.'

Sister Agnes lapsed into silence. Thinking she may have fallen asleep I felt strangely content to remain sitting there, listening to the bees attacking the lavender, while I pondered the significance of her calling me Ariadne and remembering the car. I supposed it wasn't surprising I might resemble the countess; the criteria had been so specific about size and colouring – I'd often suspected the countess had recruited in her own image. And Bertie had frequently gazed at me as at a spectre.

If Agnes had indeed been here in 1937 then she and Bertie were the only ones who knew how Isabel Ariadne Foxhill had looked as a young woman; much younger than I was now. Photographs were all very well but their two-dimensional flatness could hide the essence of their subject. Agnes suddenly said: 'She used to take me into the village in it, the Morris.'

'You knew her?' my pulse drummed in my ears.

'Oh yes, dear. I nursed her for months. Ariadne almost died having the baby; I can hear her now, begging God to take her. It was an awful night. Ariadne and wee Bridget O'Toole were in labour at the same time and many of the sisters were at Compline. I had to keep running between the two rooms so I couldn't be with her all the time.'

She sighed, tears welling in her eyes. Dashing them away she went on: 'Because of the complications, the doctor had to carry out a hysterectomy afterwards – which in those days was a dangerous ordeal.'

She sighed, looking down at her worn hands. 'I reckoned it was God's punishment for her trying to deceive her parents. And the worst of it was, I'd helped her.' Even now, her lined face crinkled into tissue paper with the memory. She looked up at me. 'Instead of its being adopted as Ariadne's parents were insisting, I'd found a couple in Clacton prepared to foster the child until.... Ariadne had been sure her parents would come round eventually.'

I didn't dare breathe. 'Yet it was adopted?'

'Oh yes. Because Ariadne was so ill and the doctor needed permission to operate, Sister Mary, the Mother Superior here then, sent a telegram to Ariadne's mother, the Countess Hampden; she arrived several days later.'

Agnes switched back from her trance-like state. 'A strange lady, hiding from herself – but then folk of her class were like that, poor souls. She was facing the loss of her only daughter and yet all she was allowed to consider was how it would look to the outside world. Anyway....' Agnes sighed, clutched the rosary which hung from her waist. 'She asked if the child had been adopted, which of course, it had, and that was that. Poor Mr Tennyson was frantic.'

'Tennyson was here? He knew?'

'Yes, he came here. But Mother Superior wouldn't admit him and the countess then threatened his father's job and had his university funding stopped and him sent down for his behaviour. He joined the air force after that, got killed during the war – a happy release, I daresay.' Agnes broke down and sobbed. She obviously still blamed herself for how things had turned out. 'I couldn't tell him. And it made no difference by then anyway.'

Despite my loathing for Fentiman, I was sorry for how fate had dealt with his grandfather. 'Tell him where his son was, you mean?

'We were forbidden to say anything.' She stared at me in such anguish. 'Ariadne's baby was dying, we had to christen it that night. So, unlike most adoptions – where the adoptive parents choose the name later – in this case I knew the Christian name; you can't ever change that, you know.'

Divorced from my voice, I asked: 'And what was it?'

'I told your young man the same thing yesterday.' Had she lapsed again, thought I was indeed Ariadne and was now referring to Tennyson?

'Came to bring us a big donation left by Lord Danhanbury who'd been a good friend of Ariadne's – wanted to marry her, you know.'

'Young man? Jolyon? Jolyon St Clair?'

'That's the one, such a handsome man. Wanted to know if this Barry Fentiman character really was Ariadne's grandson. Said the answer was crucial to his community but by the looks o' him his own life depended on it.'

I couldn't speak. This was the only woman who knew for sure; the woman who'd been there when the baby was born; whom God had spared to be here for us now.

'I christened her Endaira. I knew Ariadne would appreciate it. Her name was Greek for The Holy One – so I just wrote it backwards, from right to left.

A girl. '*Seek The Holy One, westwards*' – the countess's final criteria. She had known.

Chapter 42

Now, at the end, she was facing what she'd always dreaded. That all that sacrifice had indeed been for nothing, unless ... unless she could find a successor capable of taking Sanderling on into the twenty-first century. Someone who could preserve its force for good yet find a new way of operating to serve for the next few hundred years.

The search for the proverbial distant cousin had proved a disaster, she'd never expected that dragging the pond would produce that particular piece of flotsam; the odds against finding Fentiman had been enormous. Though she'd only been cross because her secret had been discovered: Fentiman wasn't related to her in any way.

Poor Sister Agnes, who'd tried so hard to help. She smiled, remembering the warmth of the young nun to whom she owed her life, could see her there on her knees beside the bed.

'I've done a terrible terrible thing, Ariadne. But I didn't expect her to survive the night so if by a miracle she did, and they didn't realize she was yours, she'd be easier to hide away; no one would take nearly as much notice of what happened to her if she wasn't connected with you. And if she died ... and wit' you not being able to have any more,' she'd broken off to squeeze her patient's hand, lessen the blunt truth, 'then your family would be pleased there was an heir, and a male one at that.'

'There's never been a male heir.'

'So I swapped the babies over. Took that poor child born in the next room and made him yours – and had Endaira christened and registered as the daughter of poor little Bridget O'Toole who was keen to be rid of her child fast.'

The countess remembered thinking how typical of Agnes to choose a name that sounded Irish but for someone who knew their mythology would always provide the way back ... the thread. Remembered too, how cheered she had been by this news until she'd looked at Agnes.

Here Agnes had broken down, dampening the sheets where her head lay. 'But Mother Superior was so angry when the foster parents came from Clacton demanding the money for Endaira's keep, that she immediately gave her up for adoption and tightened the rules. After that only Mother Superior and her deputy could handle such matters or access the records. I don't know where she's gone. I'm so so sorry.'

The numbness never went away. The constant ache that somewhere out there was a daughter she would never know. Pathetically she studied every child she met – searching hopelessly. And what could she have done, even if she'd found her? Adoption was a one-way transaction and thanks to Agnes's swap, no one would ever believe the child was hers anyway. They'd dismiss her claims as those of a poor crank whose mind had been turned through the loss of her only child; which wasn't far from the truth.

Hence the children during the war. Yes, it had been a noble gesture, but the countess also hoped fate might just throw up that one orphan in a million.

She'd more than once considered mounting a search for the child, especially after the detective found Fentiman. If anyone could find Endaira and her offspring it would be Edwards. But the countess was too frightened. What would the child, person, probably parent herself now, think of her when she found out why she'd been given up? She would hate the countess for what she'd done ... rightly. And anyway, what if she and her children had turned out like Fentiman? What then? And whose fault would that be – for abandoning the child's upbringing?

Even if the countess had found her years ago, the woman could easily have been corrupted by all this wealth if she thought she'd been born to it. One had only to look at the drug-fuelled sons of the aristocracy to see that. Yet if she did find her now she'd have to acknowledge her, else what would be the point of looking – her daughter wasn't a fish to be thrown back for not making the grade. No, after all this time it was a subject best left alone.

Admittedly biased through circumstance, yet nevertheless convinced that inherited genes were no guarantee of suitability for the task which awaited her successor, the countess had lighted on the criteria idea. Tonight she felt an excitement she hadn't felt for decades, that something momentous was going to happen, that she would at last set eyes on the answer to her prayers. Foolish, but then she could think of no other method by which to choose the next chatelaine. The Edwards woman was good, and she'd come up with two possible candidates.

The countess settled into bed with the files in front of her, Hildegard warming her toes. The room was bathed in a soft light and she felt at peace. The long quest was soon to be solved. She felt weary after her long talk with Edwards after dinner but she just wanted to take a quick look; she'd read them thoroughly in the morning. She opened the top cover, slipped out the contents. Natalie Frobisher – the woman had hard features, looked calculating, but then she might need to be. The countess glanced through the papers. Impressive certainly. She put the file to one side and opened the second.

Staring back at her was a picture of herself taken soon after the war by the looks of it, though she failed to recognize the background or the clothes she'd been wearing. Where had Edwards got that from? She must have used it to help find someone the same build and colouring and left it in here by mistake. Curious as to exactly where and when it had been taken, the countess turned it over. It said simply: *Synnove McKenna*, the name on the front of the file.

This was all wrong. She'd been adamant no candidate must have any prior connection with the countess or Sanderling or indeed the area or anyone in it. Yet this woman had purloined an old photograph and was masquerading as being close in likeness to herself as a young woman.

Furious she picked up the phone and dialled Poulson. Then regretted it because, like her, at this hour he must be in bed. Feeling guilty when he answered she said curtly: 'I want to see you first thing,' and put the phone down. He'd have to deal with Edwards, and change the will. If a successor was not chosen prior to her death, she'd left the selection to Edwards. She couldn't have that now, couldn't trust her.

Her feeling of contentment ruined, she was shuffling the papers back into the file when a fact sheet of McKenna's background fluttered in front of her. A searing pain tore through her heart as she stared at those unforgiving words:

Mother: Endaira, born 21 July1937 – adopted shortly after birth, becoming Endaira Connelly; married Squadron Leader Bill McKenna 1962; died of cancer 1989. One daughter – Synnove.